THE UNTENDED

THE
UNTENDED

A Novel

—

MATTEA KRAMER

SHE WRITES PRESS

Published 2025
Printed in the United States of America
Print ISBN: 978-1-64742-887-7
E-ISBN: 978-1-64742-888-4
Library of Congress Control Number: 2024927607

For information, address:
She Writes Press
1569 Solano Ave #546
Berkeley, CA 94707

Interior design by Stacey Aaronson

She Writes Press is a division of SparkPoint Studio, LLC.

Company and/or product names that are trade names, logos, trademarks, and/or registered trademarks of third parties are the property of their respective owners and are used in this book for purposes of identification and information only under the Fair Use Doctrine.

This is a work of fiction. Names, characters, places, and incidents either are the product of the author's imagination or are used fictitiously. Any resemblance to actual persons, living or dead, is entirely coincidental.

THE
UNTENDED

1

Just off the interstate at the Greenfield exit, it was humid inside The 99. There was an odor of vinyl and unwashed dishrags as Casch Abbey asked the regulars at the bar table if they wanted anything else.

"Can I use your apron for a sec?" said one with a reddish beard.

"What?" she said. She was used to a lot of clowning but hadn't gotten this before. The guy didn't answer, just reached and took a handful of black apron and wiped the last of the buffalo-wing grease from his thick fingers.

Casch took a step back. Keep it cool or they won't leave a tip. She turned, throat tight, and saw a customer waiting there— he'd seen what happened. And somehow that was even worse, someone witnessing that you were a human napkin. She could see this new guy wanted to say something. His eyes had narrowed, his hands were deep in his pockets. The tongues of his high-tops stuck out over his jeans.

She cleared her throat, gestured toward the empty table in front of him.

"Something to quench your thirst?" she asked.

Their eyes locked. She thought, Please don't say anything.

"Yeah, could I have a Red Stripe?" he said softly, and pulled out a chair.

She let out a breath. Because he got it.

"Red Stripe coming up," she nodded, and sidestepped away. In her periphery she saw the men looking at her as they lumbered toward the exit. She needed a cigarette. But she had the entrees coming for her four-top, and this guy needed a beer.

"This might sound weird," he said as she placed the sweating bottle on a square napkin in front of him.

And Casch felt a bloom of heat in her chest. With the inside of her wrist, she brushed away a strand of hair that had slipped from her ponytail, and waited for what he would say.

"But you have strong hands," he said.

"What?"

"Your hands, I couldn't help noticing. Look."

Tentative, she brought her arms forward.

"See?" he said. "Look at the veins."

The two of them studied the raised veins that snaked down her wrists and disappeared between her knuckles. She flipped them so her palms faced up and saw his eyes catch on the three blue dots inked inside her left forearm.

"You do some kind of work with your hands? I mean, besides waitressing," he added, shaking his head at himself.

"When you're a single mom you do every kind of work with your hands. My son's seven, my daughter's ten," she said, and managed a smile. But social services is trying to take them from me, she didn't say, and just thinking it made the dread open in her stomach like ink.

"Anyways," she said quickly, "I'm not sure that has anything to do with my hands. I do also hit the heavy bag."

His face was blank for a second.

"Wait, you box?"

"Just the punching bag at the YMCA, I'm talking about," she said, shrugging one shoulder. But she saw his eyes deepen with interest.

"What's your name?" he asked, sitting forward, and she told him.

"Like cash money?"

"Sounds the same but it's C-A-S-C-H."

"Never heard that before."

"I'm the only one," she said. My daddy named me before he ran off to Florida, she didn't say.

"Casch, will you show me how to box?"

"Show you—right here?" Her forehead wrinkled.

"I've never boxed."

"Hold on," she said, and ducked away.

At the server station, Gabi was tapping an order into the greasy touchscreen, and Casch came up close enough to say quietly, "Some guy wants me to teach him how to box."

"What? Which table?" Gabi asked, gold hoop earrings swinging as she glanced around.

"Eight but don't look."

"Oh he's cute."

"I said not to look," said Casch, hiding her smile as she continued back to the kitchen, where it was ten degrees warmer and someone was shouting at Rick, who washed dishes. She grabbed the two plates that were under the heat light at the window.

After she'd delivered the chicken tenders and fried shrimp that came up next, Casch weaved back to his table.

"K, stand up," she said from behind, and he jerked around. Then he pushed out his chair and got to his feet. She was half smiling as she said, "I do it like this."

She looked down at her busted black sneakers as she bent her knees and folded her arms into her chest. Then she swiveled, her left arm emerging and crossing the space between them.

"Jab," she said, her fist grazing the stubble on his jawline, and she looked at his eyes, brown.

Then she swiveled again, her left arm retracting toward her snug black V-neck shirt, and she pivoted the other way. This time her right arm emerged, came sailing toward his midsection, and tapped his belly. She felt his stomach tighten, the sweatshirt's bronze zipper pinned between her knuckles. She could just catch his smell, like pine air freshener. He seemed genuinely nice—which meant he probably wasn't, because she was always wrong about people.

"Anyways, that's how I do it," she said, and turned toward the couple that had just sat down at the next table.

After she'd brought his burger, Casch came to check on him and found that he'd eaten and was gone. You're kidding me, now this guy dined and dipped?

But no, no, here he was. He had only gone outside.

"You need anything?" she asked as he crossed in front of her and sat back down.

"Yeah, could I have a piece of tinfoil?"

She looked at the basket where his burger had been, there were a few soggy fries.

"Okay."

When she returned and handed him the foil, he said, "This is for you."

And in the calloused palm of his right hand was the largest reefer bud Casch had ever seen.

"What, really?" she said, glancing to see if anyone was looking.

4

"Yeah, I'm wrapping it for you," he said, and crinkled the foil around the nearly pine cone–sized nugget. Then he asked for another beer and she nodded, sliding the gift into her apron pocket as she backed away.

"He just gave me weed," she said as she printed the check for the four-top and Gabi passed her carrying an order of wings. Gabi's eyebrows lifted but neither of them stopped moving, Casch tearing off the slip and Gabi already delivering the basket at the corner booth. Casch dropped the bill, refilled their waters, and thought to herself that this guy had done something nice for her.

After he'd paid and she'd brought his change, he said, "You're going to be a prizefighter."

"Ha." All her weight gathered on her right foot as she shook her head and said, "No, actually I'm trying to go to nursing school."

His faced changed. "Really? That's impressive."

"Don't be too impressed, I haven't even turned in the application."

"Well good luck, that's really cool. I'm Topher by the way."

"Topher?"

"Short for Christopher."

"I take it you're not from Greenfield, Topher."

"White River Junction."

"So you don't know how special Greenfield is."

"Oh—yeah?"

"Kidding."

"Right," he said, nodding, and zipped up his hoodie. "Hey listen, I come through Greenfield pretty often. I was wondering if I could, if I could get your number?"

Smiling from the side of her mouth, she drew the pen from

her apron pocket. She flipped over his receipt, started scribbling—and, hesitating, she went with her real number.

"I saw what that guy did to you," said Topher after she'd folded the paper lengthwise and handed it to him.

"He comes in here all the time," said Casch. "He got laid off from the silver factory. All the waitresses know him, and we all know who's doing his wife, too."

Her mother was snoozing on the couch when Casch got home, head sideways at a funny angle, travel cup out on the coffee table. Casch pulled the door closed and Flora's eyes came open. She sat up, poking stockinged feet around the carpet to find her red plastic sandals.

Casch watched for a second, that drowsy face reminding her of when she was a kid—often there had still been sliced hot dog on her mother's dinner plate when she dozed off, gassed from another day cleaning houses.

"I changed the litter box," Flora said, standing up, "which is something you might want to consider doing. Looked like it was holding every poo the cat ever had."

"Thanks, Mom, bye," said Casch. She dropped her purse on the floor beside the taped arm of the couch and slipped into the kids' unlit room. She could hear the front door click as she sat gently on the edge of Dean's bed. His sandy-brown hair—same color as hers—was just a little too long and falling in his eyes. In her narrow bed a few feet away, Molly had pushed away the covers to reveal her shooting star T-shirt. Casch watched Molly's chest rise and fall, then looked back at Dean.

She'd never told anyone, but often she pictured something terrible happening to them—a bus accident, a shooting—and then it got hard to breathe. Because something could take them from her. Only she had never imagined the something would be called Department of Children and Families.

It was only a couple nights ago that she'd come home and there was a manila envelope waiting on the coffee table. "Some lady dropped that off for you," Flora had said. And both of them knew good news didn't come in packages like that.

In the morning she hustled Molly and Dean out of bed, she fixed them peanut butter toast, she flipped on the coffee maker while Dean, still in his underpants, said, "I'm feeding Otis," and spilled cat food across the floor.

Molly brought a book to the table and sat down to eat. For a second, as the coffee dripped, Casch watched her. She had been a good student, too, when she was that young.

"I could be a detective," said Molly, her fingers smudging the page.

"Definitely and you can start by finding your Reeboks," said Casch, smiling into the cupboard as she grabbed a mug.

After she put them on the bus, she got the folder from her bedroom and laid her pages across the table. It was months now that she'd been working on this application, she thought, and sat down to look it over. She knew what she had to do now was bring it in. The day after she'd gotten the DCF notice, she'd gone storming into the restaurant and told Gabi they were trying to take her kids. She suspected it was Dean's dad who called in the complaint though she couldn't prove it. She'd made the mistake of letting Dean wear Molly's old rainbow sweatshirt to his dad's house one weekend. "You turning my son into a pretty boy?" Jay had asked, and soon afterward, the DCF papers arrived. Jay didn't even want custody of Dean. But he wanted to mess with her, and there was nothing that mattered more to her than her kids.

"Oh girl, I been there. DCF came knocking on my door," Gabi had told her. "Here's what you got to do. You got to show them you're bettering yourself."

At the kitchen table now, Casch nodded and began arranging the nursing school application in order. The sheet on top was a checklist. She went down it with a pen, ticking off her items.

"Crap," she said aloud, pen hovering. She'd forgotten you had to get something stamped—if your high school transcript was more than ten years old, you needed a notary. And of course she was just past the ten-year cutoff; she was twenty-nine now, her last year before thirty. She would have to go into town to have the transcript stamped, then over to the community college to drop it off.

But what if she got it all finished and brought it in, and they laughed at her? She pictured a bunch of suits around a long table, crumpling her application, tossing it in the trash. The fear clawed up her throat. Screw them, you know?

Town hall is apparently the joint if you're in the market for a notary, or at least that's what the guy with the ponytail at Main Street Office Supply told Casch when she went in there asking. He shook his head in a friendly way and said, "Not here, try across the street."

"Thanks," she said as she turned, and eyeballed, for a second, the random merch. There were patterned socks, there were plush toys—the kids would've begged her for them. There was a sign that said *We Have Topographical Maps!* By the door was a display of maple sugar candy and Vermont gazetteers—stuff that was also available at every gas station—and for a second Casch wondered how the eff this place stayed in business.

She pushed out the door, bell sounding overhead, and trooped across Main in her faux Timberlands, across the triangle of grass that was town common, and up the steps of town hall.

The thud of the heavy door echoed behind her as she squinted in the dark interior. This place could practically be the set of a horror movie, she thought, eyes adjusting. She started down the long hallway. It wasn't until she got to the back of the building that she saw another soul, an old guy in an orange winter hat coming out of the men's room, crumpled plastic bag under his arm. She looked at him but he avoided her eyes—who wants to be seen doing drugs in the public restroom? Everyone's trying to hold on to a little dignity. She retraced her steps and this time stopped at the door that said CLERK, where she could see yellow light behind pebbled glazing, and a shape moving, like a ghost.

But no, no ghost. Just some sour woman who informed her, like it was the most obvious fact in the world, that of course this was the place you came to get some shit notarized. Casch opened the purple folder, filched from Molly's school supplies, and pulled out the sheet that needed a stamp. A stamp to make her nursing school application valid. A stamp to keep DCF away from her kids.

The clerk stamped and signed the paper and said, "That'll be six dollars."

"Six just for a stamp?" said Casch quietly.

"I don't set the price."

Casch paid and slipped out. When she was back in her van, she slid on her sunglasses. Her application was done. It was done, it was ready.

"Hey, check that out, DCF," she said, and punched the radio on. She sniffed and shook her head as she backed out and turned west toward the community college.

At the bottom of the hill the light was green and she sailed through the intersection, and on a whim hit her blinker. She would treat herself to an iced coffee, that's what she would do, extra cream extra sugar. This was the Dunkin' without a drive-thru, Casch threw it into park and stepped out into the L-shaped lot.

She ordered the jumbo iced from a cashier with a pierced lip who asked her to say that again. Casch repeated the order.

"Sorry I am braindead today," said the girl.

"No worries, don't you guys have to get up at like four in the morning?" said Casch.

"Yeah."

"See, I feel for you."

And when the girl handed back her change, Casch looked down at it. She'd paid with a ten.

"You know what? You keep it," she said.

And she had just stepped back into the sunshine and had the first milky sip through the cheery pink-and-orange straw when her purse chimed. She kept walking as she reached in and pulled out her phone and read:

hi its topher really liked meeting u

She was thinking she probably shouldn't have given that guy her number just as a station wagon came out of nowhere and she looked up to see the pinched nose and droopy eyelids of the driver in the same instant that the car rolled over her foot and she screamed and he hit the brakes and someone else was yelling and Casch was screaming.

2

A first delivery to a new guy always puts you a little on edge, he thought, sliding his phone away as the light changed. Topher eased on the gas and the ketchup-colored Ford Ranger crossed the intersection and entered the mouth of the Metro-North station, passing the long line of exiting cars. It was just after four o'clock, rush hour. He didn't turn into the parking garage. He drove around and found an open space along the fence. Just like he said he would. He paralleled in and flipped off the engine.

He was early. His foot tapped the mat. It always put you a little on edge, even if the person was vouched for. You go on your instincts, obviously. If everything feels okay, then it probably is. Go on your instincts and carry a Glock.

Anyways this is the right setting, he thought, glancing around. A car alarm blared, drowning out the loudspeaker announcing the next train. He'd figured this out when he first started coming to New York. Do the Metro-North stations at rush hour. Everyone's pouring off the trains, jumping in their cars. No one's looking at you.

A white Altima cruised by and parked two spaces up. Topher hopped out and went around to the passenger side of his truck. He stood leaning against the door, facing the chain-link fence, one foot crossed over the other. His lower right periphery registered the canary yellow of a few scrappy dandelions. You have decent options for cover in a place like this. The long chain of cars behind you, a few feet to the garage. Decent cover, if you got ambushed.

And here was his guy, emerging from the Altima. He wore a Mets jacket, had a chinstrap beard, he was saying "Hey, what's up, man." They were slapping hands, everything was fine. Topher was handing off a paper bag, the Mets fan patting a warm wad of bills into his palm. "Thanks, man." "No problem." And it was over, Topher waiting until the guy pulled away before trotting around to the driver's side and hopping back in the Ranger.

He'd made good time from the city, he saw, when the first sign for the Greenfield exit popped into view.

Was he getting off here? He was, he was doing it. When the exit appeared, he hit the blinker and veered right, rolling down the off-ramp into the empty rotary. In the parking lot of The 99, he backed the truck into a spot across from the restaurant's entrance.

Then sat there, rolling a tip between his fingers. He rolled from one side as he looked out and watched a family shuffle toward the entrance, a mom holding the toddler's hand and dad with a baby in a car seat. Topher unrolled the tip and rolled the other way. Then he pulled the gazetteer from behind his seat and took a fresh paper from the tangerine and gold sleeve of Zig-Zags. With stained fingertips, nails chewed to sunken half-moons, he pinched fluffy weed from the aluminum alloy grinder and sprinkled it along the paper. Closed the grinder and returned it to the center console.

He always felt better once he was back in Vermont—it still felt strange to have business in the city. When he'd returned from Afghanistan the second time, he and Alex used to check in on each other, and on one of those calls Topher said he was growing indoor. Alex, who was from New Jersey, said, "Let me know if you ever want to sell down in the city, we could use better weed."

"I'll grow you better weed," Topher had promised.

Gently he lifted the paper and started rolling.

Connor and Tory had been up in the field today, tilling, adding phosphorous. Of course they'd agreed to certain rules. They parked a distance from the trail, they parked in different spots every time.

He ran his tongue along the edge of the paper and sealed it closed with a fingertip. Then spun the unlit joint in his fingers.

Was he just going to sit here? His mind flipped to her fist grazing his cheek. Rugged, but cute. He was certain Gram would like her. In fact, if she weren't ten years dead, the two of them would start chitchatting, and it would be him that was the odd one out.

He dropped the joint in the empty cup holder and got out. Locked the truck, crossed the pavement. The sun wasn't even down yet but floodlights had the place lit up like a prison yard.

It was only after he'd drained a beer and ordered another that he asked the bartender if Casch was working.

"Nah," said the guy, drying a glass with a gray dish towel, "she didn't show up for work today."

3

"CASCH, I KNOW YOU'RE HOME. I SEEN YOUR VAN," said the voice outside, and Casch's shoulders jerked forward. There was a hard knock on the door.

Gripping the taped arm of the couch, she hoisted herself and limped, left foot in a hard-plastic boot, to unlock the dead bolt. On the step Gabi was wearing sunglasses and a velour track suit, the color of strawberries.

"Girl, tell me why you're not replying to my messages?" said Gabi.

"Oh," said Casch, and she looked toward her phone on the couch.

"Let's go to the community college, where's that application?"

"Yeah, no, I was planning on doing that today, actually. What time is it?"

"It's like one."

"It is?" said Casch, touching the back of her neck. Where had the time gone. "Okay, yeah, let's do it."

"Boom, I'm driving," said Gabi.

Outside it was warmer than in the apartment, Casch squinting in the April sunshine as she maneuvered her crutches down the walk. She had wedged the folder into her brown pleather purse, which swung from its thin strap as she descended the curb to the passenger side of Gabi's rusty Blazer.

"Here let me help you," Gabi said as Casch tried to get the crutches into the back seat—which looked just like Casch's van, one black booster seat and coloring books with the covers torn off. But she couldn't get the crutches to slide in far enough.

"Here, I got it," Gabi said, taking them from her.

"Thanks," said Casch softly, and climbed in the front seat. The car smelled like something apple-cinnamon—Gabi didn't smoke.

"Now we'll be all running into each other at school," Gabi said, grinning as she turned right out of Greenfield Terrace, "and the first thing I'm going to do is introduce you to Frances. I call her Frankie, she's the head of student advising. I'm like half in love with her, honestly. She sucks back Diet Dr Pepper and out of nowhere she'll be like, 'Gabi have you ever thought about maybe one day being president of this college?'"

"She really said that?" said Casch, swiveling her head to look at Gabi, whose dark hair was pinned up in a plastic clip.

"She totally said that! And I'm like, I fucking love you, and meanwhile she has a sign on her desk that says *You don't have to be crazy to work here, we'll train you.* I'm like, Frankie, we were meant to be together!"

Casch was laughing as Gabi crossed under the highway. The community college was in a stretch of flatland, not far past the rotary and The 99. Gabi parked in the horseshoe by the main entrance.

"I'll wait here," she said, "but if you happen to run into a lady with a blond perm, call her Frankie and drop my name."

Casch grinned as she climbed out and pulled the crutches

from the back. Inside the building, she followed the arrow for Admissions down a long hall with a gray-blue linoleum floor. She turned right and went through an open doorway into a brightly lit office. The woman at the desk glanced up from her screen.

Casch opened her mouth—then felt her face get hot.

She was finally here. After all this time, she was here. She was turning in the application. And it was in a purple unicorn folder. If you're applying for the fourth grade you've really nailed it, babe. She felt her cheeks blushing. You're such a joke.

"Can I help you?" said the woman.

"I—" said Casch.

Afterward Gabi drove up into town, and Casch rolled down her window for the breeze. On Federal Street they pulled in at the twenty-four-hour Grab-N-Go and parked in front of the window with the sign that said Gallon Milk $2.59.

"Special requests?" Gabi asked as she swung open the car door.

Casch shook her head and watched her friend hop out, the back of her red sweatpants disappearing into the store. The two of them had started working at The 99 around the same time, right after it opened. In a busy dinner shift it only takes a minute to see who can handle themselves and who's in the weeds. Gabi had all her tables dialed in and started helping this guy Aaron— he didn't work there anymore—and Casch saw that Gabi could run the whole floor. At the end of that night, when they were closing out, Gabi had nodded at her and said, "You know how to hustle." That was when Casch realized they'd been watching each other, thinking the same thing. A couple weeks later, when they were rolling silverware, Gabi told Casch that she and her mom had gone down to the casino in Connecticut and Gabi had blown $200. She'd needed that money for snow tires. At the time, Casch had a few hundred bucks in her bank account.

"I'll lend it to you," she had told Gabi, "I'll go over to the ATM right now."

"What? No," said Gabi, waving a hand like she was saying goodbye. "I wasn't trying to fish for anything, I just needed to tell someone."

But Casch was glad to do it—she almost never got to help anyone. She set down a roll-up and marched across the street in her blacks to the ATM in the Price Chopper plaza and took out $200. "No big deal," she'd said to Gabi when she handed her the money. And it wasn't; Gabi paid her back the next week, straight out of her earnings from the restaurant.

Just now Gabi came out of the store with an orange bag of Cheetos and a couple shiny scratch tickets.

"One for each of us," she said as she climbed in the car, and handed Casch the one that said *Wheel of Fortune*.

"Whoa thanks," said Casch. She looked down at the ticket's green sparkle.

"You know how Mike Tyson said, 'Everyone has a plan till they get punched in the face'?" said Gabi, pulling off her gold-rimmed sunglasses. A couple flecks of mascara had smudged beneath her large brown eyes.

"Yeah," said Casch.

"Well, I'm like, everyone gets punched in the face occasionally, right? In this world? I mean, you're doing pretty good if you don't get punched every day."

"You're saying just to keep getting up after you get punched?"

"No, I'm saying treat yourself like a million dollars regardless," said Gabi. Then she reached two fingers to the open ashtray that was full of change, plucked up a nickel, and offered it to Casch. "You deserve a winner," she said.

The woman who stood on Casch's front step the following afternoon was younger than Casch had pictured, with short hair and a stud in her nose.

"Social worker," she said, all friendly and chatty, "Department of Children and Families, we spoke on the phone?"

She stared expectantly at Casch, whose pulse knocked in her throat. *This* is my home visit? You can't come in my house right now—my house is a disaster.

She hadn't realized they would come unannounced. She'd told them about the broken foot, and over the phone the woman had sounded genuinely sympathetic. Casch had thought there'd be an appointment, that she'd have some warning. Gabi had told her to clean up the house really nice.

Could she say no? Could she say not right now, come back another time? What do they do if you say no?

"Can I come in?" said the woman, smiling as she hugged the papers to her chest.

"Uh, sure," said Casch, glancing over her shoulder, stepping aside. And the social worker was in her home.

"I was so sorry to hear about your foot," she said, looking down at the plastic boot as she entered. "Has it been healing up okay?"

Casch pulled the door closed and stared at her own living room—crusty dishes on the coffee table, crumbs across the carpet, a mound of laundry in the chair. One of her stretched-out bras had fallen from the pile onto the floor.

"Why are you here?" she said, turning to the woman.

"This is a Chapter 49 assessment," she replied, like it was so obvious.

"What does that mean?"

She cleared her throat. "Concern about potential neglect."

Casch felt herself freeze. The woman kept talking.

"My only priority is the child," she continued, "and the purpose of the home visit is just to ask a few questions, look around the domicile, see the child in his home environment. Then I'll be on my way."

They thought she was neglecting her children. Her throat was dry as she tried to swallow. They thought she was a person who would neglect children. Her face burned. They thought she didn't understand that having Molly and Dean was the best thing she'd ever done.

The woman kept chatting while Casch's eyes darted and caught on all the things she would find wrong. She would report it all, the kids' dirty home.

"So why don't we get started? I'll ask some questions, you'll show me around, I'll meet Dean when he gets home—he is coming home on the bus, I assume?"

Casch nodded.

There were so many questions, Casch gaping as the woman asked one after another. Some of them were easy: What grade is Dean in? What is his teacher's name? Like she was being tested on her own child. But some of them were hard to answer. How do you meet Dean's daily needs? How do you handle difficult situations?

The woman asked to see his room.

"They share," said Casch, mouth dry, as the woman went poking around the sloppy bedroom. The floor was covered in clothes, there was a tear in the window screen. On each twin bed the sheets were tangled, Molly's checkered comforter wedged up against the wall. Beside her bed was an old Chips Ahoy! box that she was planning to use for a birdhouse.

"Do you think Dean has enough age-appropriate clothing?" said the woman.

"Age-appropriate," said Casch.

"I know they grow so quick," she said, nodding her head like it was an offer of kindness.

"He does have enough. Yes."

The woman insisted on coming out to the curb to watch her get the kids off the bus, and Casch's face seared with embarrassment.

"Who are you?" said Molly after she hopped to the curb. Dean took Casch's hand.

"Does anyone else live here?" the woman asked when they were back inside, glancing at her papers. "It's the three of you—or is there someone else living here too?"

"No, it's the three of us," said Casch firmly.

The woman asked to speak with each child individually. Casch waited at the kitchen table, leaning, trying to hear any of it. But it was so quiet, the woman's voice soft and each kid hardly saying a word.

"All set," the woman said cheerfully when that was done. "I'll just have a look at the kitchen, then I'll be on my way."

Casch watched her examine the dishes piled in the sink beneath the dark brown cupboard doors that drooped crooked on their hinges. The only sound was the hum of the old refrigerator that was the color of American cheese. By the back door, Casch saw the woman note the kitty-litter box and the overflowing trash—she'd known it needed to be taken out, but it was a hassle

20

with her foot. The dumpster was on the other side of the parking lot.

"Do you mind if I have a look in the refrigerator?"

Casch stared at her. Please leave, she didn't say.

The woman looked at her expectantly.

"Okay. Sure."

Pulling open the fridge, the woman bent down and peered inside, then jotted something on her paper.

"Okay," she said, standing up, "I'm all set."

When the front door clicked behind her, Casch's head was pounding, her foot throbbing.

"Why was she here?" said Molly, standing in their bedroom doorway, arms folded over her chest.

"I don't know," said Casch. Was it her fault?

"I'm going outside," Molly said, taking the elastic off her wrist and holding it in her teeth as she used both hands to put her wavy brown hair into a ponytail.

"Me too," said Dean, squeezing past his sister.

Casch nodded and limped into her room. The meds for her foot were on the nightstand. She took two and then stood staring at the bed.

Finally she turned and went through the kitchen and out the back door. Molly was just down the sloped lawn, her spiral notebook open in one hand. Dean was gathering sticks at the edge of the forested embankment that buffered the apartments from the highway. Gently Casch lowered herself to the grass, which felt pleasantly cool through the seat of her leggings. She lay backward and cradled her head with one hand.

Soon the kids drifted over and sat beside her. They listened to the muffled whoosh of cars, and a bird calling. The call echoed.

She would never think of coming out here if not for the kids.

Like the sweltering day last August, when they'd asked her if they could walk up the river. Casch had taken them swimming that day—but not to the sandy beach, which was the town rec area; you had to pay to park there. She had taken them farther north, to the old pumping station. She'd pulled over by the covered bridge where there were only a couple other cars, and the three of them went scrambling down the dirt path in their rubber sandals. Most of the river was only about ankle deep, but here you could swim. Molly dove around rapturously in the cold pools while Casch and Dean held off in the shallow part, blue floaties on his arms, Casch's cotton shorts and T-shirt soaked and cleaving to her skin. She'd been so concerned about whether the kids' swimsuits still fit them that she hadn't even realized, till they were practically out the door, that her own suit was so old it had disintegrated. But who cares? She swam in her clothes.

It was after the three of them had waded out of the clear water, back to the pebbled shore, that Molly looked up the riverbed and said, "What's up there, Mom?"

"What do you mean?" Casch had replied.

"If you follow the river where does it go?"

"I, uh. Don't know."

"Let's try it."

"What?"

"Let's go there, let's walk up the river."

"Yeah, Mom!" said Dean. "Let's walk up the river!"

Casch peered upstream to the place where it bent gently and disappeared in the greenery. Why not? she had thought. Why *not* walk up the river and see where it goes?

They had left their towels in the grass on the bank, their sandals and Dean's floaties in a sandy pile, and started walking.

And as soon as they were around the first bend, it seemed

they had traveled somewhere else. Ordinary Greenfield, baked in the August sun, shut behind them. This new place was cool and dark under a forest canopy. The kids fell quiet as they studied unfamiliar surroundings, and the only noise, besides the splash of their own feet, was the river itself, moving over the rocks.

They walked for a long time looking at the crowds of ferns, and on one side, a muddy flat where skunk cabbage grew. At a moment when they were all peering up toward the next bend, a little bird came diving from a tree into the water in front of them. They startled back. Then, just as quickly, the thing emerged and fluttered up into the tree branches.

"Mom, what was that!"

"What *was* that?" said Casch. They all looked at one another, charmed.

The river world had seemed so private, so completely theirs, that Casch was surprised when they came out to a sunny curve and there was a family having a cookout. Dad was tall, wearing Bermuda shorts, holding a spatula over a charcoal grill. The wife, standing with a little girl, wore a ruby swimsuit. A bigger girl played in the water. They'd set up lawn chairs, there was an explosion of beach toys. The smell of cooking meat hit her nose and Casch realized she was hungry.

The parents had waved a polite hello. Casch herded the kids onward—such a perfect family, you know what they thought looking at her. And soon they were past.

They came to a dark pool, and as the kids bent over to look, two frogs leapt from the rocks into the water. Molly reached in and caught one in her fist, like it was the easiest thing.

"Look," she said, opening her hand, and the thing jumped away.

They stayed by that pool because Dean wanted to get one

too. By the time he'd caught his own and showed it proudly in his hands—it sliced immediately back into the water—Casch saw that his teeth were chattering.

"Dean, you're freezing," she said, and now she noticed his lips turning bluish.

"No, I'm not."

"Baby, you're shivering."

"No."

"It's time to turn around," she said, taking his hand, and this time he didn't protest.

But when they started back, the riverbed seemed less forgiving than before. Casch's feet were raw against the slick rocks, and Dean slipped around and held tight to her hand. Though she had been grateful for the shade when they'd set out, now Casch felt a chill under her wet shirt. She glanced at Molly, who was no longer looking for birds but just plodding ahead, staring at her own feet.

They came to the other family and Casch wanted to hurry by. But the pretty mother had looked at Dean and frowned. "Does he need a towel?" she'd asked.

"We have towels back this way," said Casch. "Thanks, though."

"No, please, take one. Look, we have a whole stack."

And the woman had unfolded a striped beach towel, luxuriously thick, and walked out into the water to wrap it around Dean's shoulders.

"You keep it, we have a million," she said.

It was a while still before they rounded the last bend—Casch couldn't believe how far they'd gone—and saw the covered bridge up ahead. Her van, its rusted wheel wells covered in duct tape, was the only car. At once both kids said how hungry they were. Of course they'd been hungry all along, but they had not complained. The three of them grabbed their things and hustled up the path. It felt good to climb in the hot airless car, and they went zooming home for food.

They had not gone swimming again after that. The kids started school; August turned to September. But they still had that coral-and-white striped towel in the pile in the bathroom, making all the other towels seem crummy and thin.

Out in the backyard now, there was a tapping sound.

"What's that?" said Molly, lifting her head from the grass. She sat up. The sound came again, like a drumroll. Casch watched her daughter peer into the trees.

"There," Molly whispered. "There, Mom, look."

She pointed but at first Casch didn't see. Then her eye caught the splotch of red and the black and white stripes of the bird in the tree.

"I see it," said Casch softly.

"Where?" said Dean.

"Right there, baby," she said, pointing. Molly lay back down. For a minute the three of them listened to the bird hammering its beak into the tree.

"Does it live here, Mom?" said Molly.

"I—don't know."

"I think it does, I think it lives here." Molly sat up again and reached for her notebook.

"What are you doing?" Casch asked, rolling her head to look.

"I'm adding it to my map."

———

It was a Friday afternoon when Casch tossed the overfull trash bag into the dumpster on the north side of the apartment complex and stood for a second, watching steam rise off the rear of the county jail that was just uphill from Greenfield Terrace. Then she climbed back in the van, engine running, and drove a couple seconds to the mailboxes. Hers was stuffed— electric bill, notices from the kids' school. And a long envelope from Greenfield Community College.

Her pulse spiked. They already—?

She tore it open. *Dear Casch, We are delighted to inform you—*

Shut the fuck up!

She jumped in the van, drove four seconds. Back in the apartment, she called Gabi.

"GUESS WHO GOT INTO NURSING SCHOOL."

"Of *course* you did," said Gabi, and Casch could tell she was smiling.

Next she called Marylouise—her mother's friend had helped her with the application, she should be the next to know. Years ago, Marylouise had been the only person who'd said anything kind when Casch was pregnant with Molly, and Casch still remembered: If anyone can do it, it's you.

The machine picked up. Of course Marylouise was sleeping, she was an overnight nurse.

"I GOT INTO NURSING SCHOOL," she gasped, then tossed the phone aside. Just recently Marylouise had told her that seeing her with Molly and Dean was how she knew Casch would be a great nurse. And she had given her a tattered softcover book, *Folk Medicine and the Spirit of Nursing.* Casch had opened the book to the middle and read one passage: *The human body has all the elements it needs in order to heal, if given the right conditions. Intuiting what those conditions are for each patient is a central inquiry of nursing.* Casch had read that same bit over and over. When she knew it by heart, she shut the book and put it away.

Now, standing over the couch, she shadowboxed, a jab and a punch. She, Casch Abbey, was going to nursing school.

She was standing outside grinning when the kids got off the bus.

"How was school, you guys? What happened today?"

She accepted the featherweight Spider-Man backpack that Dean pressed into her hands.

"Nathan peed his pants," he said.

"Okay."

When they got in the house she said, "Hey, guess what?"

"What?"

"What?"

"Mom got into nursing school!"

"You're going to be a nurse," Molly nodded, like it was settled.

When it was time to make dinner, Casch brought her old clock radio into the kitchen and flipped it on. You need music, tonight you need to jam. And they needed something good for dinner.

She stared into the empty fridge, at the wilted iceberg that was turning orange along its spine. She looked in the cupboards, at the cans of soup, at the crumbs scattered across the old floral shelf liners that were curling at the corners. She went back to the fridge. There was a jug of milk with a couple inches in the bottom. She took off the cap and smelled it.

Then she was lighting a cigarette and making biscuits. There was a little flour, there was a thing of Crisco, she was pouring sour milk into a bowl and making batter.

She and Molly and Dean ate the biscuits around the table that night with steaming bowls of chicken noodle soup, little bits of carrot floating in the oily broth, while the radio crackled.

After the kids were asleep she read the entire letter about *Twenty-First Century Nursing*. The color brochure had a glossy picture of a cluster of girls in pine-colored scrubs outside on a sunny day, their arms linked.

There was an intimidating list under ACADEMIC PROGRAM – ASSOCIATE IN SCIENCE – NURSING (NUR), which Casch did not look at, because, Jesus. And there was a back page, Philosophy. *Patients are physical, intellectual, and spiritual beings. It is impossible to separate the person from the environment. Health and illness are dynamic and ever-changing; they are separate but co-existing.* She read that several times. Then she noticed a card tucked inside a preprinted envelope.

Return with $200 deposit (non-refundable).

She stared at it. Of course there was a deposit. What did you think, it was free? Slowly she slid the card back into the envelope and pushed it aside. Last time she checked, she had fifty-eight dollars in her Greenfield Savings Bank account.

Why did she tell the kids? She wished she hadn't told the kids. You're not sending in any deposit. You'll never be a nurse.

Where were her meds? From the plastic bottle she shook two round yellow tablets into her palm and swallowed them dry.

"CONGRATULATIONS," said a voice the next evening, soon as Casch picked up the phone.

"Oh, hey, Marylouise. Thanks, yeah, it's not really—"

28

"I am so proud of you!" said Marylouise.

"Well we'll see what happens," she said, glancing at the door to the kids' room. She had just tucked them in.

"What do you mean, we'll see what happens?"

Casch slipped into her own room and shut the door.

"Honestly I'm not sure I'm even gonna do it."

"Not sure you're gonna do it! Why on god's green earth not?"

"Well for one thing they're asking for a $200 deposit. And I can't work right now, with my foot—"

"It's on me."

"What?"

"It's on me, girl. Let me put up the two hundred."

Casch, her back to the shut door, stared at her bedsheets and her old comforter, the color of wine, that had fallen to the floor.

"You, uh. Really?"

"You bet. In fact, it's an honor. I'd invest in you any day."

Casch felt the words in her chest.

"Thanks—thank you."

"You know I work nights, I'm about to head to the hospital now, matter of fact, so most of the time I'm asleep during the day. But we'll make a date when I have a weekend, okay, and you come over for a cup a coffee?"

"For sure. Thanks, Marylouise."

Casch hung up and held the phone to her chest.

"Holy fuck I am going to nursing school."

Her voice was a whisper but she wanted to shout it. That would wake the kids. She wanted to jump—get up and jump on the bed—but her stupid foot. She looked at it. Then plopped down on the carpet and pulled off the plastic boot.

"Screw that thing, I am done with that thing. I am going to nursing school. I'm going to be a nurse. A *healer*.

"And when I'm a nurse, I'm going to buy a house. We're going to live in a real house.

"Holy fuck."

Celebrate. She had to celebrate.

Slowly she got up and took the Lugz shoebox off the top shelf of the closet. Opened it on the floor and was reaching for the toy when she saw the twist of tinfoil.

That weed. From that guy.

She peeled back the foil and whiffed the big smell. Then set it on the bedside table.

From the box she lifted out the purple plaything. Haven't used this in a while. When she pressed the button to test it, she found it was dead. Oh, c'mon.

Luckily a little switcheroo—the batteries from the TV remote—did the trick. She flipped off the lights and spread her body over the bedsheets. For a minute she lay in the dark. Things were maybe going to be okay. Everything, maybe, was going to be all right.

She licked her fingers. And when she started, she went achingly slow.

Afterward she lay in bed, hands on the warm skin of her shoulders, and let out a long sigh. She didn't know when she'd last done that—and how much longer since she'd touched anyone else.

She rolled to her side. And saw the glint of the foil-wrapped reefer.

She hadn't rolled a cigarette in years, but when she turned on the light and went rummaging in the bottom of the shoebox, she found an old orange sleeve of papers. She settled in bed with *The Berenstain Bears God Bless Our Country* in her lap and pinched tacky bits from the bud into a line on the little paper. This stuff was so sticky—she'd never had weed like this. It left a shine of resin on her fingertips, like syrup.

She smoked with her shoulders resting in the pillows. I am going to nursing school. She blew smoke at the ceiling, at the swirly watermark in the corner. Then looked at the joint. This is good weed. This is really good weed.

You never used to get stuff like this, she thought, it used to be dime bags of shake. In high school kids had done anything they could get their hands on—blackberry brandy, Captain Morgan. Shitty weed that was half oregano. Hell, cough syrup. A lot of those people never eased up. They drank hard in high school and kept drinking hard afterward. But Casch knew how to take it easy; she wasn't going to be like her mother.

That one bud had to be practically an eighth by itself, she thought, looking at it. And that guy had just given it to her, no big deal. Yet she hadn't gotten the feeling he was trying to get anything from her.

And somehow he'd gotten her to box, in the middle of everything. Unlike her to do that. Not that anyone noticed, people don't care what other people are doing—there was some wisdom right there. That's why it's pointless to worry what other people think, they're not even thinking about you is the truth. Except you always forget that right when you need to remember it the most.

You're going to be a prizefighter, he had said, after putting down a tip as big as his bill. In her mind she saw him standing in front of her like he had more to say but wasn't saying it.

And when she told him she was applying to nursing school—that was unlike her, too, blurting out her business—his look was so earnest. Good luck, he'd said.

She smiled. Well, that worked out.

And didn't he send her a message? She'd never replied. She patted around the sheets for her phone.

hi its topher really liked meeting u

She took another pull on the joint.

hi its casch do u remember me

4

The sun was high over the mountain by the time they'd gotten everything up to the field and started planting. In his own row, out of earshot from Connor and Tory, Topher fell into a rhythm. Slice shovel into soil, loosen sapling from container, kneel to the ground. Before placing the plant into the earth, he untangled the roots that had hit the plastic bottom and grown around in circles.

That last part was important; you can't leave the roots stifled like that. The plants are alive, they're breathing. They have to know there's room to grow. Once you've pulled off the tangles and roughed up the root ball—so it's ready to spread out and take nourishment—*then* you lower it into the ground.

He sat back on his heels and wiped his forehead with the side of his wrist. He was facing west-southwest, sun off his left shoulder, looking up toward a spruce-covered crag. At their highest point, the Green Mountains only rose to about 4,000 feet. But if you walked due west from where he was sitting, you'd hit the Appalachian Trail. From there you could hang a left and follow it all the way to Georgia. Or, hang a right, go a couple hundred miles, you'd get to Mount Katahdin, Maine. Topher had never done either.

He stood and paced out three feet, then sliced the shovel

into the ground. Grabbed the next plant and shook it gently from its container. This one was smaller than the last; roots hadn't hit the bottom. He tried to keep the root ball intact as he gently transferred it to the ground. If Gram were alive she wouldn't mind him growing weed—I don't need the man telling me what I can or cannot grow, she'd say something like that. But he wouldn't let her know the extent. She was tough but she would worry. Early this morning, after they'd unloaded the plants at the gate and Connor and Tory went to move the cars, Topher had waited, crouched by some mountain laurel. And suddenly a green police cruiser had come crunching along the gravel.

Topher's pulse had spiked. Why was a cop way out here? His neck had gotten hot; he prickled with sweat. That cop had to be driving backroads till the end of an overnight shift, that's what Topher figured. Had to be killing time. Still, he had let out a breath when the cruiser disappeared. From that spot on the gravel road, an access trail skewed off behind a rusted gate with a weathered sign that said Private. You follow it far enough, and bushwhack a little, eventually you'd hit this field. But no one came out here. It belonged to a guy with a New York address—Topher had looked it up. Land deeds are public info; Gram had taught him that.

Gently he filled soil around the plant's stem and patted it nice and firm.

By eight that night they were sitting shoulder to shoulder at Shea's, draining a pitcher. Dim lights hung low over the bar, a single TV flashing local commercials. Topher sat facing an old framed *Sports Illustrated* cover of Robert Parish.

"Solid," said Tory, "solid day."

"No doubt," said Topher, having a cold swallow. "Hey, actually, I've been meaning to tell you guys," he said quietly, setting the glass down, "we got a new customer, I got money for you."

"Oh, you were trying to hold out on us?" said Tory, winking.

"Shut your mouth," said Connor, "you know you're lucky Topher cuts you in as much as he does."

"I'm just kidding. Anyways I've told you a million times I'd make city runs."

"I would too," said Connor, glancing at Topher.

"Nah don't worry about it," said Topher, though he liked that they always offered. Obviously Tory didn't have the smarts to do it, and if Connor ever got popped for dealing, Topher would never forgive himself. Connor's mom was the closest thing to a mother Topher had, and he wasn't going to repay her by letting her son be the mule. He was going to handle it himself. He liked it, actually.

"Business is good," he said softly, glancing at the TV, "and you know the way to keep it good is by keeping your head down."

"Oh, here comes the lecture," said Tory. Connor punched him in the shoulder and then rose from his stool, crossing the checkered linoleum to the bathroom. Topher and Tory watched the start of the Sox game as they drank down their beers.

"Michaela is asking if you're single," said Connor when he sat back down.

"Me? Or Topher?"

"Who do you think?" said Connor.

Topher didn't say anything.

"What should I tell her?"

"You should say sorry but Topher's trying to set a personal record for how long since he's been laid," said Tory, leaning in front of him, "and his previous record was like two years."

"Shut up."

"There's nothing wrong with being picky," said Connor, pouring out the last of the pitcher.

"Michaela's not bad."

"Not my type," said Topher.

"Oh yeah, what's your type?"

"Oh I know," said Connor, "the chick in the army, right? The mechanic?"

"I never heard that," said Tory, looking at Topher.

"There was no one in the army."

"Yeah there was, you told me—"

"There was no one in the army."

"Whatever, let him be pissy," said Tory. "My only question is like, why do girls hit on him? Helloooooooo, does anyone wanna give Tory some love?"

"Good luck with that," Connor laughed.

"Oh, you think you're the expert because you've had the same girlfriend since you were twelve? That makes you the opposite of an expert."

"Whatever you say."

"All right then, you tell me," said Tory, "what's my problem?"

"Your problem is that you're a dipshit."

"Thanks."

On his hip, Topher's phone vibrated. He slid it out and looked at the screen.

"Look at that, more orders coming in right now," said Connor. "I'll drink to that."

"Hey, you know we got another big day tomorrow," Topher said, shifting to put his phone away. "What do you say we finish this beer, call it a night?"

5

He remembered what he'd thought when he first saw her, she's one of these that's pretty without putting in one ounce of effort. Her tits in the black V-neck hadn't hurt. He had suggested they go for a walk—only problem was, he didn't know Greenfield, he didn't know the trails.

He'd texted, Where's a good spot? And she said Poet's Seat, the stone tower above the ballfields. She was right; this place was perfect.

Topher peered out the window of the Ranger toward a cluster of black birch, then leaned to look up at the tower. His foot strummed the floormat.

He remembered how she'd gotten low and swiveled, the apron bunching around her waist before she threw the first jab, and he had noticed that she made one mistake. She looked down at her own fists, instead of keeping her eyes up to watch her opponent's next move.

He took out his phone to check the time. But right then a busted old van with tape on the wheel wells came rolling up the dirt road. He saw it was her and felt a shot of nerves. He climbed out and stood there, casual. Look at that rattletrap, he thought, and loved that that was what she drove.

Her door swung open and her feet appeared, the laces of her Timberlands undone.

"Hey!" he said.

"Hey," she said as she slammed the door, and for a second they stood looking at one another. Then she smiled and pointed at his phone holster.

"Are you a drug dealer from the nineties?"

"Listen," he said, smiling, but he had no rejoinder. There was a beat of silence.

"There's a trail that goes out that way, we could try it?" he said. "I checked the map, there's a stream, it could be nice."

"Sounds good," she nodded, peering at him, smiling from her eyes—honey-brown, no makeup.

But when she took a couple steps, he double-taked at her. Something was wrong.

"You okay?" he said. He wanted to offer his hand but held back.

"I broke my foot, some jerk drove over it."

"Are you sure you want to go for a walk?" he asked, forehead creasing.

"Yeah, I've got to start waitressing again, might as well get back in shape."

"You're sure?"

"I'm sure," she said, like no big deal, like it was no problem whatsoever to hike on a busted foot. Just like Gram.

There was a yellow blaze on a beech tree and they set out. Late-afternoon sun filtered through the canopy, the flute song of a wood thrush echoing overhead.

"Who's with your kids?" he asked, hands in his pockets.

"They're with my mom for a couple hours. Molly actually got invited to a sleepover but didn't want to go."

"No?"

"No, and she's a great kid. I don't understand it. Add that to the list of things to worry about."

"I can tell you're a good mom," he said, his eyes on the ground ahead of them. She laughed.

"What?"

"If Molly was out here with us, she'd know some of the plants and she'd be all asking me about ones she doesn't know. And I have to be like, oh sorry baby, you're ten years old and you're already smarter than me."

"You don't have to know plant names to be a good—"

"That's not—"

"But here's a cool one," he said, stopping and squatting down to reach a finger under a tiny flower. He propped it slightly so that she could see.

Then he watched as she bent and really looked at the blossom. It was only the size of his thumbnail, its tiny yellow petals curling back toward the stem.

"I wouldn't have noticed that," she said, hair slipping from her ponytail and falling forward into her eyes.

"See the speckled leaves? That's how you know what it is, it's a trout lily. And actually, would you look at that," he murmured, his chest thumping—he was close enough to smell her cigarettes. He stood up and took a couple steps off the trail. "These are wild ramps!"

He plucked a leaf and tore it in two. "They're spicy," he added, popping one piece in his mouth and offering the other to her.

"Yeah?" she said, looking at him curiously before accepting the gift from his outstretched hand.

When they got back to the parking lot they stood dawdling.

"Hey that weed you gave me was amazing," she said. "Thanks for that."

He brightened. "Glad you liked it."

"Like the best I've ever had."

He grinned. "Aim to please."

"Do you want—do you have any with you?"

"You're pretty much not going to catch me without it."

"Want to smoke?" she said.

"10-4."

They climbed in the Ranger. He had parked so its nose faced the view over Greenfield, and as he arranged the grinder and paper on the gazetteer in his lap, he saw she was looking out at the town below.

"Did you say you're from White River?" she asked, turning and watching him lift the paper and start rolling.

"That's right, you remembered."

"I—yeah. And what do you get up to up there?"

"I do a couple different things. I drive organic produce down to New York. Rich people will pay anything for it."

He glanced at her and they both smiled.

As his hands worked she seemed to study the old truck's interior. He looked at what she was looking at, the dash and the knobs of the radio that were polished and gleaming.

He finished and ran his tongue along the paper's edge. Sealed it with a fingertip and held finished product between right pointer and middle finger as he lifted his hips and patted his pocket for a lighter. Clicked a flame and took a couple puffs until it was lit, then passed to her.

She was quiet, gazing out the front window as she smoked. But after she passed it back, she sat watching him, watching his lips tug on the filter. They burned most of it down and then Casch was grinning.

"What?" he said.

"Nothing."

"What?"

"Nothing."

"It's gotta be something."

"Dude, I'm high as fuck."

He smiled at her and she laughed.

"This weed is ridiculous," she said.

"A hundred percent natural, from the earth."

"So this is like health food you're saying?"

"Yeah, that's right, this is like carrots and apples."

"What are you, a horse?"

He laughed and shook his head.

"No this is great because groceries keep getting more expensive, so screw eating; who needs it? I'll just smoke these greens. I'll be all set," she said.

"Maybe that's how it gets legalized? It's like a public-service announcement, eat your vegetables!"

"Smoke your vegetables!"

"Smoke your vegetables, kids!"

"Hey hey hey let's not get carried away, pusher-man, I have kids at home."

"True," he said, face dropping, "I didn't mean it like that."

"I'm just kidding," she said, poking him. "Weed is the last thing I'm worried about."

For a second they were quiet. The spot she'd touched, just below his ribs, was warm.

"You all set with this?" he said, waving the joint.

"Yeah, definitely."

He reached to the floor and plucked a Red Stripe cap off the mat, his arm grazing her black stretchy pants. He sat up and pressed the joint into the cap.

"Yeah, so guess what," she said.

"What?"

"I got into nursing school."

"What!" He swiveled to face her. "Hell yeah you did, congratulations!"

She shrugged like it was nothing, but she was smiling.

"See, I knew it when I met you at the restaurant," he said.

"Knew what?"

"That you have follow-through," he said, and mimed a punch.

"Ha."

"No, I'm serious, that's inspiring."

She laughed. "Really, inspiring?"

"Yeah. It is."

"That's gotta be the first time anyone's called me that."

"It's inspiring to see someone who's—" he stopped.

"What?"

"Building something. Instead of staying stuck where they are."

Their eyes met.

"So, when do you start?"

"Uh," she said, squinting out the passenger window, "August maybe?"

He was watching the side of her face.

"I love how you wait two hours to tell me," he said softly. "If it was anyone else, that would've been the first thing they said."

———

That night Topher drove northbound with the radio off, the evening so lit from the rising moon that he could've turned the headlights off, too.

"Gram, you would like her," he said aloud. "If you met her you'd say, 'Now *she's* smarter than the box.'"

He remembered when Gram coined that phrase. He had brought in a load of firewood and was crouched on the braided rug in front of the cast-iron stove—he could see it so clearly, he had been transferring wood to the plywood box. But one side of the box was broken. The weight of logs pressing into it had pushed out the nails. Instead of fixing it, though, Topher, maybe fifteen years old, had just loaded up more wood. Which was obviously going to break the thing even worse.

"Are you smarter than a plywood box?" Gram had asked, leaning over him, oversized denim shirt hiding her wiry frame. She just meant don't be a dumbass. Go get your hammer, bang the nails back in, then load up your wood. This isn't astrophysics. It became their saying: Are you smarter than the box? No one else knew it; it was theirs alone.

Gram was the one with the original grow operation, he thought, leaning back into the seat, a couple fingers on the wheel. Not weed, of course. But she was always outside pulling suckers off the tomatoes, guiding cucumbers up the trellis. By July every year she would start putting up the harvest—the pickles were Topher's favorite. As a kid he hadn't thought about it but of course that was how she did it. She didn't plan on her husband dying and then having to raise her grandson because her daughter and daughter's man would be the type to abandon their fourth kid, just leave him like it was vacation and never come back. But Gram did it like no problem, like it really was her plan. And it had seemed that even in mud season, after all the snow had melted and it was almost time to start planting again, there was always one more jar of Gram's tomato sauce to be requisitioned for a spaghetti dinner.

He waited a day, and then one more day, before texting her. It was at night, lying in his boxers on top of the sheets, that he pressed send and immediately wished he'd said something better.

But then he had a rush of energy, because she wrote right back. They settled on Saturday. She said he should come pick her up. And sent her address.

When he got off the highway at the Greenfield exit, he went east, the gazetteer open on the gray upholstery of the passenger seat. He passed a Dunkin' and the road started uphill. Last time, to get to Poet's Seat, he'd taken Main Street. There was a plaza with a liquor store and a check-cashing place, then one traffic light. There were little storefronts, mostly empty. Though he was always going by on the highway, he'd only been into the center of Greenfield a couple times. The place didn't have the best reputation. But to him it didn't look so different from any other place in Vermont.

Today he turned left before he got to Main Street and found himself in a little neighborhood. Up ahead was a sign for Greenfield Terrace. Which was a cluster of low-slung apartments, he saw, as he made the left-hand turn into the parking lot. He cruised by a grassy island with a swing set, one swing gone from the end of its chains. There was a shopping cart abandoned to the curb.

And there was her number, and her van right there. He pulled in beside it. His heart quickened as he went to her door and knocked on the vinyl.

She opened it immediately, slipping out to the step so quickly that he didn't see inside.

"I bought us some time," she said. "My mom's taking the kids shopping in New Hampshire."

He felt a ripple of anticipation. "Oh, yeah?"

"Yeah, and I'm showing you a locals' spot today, okay? But you gotta keep it a secret," she said over her shoulder, already walking to his truck.

"I am excellent at keeping secrets," he said, running around to the driver's side.

"I believe that about you."

They climbed in and he fired the engine. "Where am I going?"

"Left out the parking lot."

He stole a look at her. Her cheeks were full and flushed and she was wearing a gray sweatshirt, like you'd wear to the gym, with an upside-down triangle at the neck.

When they came to a blinking light at a T, she had him turn right. They passed an old lot where it looked like a building had burned down, and then a place—not much more than a shack—with a cursive sign that said Bintliff's.

"Strip club," she said, looking at it as they went by, "people call it porn in the corn."

After that it was just farmland. A pickup truck passed them going in the opposite direction, a Confederate flag mounted to its rear and flapping in the wind. Topher glanced at her and they made eye contact.

A few more minutes and she had him make a left on a dirt road. Trees closed around them. Up ahead was a covered bridge.

"Pull over here," she said.

"That foot bothering you?" he asked when they got out.

"A little. It might have been dumb to go hiking on it. But that's why we're here, we don't have to go anywhere else." She gestured toward the river. "Come on."

They settled on a flat rock. Beneath their feet the clear water poured over pebbles, and across the way was thick green sumac and one speckled alder tree.

"This is where I take the kids swimming. I figured I needed some sort of cool spot to bring a guy like yourself," she explained, smiling without meeting his eyes.

He grinned. "Oh yeah, what sort of guy is that?"

"Knows plants and shit."

His eyes closed for a second. When he opened them, he wanted to touch her hair.

"How do you know about that stuff anyways?" she asked.

"Just grew up with it. My Gram was big into gardening, always growing something."

"And now you're the one always growing something."

"What do you mean?"

"Weed."

He blinked at her. "Oh. Well. Just don't, you can't be telling anybody that, okay?"

"I am excellent at keeping secrets."

He looked at her.

"I believe that about you," he said.

When they climbed back in the Ranger, he drove the gravel road and turned back the way they'd come. The radio was on low, just a bass thumping softly.

"That was it, you were supposed to turn there," she said, pointing, looking at him.

"Oh," he said, meeting her eyes, "what street is this?"

"Silver."

He kept going.

"The high school's over there," she said when they passed a turnoff with a sign.

"High school suck as much for you as it did for me?" he said.

"I'm not trying to remember it," she said.

They came to an intersection and he turned right.

"Federal," he said, reading the sign. They passed a big gas station, and across the street a huge brick building with boarded-up windows.

"That's the old silver factory," she said.

"The silver factory isn't on Silver Street?" he asked, looking at her, and again their eyes met. She was watching him. Probably wondering where he was taking her.

They went by a pharmacy and a funeral home and an Elks Lodge, and when they came to Main Street he turned right. He could feel her watching him. When he got to the plaza with the check-cashing place and the liquor store, he flipped on his blinker.

He parked and turned off the truck. The engine made a clicking sound as it cooled.

Suddenly Topher turned toward her. He slid a hand behind her seat and grabbed the dented gallon jug, mostly empty, and drank a few swallows of water.

"You want?" he said, offering it out to her.

Slowly she took the jug. A couple drops dribbled as she drank. When she had finished, he reached and gently wiped her chin with his thumb.

"Are we driving around in circles?" she said softly.

———

She led him by the hand through her living room.

"Don't look, my place is disgusting," she said.

"I don't see a thing," he said, and she looked away smiling as they rounded the couch and she pulled him into her bedroom. This is happening, please let this happen, she thought as she pressed the door closed. Please don't be an asshole. She turned and he was there, pushing back strands of her hair with the side of his hand and kissing her with warm lips. He pulled her sweatshirt over her head and she reached for his T-shirt, and when it came off she saw there was a tattoo on his ribs and a chain around his neck. He sat on the edge of the bed and pulled her into him and stroked her cunt with a knuckle. She was already so wet. Can you be too wet? So wet it's embarrassing. Like, someone lay this chick already.

She leaned to kiss him just as he reached up to touch her face, and he accidentally knocked her in the chin.

"I'm sorry! Shit, that was dumb," he said, touching her jaw with a thumb, "I'm sorry."

"No prob," she murmured, looking at him. She saw how much it mattered to him—that he didn't want to mess this up.

"What's this one?" he asked afterward, running his finger down her bare arm to the three dots inked inside her wrist.

"It's homemade, a friend did it. In high school," she said.

He nodded, gazing at her.

"The first time Molly ever asked me about it, I was like, it's three dots for the three of us, see? It's you, me, and your brother.

I was just making that up. But now I'm like, maybe that really is it, you know? I just didn't know it at the time. Three dots for my little family."

He closed his eyes. Under the sheet, his legs were warm against hers.

"Is this your only one?" she asked, touching his ribs, her fingertips grazing the dates branded there.

"Yeah." He looked down at it. "That's for my Gram, the day she was born and the day she died."

That night, after the kids were in bed, Casch sat on the couch sipping a Red Stripe and smiling at the muted TV. She had been feeling so good, after they were dressed and saying goodbye, that she'd pressed her nose into his shoulder, as if they'd done this a million times, and said, "I like your smell."

And his face had lifted. "What do I smell like?" he asked, his eyes holding her.

"I don't know, it's like, wood chips?"

"Sounds right," he said, grinning.

She could tell he had been nervous with her for the first time. But she had made like she didn't notice. And then they were just, comfortable. Maybe she'd never known what people meant when they said chemistry. Chemistry is when a thing you've done before feels better than it ever has.

Still, she made sure he left before Flora got back with the kids.

Casch set down the beer and reached for the pack of Parliaments, held one with her lips as she clicked the lighter.

If she could have, though, she would've had him stay. Who wouldn't want a guy like that around? You know he'd help with anything.

Imagine DCF getting wind of that, she thought, exhaling. They'd be looking him up, looking at his record. She squirmed on the cushion.

But you know what? Kids don't need some boyfriend around anyways. Long as she lived, she would never forget her mother chattering to her about Russ, suddenly everything was Russ. She would never do that to her children. See, it didn't matter. She could hang out with Topher, and the kids didn't need to know he existed. Kids can be kids.

Although Molly was getting older, you could not not notice. Her questions were getting harder. She was wanting to know more about her dad. And Casch did not want to be like Flora, and have no answers. She remembered standing in the bathroom of their old apartment, watching her mother apply jam-colored lipstick. "Let's hope Russell really likes me!" Flora had said to little Casch. Casch had nodded gravely, though she didn't understand; the question of whether *Flora* really liked *Russell* was never raised. Which confused young Casch, because in her world Mom was this mighty creature who zoomed them around cleaning people's houses and turned up the radio for all the Tracy Chapman songs so they could belt out the words together.

But then Flora and Russ were engaged, Flora and Casch were packing up and moving into his ranch. Casch had been about the age Molly was now, she was eleven when Flora got married. For his part, Russ made a big show of winning her affection.

She took a long pull on the cigarette as she felt the old rage quiver.

What could she say to Molly? The girl wanted to know about her father, we have to know who our fathers are. Molly had Carl's pretty eyes. His front teeth were crooked, but he hadn't seemed to care what anyone thought. He and Casch never talked at school; it was at a party in someone's basement—her last year of high school—that he started telling her jokes. He got in a fight later that same night. Casch heard the shouting outside the bulkhead. Afterward, Carl came back in and the two of them made out, his lower lip bleeding a little and giving a taste of metal.

Then she started going over to his place, which was here. In Greenfield Terrace. He lived with his mom in an apartment that was the mirror image of this one. When you came in the door, the bedrooms were on the right side instead of the left. For some reason his mom let him have the bigger room. Casch started coming over and they would have sex, that became their routine. One time she had a headache and asked if there was Tylenol, and he reached under the bed and offered her the plastic handle of vodka instead.

And then she, Casch, just sort of lived with them. That was her escape. No drama. One day she left Russ's house with a duffel bag. And she didn't go back until she was pregnant.

In the living room now, Casch pressed the butt into the empty coffee mug on the table and sat staring at the silent TV. She pulled her purse to her lap.

There were four round yellow pills left in the bottle and she tapped two into her palm. She had an appointment for her foot tomorrow, she could get more then.

The sound of a door opening and closing in the YMCA basement echoed all the way up to the second-floor stairwell the following morning as Casch dropped her little blue duffel in a cobwebby corner, shed her hoodie, and started wrapping her fists. It's a silly place for it, she always thought, it's dumb that the punching bag is in a stairwell. Anyone who's going to the old basketball gym has to pass right by, which always made Casch freeze up, she always paused for a second and bobbed in the corner until the person was gone. She started bobbing now. Not to avoid anyone's eyes, just to feel it. She bounced and threw a couple swings in the air. Then she reached down and grabbed the pair of cherry-red Everlast boxing gloves that she'd checked out from the front desk.

She made an exploratory jab at the bag. Then another. Then up from her hip came a punch. One, one-two. This bitch is getting laid.

Clockwise around the bag. Then counterclockwise. One, one-two. Her upper lip prickled with sweat.

Picture Russ's face, she thought, as her right hip bloomed into movement that flowed up into her shoulder through her arm and into her fist, slamming the bag.

"I win," she said.

An hour later and a half mile away, Poet's Seat Tower was visible on the hill to the east as Casch climbed out of her van and crossed the hospital parking lot.

When she finished nursing school she would get a job here, she thought, peering at the old brick building, mostly window-less. The glass doors slid open and a woman in a yellow shirt came outside folding a piece of paper. She looked up at Casch and said hello.

"Hi," said Casch. It was funny to think about: You'll be a real nurse, you got a job with benefits and everything. And maybe the nurse she saw today would become like Gabi to her, maybe they'd take lunches together. That was a strange idea. Future friends.

She passed into the warm vestibule where a stray wheelchair had been abandoned, its gray pleather backrest spray-painted GMC. Following arrows down a wide hallway, Casch checked in under the sign for Internal Medicine. In the waiting area she took a seat across from a guy in a Dee's Trucking shirt, his foot tapping anxiously. Drug test, she figured.

The nurse who called her name wore pink scrubs and brown leather clogs, blond hair pulled back neatly in a twist. "Casch is your first name?" she said, looking down at the chart.

"Yep."

She waited for the woman to look at her, but instead she turned, and Casch followed her through an open doorway down a hall to a tiny exam room.

"I'm going to take your blood pressure," she explained, pulling open a navy Velcro cuff. "You're a smoker?"

"Uh. Yeah."

"The doctor will be in shortly," the nurse said when she'd finished, and closed the door.

It was almost twenty minutes before the same doctor Casch had seen in the ER appeared, wearing a tie, looking down at a tablet.

"So, a broken foot? Let's have a look," he said. He seemed to have no memory of ever seeing her. "Stand up for me?"

Gently Casch slid off the table, ripping its protective paper.

"On the pain scale—are you familiar with the pain scale one to ten—how much do you hurt?"

He hovered the electronic pen over the device, waiting to tap her answer. On his left wrist, Casch saw, was a large gold watch. She stood silent for a second. This guy wants me to give my pain a number. How much do I hurt—which pain are you talking about? The foot?

Or are you talking about the pain of maybe losing my kids? she thought, looking off to the side. Or, ha, the pain of being so broke I start looking for butts on the sidewalk that maybe have a little left on them—is that what you want a number for?

Or you want to go way back? she thought. You want me to pick a number for Russ? For Mom choosing him, my stepdad, over me? Or we can go all the way back. My dad abandoning me and Mom, you want a number for that?

"Do you understand the question?" asked the doctor. "On the pain scale, which is a scale that goes from one to ten, with ten being the worst—"

"Eight and a half," she said.

He looked up. "Are you having trouble sleeping?" he asked.

"Of course I'm having trouble sleeping; did you hear what I said? I'm in pain."

He used the pen to write something on the little device and he didn't look up again. "I'm increasing your dose to thirty milligrams, come back in four weeks," he said.

"*Thank* you," she said.

6

The early morning was cool but humid as they hiked single file to the field, ovenbirds and red-eyed vireos talking in the canopy overhead. Connor led the way, shaggy hair waving out from underneath his backward hat, followed by Tory, the square of his wallet visible through the worn back pocket of his jeans. Topher was bringing up the rear. Each of them carried a backpack loaded with supplies—and this was the moment of truth. They had finished planting three days ago. Now were the little guys okay? Last night he'd woken up thinking maybe they hadn't watered enough, maybe all hundred plants would be shocked and wilting.

They moved at a good clip, but their footfalls were quiet in the wet leaves. Connor turned right off the old jeep road and they started uphill, Topher's eye catching a spotted newt crawling away. Spring was hands down the best season in the woods. The birds were noisy, building nests. Plus you had wildflowers everywhere. A minute ago he'd seen a huge striped jack-in-the-pulpit. By summer those would be gone, the forest floor would be all ferns and skunk cabbage.

They trooped into an aspen grove, sunlight filtering through the young leaves. There was a noise in front of them and the guys startled back as a ruffed grouse beat its wings and lifted off. Tory mimed his finger on a phantom trigger. Then they kept on, toward the last uphill stretch.

Topher watched Connor and Tory pass through the gap in the stone wall and stop at the edge of the field. Here we go, how do we look? He held his breath as he stepped into the sunlight. And he saw that the long rows were bright green, their foliage fluttering. His fear dissolved.

"Holy crap, they're happy," said Connor softly.

Topher stepped forward and knelt at the first row. You could see there was already the beginnings of new growth, they were already budding new leaves. Thanks for all this space, they were saying. Thanks for the super-rich soil. You are so welcome, Topher thought. Actually, thank you.

"Celebration round," said Connor behind him, and Topher stood. With wide fingertips Connor packed a glass bowl whose pattern was red and orange swirls, like a lollipop. He hit it first and passed to Topher, who passed to Tory.

Then they went up and down the rows, trimming off the lowest leaves. That told the plants to grow taller and helped prevent mold. They mostly didn't talk while they worked, which is one way to know you have the right team. Of course they could have grown more—outdoor and indoor both—if they had more than three guys. But don't bring in any motherfucker you can't trust completely. When Topher first got back to Fort Benning, Connor was the only person he called. He had finished his medical evals and was up against his ETS date. He had to decide, was he going back to Vermont? That was when he phoned Connor, from a windowless hallway on base, and Connor's mom picked up.

"Oh, honey," Lynn had said when he told her who it was.

"I'm coming home," he said to Connor when she gave her son the phone. "I'm flying into Burlington."

"I'll meet you there," he replied, no hesitation.

When Topher got off that plane, in uniform for the last time, Connor and both his parents were waiting with a home-made sign. Topher hugged Connor, shook his dad's hand, hugged Lynn. It was hugging her that almost made him cry.

"You're staying with us," she said, "you hear? You're coming home and staying with us."

He and Connor had worked for the same roofing company after high school, the summer before Gram died. One day it was the two of them and one other guy up on asphalt shingles in ninety-something degrees. The other guy ran his mouth the whole time, talking shit about the boss's son who was going to take over the business. Topher hardly said a word, that was his usual. But Connor didn't say anything, either—he kept his head down and worked till the job was done. That was how Topher knew about Connor.

So it was Connor and his dad who had driven him to Rutland when he'd shipped out for basic training; Gram had died only months before. The cabin had been repo'd by the bank. At that time there was a recruitment office in the strip mall, where the Verizon store was now. Topher signed the papers and had to pick his MOS.

"Where would I—be needed?" he'd said. He didn't have a clue.

The intake officer had nodded his dimpled chin and said, "11-B. Infantry."

Every new recruit Topher met at basic said they wanted to make a difference. Some people wanted to make a difference and also pay for college. It was crazy because, only a few weeks before that, Topher had nothing. No one and nowhere to go.

Now he had a career. Right at the beginning, he felt sort of bad for people back home. They didn't know that they didn't have to work at Subway. They didn't have to be sandwich artists.

But then in basic your job is just to endure shit you can't control. One of the first mornings a kid slept through cleaning duty and the drill sergeant made him stand in the bathroom and point into the mirror and say, "You're a moron." Then he had to point back at himself and say, "No, I'm a moron." He had to keep on like that for two hours, "You're a moron, no, I'm a moron. You're a moron, no, I'm a moron." Topher and three others did push-ups for laughing.

He remembered one night late in basic when they had to do an obstacle course with a final stage that required zip-lining from a tower. There were a couple drill sergeants up there, one of them putting a harness on each recruit. At the top of the tower, waiting his turn, Topher watched the kid in front of him. The drill sergeant who was doing the harnesses got distracted and started yelling at guys down below, while the other DS yelled at the kid to step forward and jump. This was after like nine weeks of being screamed at, trying to follow every order. And that kid actually stepped forward to jump. Topher saw it and almost cut out of line to pull him back. But the DS did it first, grabbing the kid's arm, asking what the fuck he was doing. He'd almost stepped off a thirty-foot ledge with no harness. He could have been paralyzed.

But then you're done with training. You're infantry now. Before you touch down at Bagram, you get a look at the Hindu Kush. These are not the Green Mountains.

In the field now, he trimmed away the small yellowish leaves. With his thumb he flicked one that got stuck in the clippers.

He remembered getting briefed on their first assignment as

the sun broke over a slate-gray horizon. His team had waited hours, standing out in the airfield in a hot wind. He remembered hearing over the radio, IED, medevac, some guy was a triple amputee. He got so scared his legs shook. You can't turn back at that point. Not that he would have. They had loaded into the Chinook, lifted off, and he had looked around at the other guys. Alex, sitting across from him, had told Topher a few weeks ago that he was his family's fifth generation in the service. Topher had said softly, "That's cool you know your history like that, I don't even know my mom." Sitting to Topher's left was Josh, who had a tattoo that said Fuck Em All. This was a guy who had gotten on his nerves from the second they met. But now they were less than forty miles from their AOR, fear heaving in his chest, and Topher had this rush of clarity, I would die for these guys. It was strangely beautiful, I would even die for Josh. But then what happened, months later, was that Josh died anyway. Alex and Topher shipped home together.

The trimming didn't take long, and he and Connor and Tory put away their clippers and grabbed the red water jugs. This was how they were going to have to do it the whole summer, filling up at the stream. Ideally they would have run hoses right to the field and let gravity do the work, but that would require the field to be at a location down-mountain from the stream, which isn't what they had. Next year they would come up with a better system—maybe a water tank with slow drip—but this year it was five-gallon jugs. If they messed up on anything, it was going to be the watering.

But there was no reason to think they would mess up. The three of them had had more successful batches, mostly indoor and some outdoor, than Topher could even remember at this point. When he'd first come back to Vermont he had slept on

Connor's floor, on the foldout cushion thing that Connor's older brother called the flip-and-fuck. For a while all Topher did was sleep, for weeks he slept all day. At night they went to parties in the woods with people from high school, and Topher hardly said a word. But there was weed.

After a couple months of sleeping and smoking, Connor got him a job with the landscaping company where he worked, and they built stone patios together. Eventually Topher moved into his own apartment and right away he started growing weed in his closet. Just for personal use. But that spring he and Connor asked Tory—Connor's cousin, a couple years younger— if they could put a grow tent in his parents' old barn. That was the beginning. A black tent, twelve plants, and a yield of more than a pound off each one.

It was slow filling the water jugs. When Topher had his as full as he could get, he started back to the field. A gallon of water weighs eight pounds. Five gallons weighs forty. Forty pounds in each hand, eighty pounds of water.

It was spring, the end of rainy season, his first weeks in Afghanistan. On patrol outside of Nakhonay he saw a man and two boys working a field, harvesting and slicing green pods. Before that, Topher had always pictured opium as the flowers themselves. But no, the flowers produce the pods, the pods contain the milky stuff that becomes the opium. Only right at the beginning would he not have understood that. That's how cherry he was those first days—at that point he also hadn't questioned the official mission. Free the oppressed. You only have to see a couple kids blown in friendly fire, or one farmer gunned down in an apricot grove, his blood running back to the soil from where it came, for the doubt to start edging in.

He came up through the trees to the field and began watering at the southern end. He remembered coming back to base after his first time outside the wire, he remembered one morning he'd seen an armorer praying over some artillery. He had stopped and watched her touch her palms together and bow her head in prayer. He'd glanced around—was anyone else seeing this? She would get her ass teased hard if anyone was watching. But no one was. A puff of hair came untucked from her patrol cap as she prayed over an M777. He had wanted to go talk to her, suddenly he wanted to talk to her so bad. But he was a distance away, and he didn't go over there. He told himself he didn't want to interrupt because she was praying.

His platoon went back to Nakhonay after that; they camped out in the shell of an old schoolhouse. But he kept thinking about her. He spent so many hours waiting around, hot, trying to clean sand from his rifle, and he would think about her. He promised himself that when he got back to base, he would go talk to her. He thought about her at night when he was trying to sleep, this girl whose name he didn't even know. And they never met. When he finally got back there, weeks later, he couldn't find her anywhere. He tried asking after her—you know that girl armorer? But guys just shook their heads.

He was stateside for a year between deployments, or maybe it was longer, it felt longer. You're training with your unit, time trickles by. Until suddenly it speeds up. You're shipping out. The second deployment was different, there was way more confusion—why are we still here? The war was old but the insurgents hadn't lost an inch; they had resupply coming from Pakistan, they would fight forever. Official plan was to get the Afghans all trained up, let it be their war. But you could already see that when the last joe lifted out of here, the Taliban were just gonna take this bitch over.

What made the time pass was kicking it with Alex, who had a duffel bag of paperbacks on military history and would smoke cigarettes at night while he read.

"In Vietnam the medics would give soldiers morphine shots," Alex told him one time. "Not for their injuries, I mean. But just so they could deal with the war."

Topher had turned that over in his mind for a second as he nodded slowly at Alex, who had a scrappy mustache on his upper lip.

One morning after an airstrike three elders from the village came to their platoon camp. Someone got the translator, and the translator got the sergeant, who told the guys to gear up. Then the elders led them down the hillside to a house. Outside the door, three small bodies had been lain on pallets, each of them covered in a white cloth. Sergeant sent a few guys to sweep the area for weapons and told everyone else to stay with him; Topher and Alex were among those who stayed. Pausing every few sentences for translation, the sergeant apologized and started explaining what had happened, why children had been gunned down. The translator gesticulated as he spoke, sweating through his linen shirt. But the elders just looked straight ahead.

When the sergeant motioned that it was time for them to go, a man with a long white beard pointed at Alex—the only Black guy among them—and said something to the translator.

"What, what's he saying?" said Alex, looking at the translator.

"He said that you should know better," said the translator.

That night Topher and Alex had stood outside the MWR tent, the sky hazy and reddish. Alex took the last draw on his cigarette and said, "You know I told you I'm fifth-generation Army?"

"Yeah?"

"My dad's great-grandfather was the first one to serve. Born enslaved."

Alex paused.

"He enlisted as a free man. Served in the Spanish-American war."

"That's—" Topher started to say. But he couldn't figure out the words.

"My grandpa was in World War II," Alex went on, "drove a truck in Germany. And he actually didn't want my dad to enlist, because of the way Black soldiers were treated. They didn't get the same sort of support that white soldiers got."

For a second Topher didn't say anything. Then he asked, "Why did you enlist?"

"Why did you?" said Alex.

Topher stared at him. Then nodded.

Alex gestured with his chin and said, "We're in the middle of a history book right here, you know that?"

"What, what are they going to write about this one?" Topher asked.

But Alex had not answered.

Their deployment was involuntarily extended. The date they'd been counting toward suddenly dissolved, and a new date was stuck like a flag in a distant month. After they got the news, the two of them had walked away in stunned silence. They passed a guy from another team, Andrew, who lowered himself onto an overturned crate and pulled a photograph from his pocket. He had three kids. A couple other guys walking by immediately started ribbing him—put your little photo away, bud, and pull up your big-girl panties.

They had six weeks to go on the day their squad jumped an earthen wall and filed down a footpath to an abandoned town.

The temperature was way north of a hundred, everything still and silent. They passed piles of rubble, crumbling mud homes. Didn't find anything. They had just started back toward camp —Topher's mind flipped to food, to the strawberry Pop-Tart he was going to eat when they got back—when machine-gun fire opened on them. It seemed to come from every direction, so loud it rattled his skull. His hearing never fully recovered after two tours.

He emptied the last drops from the second jug at the base of a plant, grabbed the other empty jug and started back toward the stream. Connor and Tory were watering in the next row.

You come home and you keep thinking about it, that's how it goes. If he wasn't sleeping, he was thinking about it. Please stop thinking, you will go batshit if you keep thinking about it. He should've died instead of Andrew, that guy had three kids. So you roll a joint. But then you'll be stoned, you'll be sitting there, and out of nowhere you get the idea that you should write a letter to Andrew's wife. You should apologize, because you lived and he died. You're sitting there, stoned out of your head, cheeks wet, nodding to yourself. You will write her a letter, that's how you will make this right. You actually peck out a text message to yourself so you won't forget.

Later you read the message and smash your phone against the door. You coward, you can't write her a letter. She's not a dumpster for tossing away your guilt.

At the stream he squatted and dipped the jug at the place where it flowed fastest.

A lot of guys had these specific scenarios of what they were going to do when they got home. Strippers and an eight ball every night, then propose to your girlfriend and take your parents for a pancake breakfast. Most guys had families, so they figured if they could make it home then things would be okay. But Topher always knew he was returning to no one.

He remembered being at Shea's that first year back, the bartender trying to pour him a free drink. Thank you for your service. Some guy overheard and came up to Topher toting his bottle of Bud. Said he worked the line at one of the plants— Vermont had a couple of them, aerospace and arms manufacture.

"Ordnance," the guy had said, with a conspiratorial nod. "Let me buy you a drink."

"Nah, I'm okay," Topher said.

The guy had started asking questions, but Topher just shrugged, shook his head. That sort of thing used to happen all the time. Never talk to a civilian about the war. They will never understand.

He capped the second jug and wiped his hands on his pants. On the ground a few feet away, he saw some scat and bent to look. Two turds, one of them tapered to a point as fine as hair, had been dropped on the mossy crown of a rock. That right there was courtesy of a fox.

He picked up the jugs and started back to the field.

Basically you come home and spend the next four hundred days high. You think about the lies. That you're never going to make it okay. But at least what you can do now is keep your head down and grow some weed. Because fuck it.

Connor's parents knew they were growing. They didn't know the extent. But this was Vermont, everyone smokes pot. Or almost everyone. There was one time that Lynn had cornered him; he was in her kitchen eating from a box of cookies and looking at the photos on the fridge. He always looked at the one of Connor as a little blond kid with his arms around his brother.

"Toph?" Lynn had said gently.

He had swiveled around and saw how concerned she was, her forehead creased as she studied him. Lynn had a lazy eye, one eye looking slightly outward, which for some reason made him love her even more.

"Yeah?" he said, mouth full.

"Honey, I'm worried about you."

"What, why?" He wiped his face with the side of his wrist.

"Well. You know."

Pause.

"You know you're like a son to me."

He inhaled and his breath brought her words to the center of his chest.

"You don't need to worry about me, I'm fine," he said.

"I know it's been hard coming home and all. But don't you maybe want to do something else?"

"What do you mean?"

"Besides grow pot?"

He twisted the end of the plastic sleeve of cookies. It was true that he'd quit building stone patios. He was growing full-time.

"Sure, at some point," he said, shrugging, "but this is okay for now."

Her eyes searched him. "For now?" she said.

"Yeah," he said, and at last she nodded.

"Okay, honey, you know I just want the best for you."

She had hugged him and padded out of the kitchen.

At the edge of the field now, he set down one of the jugs and carried the other into the last row.

"Start from that end and we'll work toward the middle," Connor yelled, and Topher nodded.

What he wanted was to see Casch with her kids. Molly and Dean. You know families have their own ways of doing things— he and Gram had that. You have your little jokes, your own world, almost. Of course Casch had that with her kids.

You wonder, a little bit, what it's like for someone like her. Alone, raising two kids. She was tough, but who couldn't use a little help. And how many people tried to take advantage of her. He wondered about that.

7

The big Kramer Scrap sign showed in the rearview as Russ pulled out of the yard's main gate onto River Street, the late-afternoon sun high overhead. He opened the moonroof; he rolled down the windows. Hung his arm out and whiffed the perfume of a couple giant lilac bushes as he passed. He and Ronnie were meeting for an early dinner, but he had a little time to kill first.

He passed the turnoff to Poet's Seat and cruised down the hill, through his own neighborhood, then up to Federal Street. He would make a loop. He turned right and passed the silver factory.

Just a day or two ago he'd read in the paper that a developer was looking into buying that building, for purposes unknown. I'll believe that when I see it—look at that monstrosity, what are you going to do with that? After that place closed, Ronnie had spent more than a year hunting around for a job, had stooped to filing for unemployment. Russ had felt awful for his best friend, but what can you do. Finally Ronnie had put on an orange apron and went to work for Home Depot.

Diagonal from the old factory, Russ passed the Grab-N-Go. There was always a steady line of kids coming in and out of that place, a lot of them pushing baby strollers, reminding him of Casch.

When he pulled open the door that had SEVENS stenciled

across the glass, and trooped down the stairs, shoes squeaking on the rubber treads, he found that Ronnie was already there. He had a booth by the bar, a cold pint sitting untouched in front of him.

Ronnie nodded at him and looked back to his hands that were interlaced on the table.

"How's the kid doing?" Russ asked, sliding in across from him.

Ronnie exhaled from the side of his mouth.

"It's four times now we thought we got him sobered up, then come to find out he's using again."

"Ah shit man, I'm sorry."

"He's going to kill his mother, all the worrying she's doing."

"Ronnie, man, I'm sorry."

"I know you are, Russ."

Ronnie kept looking at his hands but didn't say anything else. Russ watched him for a second, then opened the menu. He read the plastic sleeve of specials.

"There is actually a piece of good news," Ronnie said, and Russ looked up.

"Yeah?"

"Yeah. They pulled the drug."

"What?"

"The drug, the pills. They pulled it."

"What do you mean?"

"They're not available no more."

"You mean—?"

"You know what I'm talking about? How Aaron got started?"

"Right, of course," said Russ.

"If you went to the doctor last week and said you hurt your back at the scrapyard, they'd have given you a 'script of it, no questions asked."

"Is that right?"

"But you know what they don't tell you?"

"What?"

"Stuff is twice as strong as morphine."

Russ's forehead wrinkled. "That can't be right," he said.

"It's not right but it's true."

"Morphine is what they give dying people."

"I know it."

"You're saying if I went in for a bad back, they'd give me pills twice as strong as what dying people get?"

"That's what I'm saying. Well, I'm saying, a week ago, they would have. But it's not available no more. You hear about the pharmacies getting robbed?"

Russ squinted.

"Down in Mass," said Ronnie. "That was for pills, they were holding up pharmacies to get those pills."

"That's—" said Russ, blinking but he didn't finish.

The waitress came and he asked for a Pepsi. Then they both ordered the dinner special, corned beef with boiled cabbage. She came back with his soda and Russ took the torn paper sleeve off the straw and rolled it into a little ball.

"Cindy found these other parents over the Internet," Ronnie said, sipping his beer. "Their kid's addicted too; they did all this research."

"What do you mean?"

"About the pills. They come from right down in Connecticut, actually, place is called Olson-Abrams Pharmaceutical. A family-owned business, if you can believe that. This woman that Cindy's been talking to, she thinks they lied to doctors."

Russ sat forward.

"Because it was just this little company. Then they come out with this painkiller, they call it a miracle drug."

"Yeah?"

"Yeah, and guess how much they're worth now?"

But the waitress arrived with their dinners, and for a while they ate in silence.

"We've been going to Al-Anon," Ronnie said, breaking the quiet, wiping his mouth.

"Really."

"You know what that is?"

"AA? Course I do."

"Not AA, Al-Anon. It's for family and friends. Of the person who's addicted. To drugs, alcohol, doesn't matter."

"Oh?"

"Yeah." Ronnie paused. "Would you ever want to come to a meeting?"

"Why would I come to a meeting?"

Ronnie didn't say anything.

When Russ finished, he crumpled his napkin and dropped it on the plate. "In AA don't they have to apologize to everyone they hurt?" he asked.

"That's one part of it. Why?" said Ronnie.

"They make you do that in your thing too?"

"Well they don't *make* you, but that's the idea. You make amends, for any harm you caused."

"Seems—like a tall order."

"That's the point," said Ronnie.

When the waitress came back, Russ said, "We'll have the key lime pie."

"Ooh good choice, boys," said the waitress, waving her pen, "that's a graham cracker crust. Two forks?"

Russ blinked at her.

"Two slices," he said.

8

Didn't miss this place, she thought, pulling open the door and whiffing the dishwater smell for the first time in weeks. She squinted in the dim interior. The manager was behind the bar.

"Whoa, Casch, how you holding up!" he said when she came over and grabbed a stool. Chris was always this enthusiastic—the servers ribbed him behind his back, asking what kind of meds he had.

"Heard you busted your foot really bad!" he said, sliding a pen behind his ear. He had red curly hair and would've been cute if not for his personality. Apparently he used to manage another 99, down in Mass, before they assigned him this place. Now he commuted an hour just to come up here, work doubles, remind everyone about every little corporate rule, like no visible tattoos. This is really what you're excited about? she always thought. Food delivered every Wednesday from the midwestern distribution center?

"I did but I'm better," she said. "I wanted to see about getting my shifts back."

His gaze dropped to the bar top where he wiped an imaginary spill.

"We did hire someone," he said.

She stared at him. "Well can you get me back on or not?"

"I've already done the schedule out two weeks, I can maybe see about getting you on after that. How does that sound?"

"Okay," she said. She waited, but he offered nothing else. She backed away.

The kids were outside that afternoon while Casch lay on the couch texting with Gabi, who said she was going straight to Chris to tell him Casch was their best person. Which was sweet, but he wasn't going to listen to her. Back in the winter Gabi had told him she couldn't work lunches during her final exams, then he scheduled her for two anyway. Of course Gabi wanted to help, Casch thought, pressing her eyes closed. But sometimes there's nothing you can even say to make things better. A few weeks back, they'd been shoulder to shoulder at the server station, Gabi grabbing a water pitcher, and she'd said quietly to Casch, "Wow, I literally never get tired of white people asking where I'm from."

Casch heard the stitch in her voice. Gabi was looking at the floor, holding the plastic pitcher with both hands. Her parents were from Mexico, her skin dark enough in white Vermont that people's eyes lingered.

"You should be like, 'The USA, have you heard of it?'" said Casch.

Gabi shook her head. "I don't need to be pissing anyone off. I just want my girls to be safe at school, you know?" she said softly.

In the living room now, Casch dropped her phone to the floor beside the couch. Then her head jerked up at the sound of a knock on the door.

No. Shit no.

Was it DCF?

Who else could it be.

Please not now. You could not pick a worse time.

Could she just let the lady knock, pretend no one's home?

But all that woman had to do was walk around back and she would find the kids. "Where's your mother?" she would say. "Are you all alone?"

Casch heaved herself from the couch and pulled open the door. And there was the perky social worker on her step.

"Hi Casch, I'm just stopping for a quick check-in, mind if I come in?"

"Kids are out back," she murmured, stepping aside and closing the door behind the woman. And she didn't even care, this time, about the grubby apartment. She pushed aside the stale blanket, and they sat down together on her couch.

She asked all the same questions as last time, and Casch gave the same answers, watching her scribble notes. She was wearing a silky shirt, Casch noticed, but the sleeves were a little too short, and they rode up her forearms as she wrote. Casch could see a tattoo on the inside of one arm, a bird with a piece of string in its mouth.

"So it sounds like everything is the same?" she said, glancing up. "No changes?"

"No."

"Then I'll just go ahead and say hi to Dean and Molly and be on my way," she said, standing up.

"Actually, wait," said Casch. "There is one thing."

The woman stopped. "Oh?" she said.

Casch felt her chest lift.

"Yeah, I got into nursing school. I'm going to be a nurse."

—

The next day, under fluorescent lights at the twenty-four-hour pharmacy on Federal, Casch watched the balding pharmacist study his computer screen. His name tag said Gerald George.

"You're sure you had a refill?" he said.

"Yeah, I'm sure."

"Well it hasn't gone through. You want us to phone you when it's ready?"

"No, I'll wait."

"Okay, then I'll call your name," he said, gesturing at two vinyl chairs off to the side and looking over Casch's shoulder to the next in line.

She sat down and watched the steady stream of people who came for their meds. One guy with a walker paid entirely with change, pulled handfuls of coins from his brown polyester pants.

Finally she got back in line.

"Oh, right," he said, plucking a sticky note off the counter, "there's an issue with this, we've had a few with this problem."

"What problem?"

"There's a freeze on this for outpatient 'scripts."

"What?"

"There's a freeze, we can't dispense this."

"Meaning, you have it? And you can't, just, give me my refill?"

"That's right, I can't."

"What if I call my doctor?"

"They can prescribe something different."

She threw up her hands. Everything was a runaround. She drove across town to the Price Chopper, where there was another pharmacy.

"Can I transfer my 'script to you guys?" she asked, holding out the empty amber bottle.

"Of course, dear," said the woman, "it should take about a half hour."

"Great, thank you."

But after the woman set the little bottle beside her keyboard and clicked into her computer, she frowned, and said, "Just one second." She disappeared past the racks of bagged prescriptions.

When she reappeared, she was shaking her head.

"I'm sorry, dear," she said. "We can't fill this. You'll have to see your doctor."

Casch, stomach hollow, stared at the woman's lined face, her pink lipstick. Were they cutting her off? The meds were the one thing that made her feel better. She would go to the hospital. She would get this figured out.

An hour later, at a desk partitioned on either side with fabric-covered dividers, a nurse in seahorse-patterned scrubs peered at Casch over reading glasses.

"This is for a broken foot?" she said.

"Yeah."

"And how is the foot?"

"Hurts."

The woman studied her.

"Pain medicine can be habit-forming," she said slowly. "Are you experiencing any cravings?"

Casch stared at the blue seahorse on the woman's left shoulder as she thought, Why would I tell you that?

"I know you got people looking for drugs," she said. "That isn't me."

"I'm going to recommend ice and ibuprofen," the nurse replied.

Eat my twat, Casch didn't say, rising from the chair.

On Saturday she woke up scratching. In an oversized Garfield T-shirt, she padded to the bathroom, and on the toilet scratched her neck and wiped her nose. She sat there with her underwear at her knees and looked at the black mold climbing up the inside of the shower curtain. She reached and pulled the curtain closed.

She was spooning coffee into the maker when Molly came out to the kitchen and said, "Mom, I'm going to plant the garden."

"Oh," said Casch, rubbing her face. "Right."

Molly had come home from school the day before with a box of garden stuff and asked if they could make a garden. "Well, I don't know, baby," Casch had said. "We can't just go digging around the apartment complex; we might get in trouble."

But Molly had taken her by the hand and brought her outside to show her how the other units had little beds. Some were by the front doors, others by the back step. Two doors down, their neighbor Miriam had pink geraniums—Flora planted those same flowers. Casch thought it was funny she'd never noticed. She had looked at Molly and half smiled.

"What?" Molly had asked.

"You're teaching your mom," she'd said.

In the kitchen now, she watched Molly tying the laces of her Reeboks.

"I'm coming too," said Dean, and plopped down to the dirty linoleum to pull on his Velcro shoes. He needed new ones, Casch saw, those were almost too small. Otis crossed from where he'd been sitting by the refrigerator, tail in the air, and purred at Dean, who stroked his dark fur. "Good kitty," he said, "good kitty."

When they had gone outside, Casch sat at the table with her

coffee. She scratched her clammy arms as morning light angled into the kitchen. But the kids came right back in, already disputing who got to do what with the garden stuff.

"Guys I can't deal with this right now," she said, closing her eyes, "I'm sick, Mommy's sick."

"Do you have your medicine?" said Molly.

Casch looked at her.

"No," she said, "I don't."

Then she went in her room and closed the door.

She felt no better on Monday. She watched an infomercial on TV about a personal injury attorney in a shiny suit. "Do you have a case?" he said, looking out at her through the screen.

"Wish I did," she said. Of course she'd thought about trying to sue the guy who ran over her foot. But someone—maybe the cop who'd shown up?—someone said the guy didn't even have car insurance. Even she had car insurance. That guy was broke *and* dumb. They'd arrested him.

Midafternoon, she went to The 99. She didn't say anything to Chris, who had papers spread out around him at one of the bar tables. She went back to the kitchen. She passed the guys in black cooks' gear who had the rock station at top volume and went all the way back to the dishwasher. Rick was in a dirty white T-shirt, towel hanging off the pocket of his sagging jeans. He had crooked front teeth that reminded her of Molly's dad.

"What up Casch," he said, pulling the washer's stainless steel lid over a load of smeared lunch plates. He glanced at her street clothes—she had never been in here in anything but her waitress blacks.

"When's your smoke break?" she said.

"Uh, I don't know, twenty minutes. Why?"

"I'll meet you outside."

She was sitting on the picnic table by the loading dock when he came out.

"Hey, maybe you can help me with something," she said.

9

"You don't have to knock, girl!" said her mother's best friend, pulling open the door of her little ranch and throwing her arms around Casch, who tensed up from the surprise embrace. She'd been sick all week, hot and cold, joints aching.

She followed Marylouise across the cream-colored living-room carpet into the sunny kitchen.

"How're things at the hospital?" she asked as Marylouise took a red mug off a hook and reached for the Mr. Coffee.

"Never a dull moment—you want cream and sugar? Actually, last night, listen to this, last night we have this older gentleman come in, thinks he's dying. Men always think they're dying. He's got abdominal pain, he's moaning, clutching his stomach. So we decide to image him. Which means we need him in a gown, right?"

"Okay."

"Then suddenly he's angry, says he's not changing his clothes. He starts cussing and telling us we're quacks."

Marylouise set two mugs out on the blond tabletop, which was lit with sunshine from the bay window, and they sat down in the wooden chairs.

"At this point, of course, the abdominal pain is secondary," she went on, "because now we're worried we've got something dangerous on our hands. So we actually, we sedate him."

"You're kidding."

"Completely serious, and when you get into this work, you'll see how you never know what's coming. So now he's sedated, and he forgets about refusing to change into the gown. We say, 'Take your boots off, sir,' and he's a lamb, he starts untying the laces. He's got the big Chippewas on, they go halfway up his calf. So he gets the boots off, the white tube socks off, and get this. *His toenails are painted red.* The whole reason he was refusing to get undressed was he didn't want us to see his feet. The man thought he was dying, for chrissakes, and still wouldn't show off his pretty red toenails!"

Casch's shoulders came forward as she laughed.

"So how are those cute kids of yours?"

"Good. Dean's at his dad's this weekend; Molly's home alone like a big girl. She'll be eleven in July."

"Hey, I have tomorrow off, what if I picked Molly up and took her for some girl time?"

"Sure," said Casch, shifting in the chair as she thought about how Molly hardly ever had time with other grown-ups. "That'd be great."

"Then it's settled. And I have a little something for you," said Marylouise, and she stood up. From the cupboard behind them she took a Chock Full o' Nuts can off the top shelf. Sat back down and with her thumb uncapped the yellow lid. She pulled out a thick wad of money, counted out ten twenties and pushed them across the table.

Casch looked down at the bills. She thought about saying, You don't have to do this.

"Thank you," she whispered.

"Girl, you're going to nursing school!"

She drove south from Marylouise's to the edge of town. Turning in at the golf course, she parked in the lot overlooking the green that spread out in the river's floodplain and watched as guys pushed around bags on wheels.

She knew she couldn't wait for The 99. She was behind on bills—she had to get a new job. She should have started looking already, but then she'd gotten sick. The only option was to go back to her old waitressing job at Sevens. There was nothing else. Sevens was where, years ago, she'd met Dean's dad.

She leaned her head back into the headrest.

Jay had been the bartender when she first started working there. He'd seemed so charming, winking at her from behind the bar. Which he treated like his personal kingdom. These days he had a job selling insurance. He had an ugly sedan.

Her phone buzzed and she grabbed it. She looked at the message and a fist-sized region in the middle of her chest lit up. She tapped her reply and started the engine.

Rick knew every weirdo in Greenfield. His message said the guy's name was Morty, and she should just go to his house, an address on Amity Street.

When she got over there not ten minutes later, she pulled to the opposite side of the street and looked at the place. A drab duplex. Somebody in there could get her meds, but not the pharmacy? She remembered the nurse judging her over a pair of reading glasses. What kind of nurse are you that you don't see I'm in pain?

The door on the left side of the duplex swung open. Casch

slipped her hands, which were sticky and cold though the day had cracked seventy, into her hoodie pockets, and watched as a mud-colored pit bull burst out the door and, behind it, a woman with a cigarette in one hand and the loop of the leash in the other. The dog lifted its leg in the grass, then turned and ran back up the steps. The woman followed, pulling the door closed behind her.

Casch was aware of her heartbeat. It was another minute before she got out and locked the car. She crossed Amity and knocked on the left door.

It opened partway to reveal a guy with acne scars.

"I'm Rick's friend Casch," she said.

"Good timing," he said, pulling it all the way open. "I'm Morty."

She followed him into a dim living room where the shades were drawn over the windows. There were two other guys standing there. No sign of a woman or dog. Without saying anything, Morty disappeared up the stairs.

Casch kept her face blank. One of the guys wore a Dolphins hat, the other a blue windbreaker and a backpack. It's fine, she told herself, these guys know Rick, everything's fine. She was about to get what she needed. She felt better already.

Morty came back down the stairs.

"If you guys were any later, I'd probably be cleaned out," he said. "There'll be a crowd here in like an hour."

"You pumping it up cause you're gonna overcharge?" said Dolphins hat.

"Fuck you, Stevie. These're thirty milligrams, thirty bucks each. If you don't like it, you can go fuck yourself."

Did he mean thirty a pill? That couldn't be right. Casch and the guy with the backpack made eye contact.

"You going for a hike?" she said.

"What?" he said.

Morty plopped into a chair and the guy took off the backpack and sat next to Dolphins hat on the couch. Casch didn't move.

Morty gestured at the other chair.

"Casch, take a seat, you're making me nervous."

"Your name is 'cash'?" said Dolphins hat.

"Yeah."

Morty opened an envelope and extracted four round yellow pills. Just eyeballing them, she could see these were the ones.

Blue windbreaker was carefully tearing a piece of tinfoil.

? thought Casch.

He rounded the foil on two sides and placed a pill in the center. Popped a short black straw in his mouth.

Oh oh oh we're *smoking* them was the headline that spooled across her mind as the guy produced a Bic and clicked a flame beneath the foil. The pill sent up a white plume, and he leaned in with the straw.

For a while at Morty's Casch felt the most beautiful thing, like she'd had the most sublime fuck and was curled up with her lover, like he loved her and they were totally connected and were drifting to sleep in one another's arms.

Except there was no lover, there was just Casch on the chair in Morty's duplex, the other guys nodding off on their own. The peaceful stupor was eventually disturbed by a knocking, quiet at first and then more insistent, and the muffled sound of a dog barking.

Casch blinked in the dimness. Morty got up and went to the door. Apparently there were other people wanting these.

And one clear thought hit her, that she needed them for herself.

"Lemme get some for the road," she said, groggy, sitting up, when it was quiet again. For once everything was simple, everything boiled down to just this one thing. Make sure you have your meds and everything will be okay.

And it was okay. Because she reached in her purse and, like a miracle, her fingers found a wad of twenties.

When she got home, Molly grabbed her hand and took her out through the back door to the garden she'd planted beside the steps. She crouched and pointed.

"See, Mom?"

Casch, hazy, looked where Molly was pointing, but at first didn't see. There was soil and little rocks. Then she saw. It was so small. But a row of somethings had sprouted.

"What is that?"

"Peas," said Molly.

Casch could see that the shoots had pushed aside clumps of dirt. The little green shoots had heaved aside the dirt in order to sprout.

"Look at that," Casch murmured. Her eyes tracked over the other plants. "Lettuce?" she said, pointing. Molly nodded. "You don't even like lettuce."

"Mom, this is different."

"What are these ones?"

"Cucumbers."

"You been watering all this?"

"Yeah."

"Look at you, girl," she said. And she did, she looked at Molly, wearing her Mickey Mouse baseball jersey, arms folded proudly over her chest. Casch's mind was humming, but Molly glowed at her through the fog.

That night the two of them had peanut butter crackers for dinner. Dean was still at his dad's and wouldn't be home until tomorrow. After they ate, Molly put a movie in the DVD player and climbed into Casch's bed while Casch took a shower. Then she stood at her dresser, brushing out her wet hair.

It crept in slowly.

She knew what she'd done. She set down the brush and got into bed beside Molly. On Monday she would go to Sevens and ask for her old job back, that's what she would do.

The money wouldn't be as good as The 99. But it was something. She would get back to working, she'd catch up on bills. Eventually she would find the money for that deposit, and Marylouise would never know the difference.

When Molly dozed off beside her, she reached for her phone and texted Topher.

She could barely look at Marylouise when she arrived in the morning. She tried to give Molly a jacket but Molly shrugged her off and followed Marylouise out the door.

She was sitting on the front step, fingers interlaced and forearms resting on her knees, when the red truck came rolling into Greenfield Terrace. She watched Topher climb out and reach for something in the cab. Then he came striding up the walk in a black T-shirt, coffees in both hands. She tried to smile as he handed her a coffee.

"You okay?" he said, studying her face. She shrugged and slowly he sat down on the step beside her.

"I was out in the field yesterday," he said after a pause, "and the plants look so happy. You get out there and it's like, they're doing what they were meant to do. Wouldn't it be amazing to feel that way?"

She nodded, swallowing a hot sip. "That's the feeling I have every time I waitress."

He looked at her and they laughed.

"You promised to keep that a secret, right? About the field, I mean?"

"I told you, I'm good at secrets."

"I trust you," he said, but that made her gaze drop to her rubber flip-flops.

When they finished their coffees, he got the weed and grinder from the truck and went inside. At first she sat with a whole couch cushion between them, watching as he rolled a joint. His hands were sexy. The palms were calloused, and there were hairlines of dirt around the nails, which he'd chewed to nothing. He worked with those hands.

After they smoked, he seemed to study the kids' school pictures that were on the wall above the TV. Dean was just starting kindergarten in that picture, Molly a third grader in her stars-and-planets sweatshirt. The cheapo frames were a little too big—Dean's picture was crooked inside it, and there was white space showing on either side of Molly's.

Casch stretched her legs across his baggy blue jeans into his lap, which for a second seemed to take him by surprise. Then, gently, Topher rested his hands on her shins.

"Oh hey, check this out," he said, shifting his weight and pulling something from his pocket. He held it out to her.

"Are you showing me—a rock?" she said, grinning at him.

"No, look at it."

She looked again.

"Oh, it's?" She glanced at him. "A heart?"

"Yeah, see that? I found it in the woods yesterday. It's for you."

He kept his hand outstretched, and she hesitated before taking the small gray stone in her fingers. It was warm. Her throat jammed, then finally she managed to laugh.

"You are the funniest person I ever met. Hey everybody, I have this new boyfriend, he brings me rocks!"

"Boyfriend?" he said, bright, looking at her.

"Well, you know. Whatever you want to call it."

"I'd be okay with calling it that."

He said it like it was the simplest thing. And she closed her eyes for a second, to remember that.

In the morning she was awake before the alarm. It was Monday, she was going to get a job. She had to go back to Sevens. That was the only thing to do.

She got the stuff off the nightstand and put her last pill on a square of tinfoil. Clicked the lighter and leaned in.

Afterward, she dropped the foil and lighter to the soft matted carpet, marshmallowy taste in her mouth, and let herself lay backward on the bed. It was a cozy feeling.

A long sigh released itself. Things were going to be okay. She was going to be working again, everything would be okay. Soon she would wake the kids. But for a while she lay like that, gazing at the ceiling.

A few hours later she parked on Station Street and walked

up the block toward Main, where the entrance to Sevens was just off the corner. She had spent years working in that dingy downstairs restaurant. She had worked there so long that the regulars got bored of grabbing her ass.

The thought of that slowed her down. If she went back, it would be the same lowlifes, and they would laugh at her. They would say, Oh, you thought you were better than this?

She glanced down the alley as she passed. The Sevens back door opened into that alley. How many cigarettes she had smoked out there you probably couldn't even count—and how many was she going to smoke there again? And, Jesus, there was Troy in his chef's gear, smoking a dog right now. He must have worked there fifteen years and was barely older than her.

"Troy?" she said, stopping.

He looked up, squinting in the sun. "Who that?"

"Casch."

"Casch, what the hell!"

She came down the alley and hugged him.

"Haven't seen you in forever, what you up to?" he said.

"Well, actually—" she started to say. And felt her face flush. Was she really going back there.

But just then a rusty Isuzu came backing into the alley. The engine cut and a guy jumped out.

"Troy, what up, bro," he said. They slapped hands and the guy opened the hatch.

"Good delivery today?"

"Course."

Troy flicked his cigarette. Casch watched as the other guy handed off a pile of steaks, individually shrink-wrapped on Styrofoam trays. Troy carried them inside. He came back out and slapped money into the guy's hand.

"That's your distributor?" she said when the Isuzu had driven off.

"You could call him that."

She looked at him.

"Would you—?" she started to say. "Would you, what if I rolled up here with a bunch of steaks, and, and, seafood. Would you buy it off me?"

Troy looked at her.

"You got inventory?" he said.

"Maybe I do."

"Well let me know, girl. I'd do business with you any day."

10

At the big Price Chopper across the state line in New Hampshire, Casch pretended to consider the giant display of Lo-Fat Ranch as she watched the cashiers. Only two checkout lanes were open. Her eyes followed customers pushing their bagged groceries toward the exit. She looked back at the cashiers. They weren't watching. No one was watching.

She went down the pasta aisle, then over to frozen. Bags of shrimp were $19.99 apiece. She tossed several in the cart. She held the freezer door open with her hip as she grabbed a bunch of salmon filets. At the back of the store, she took a pile of steaks individually shrink-wrapped on Styrofoam trays.

After she'd filled her cart, she stood for a second, staring at the pile of stuff. A lady in khaki shorts wheeled by holding the coupon mailer. Casch kept her gaze down.

It must have been obvious what she was doing; of course she couldn't afford all this. She watched the backs of the woman's pale legs amble toward dairy.

Then she looked back at her cart. She felt dirty. She would put the stuff back; she would put it all back. She reached in for the steaks.

But suddenly a guy's shoulder was in her face—he was

leaning in front of her, like she wasn't even there, and grabbing himself a rib eye.

"Sorry," she muttered, stepping back, though he didn't acknowledge her. He was wearing plaid shorts and a yellow polo shirt. She watched him walk away.

When Casch got out to the parking lot, her pulse was jackhammering in her neck. She opened the van's hatch and loaded everything in. Then pushed her cart into the cart return.

Morty let her in and disappeared up the stairs. Casch stood waiting in the dimness. A light-skinned Black woman sat smoking a cigarette on the couch. The pit bull at her feet was watching Casch.

"You wanna sit?" the woman said, gesturing to the empty space beside her.

"Oh? Thanks." She came over and offered her hand to the dog, who sniffed it and licked her palm.

"Hey, I'm Casch," she said, sitting down.

The woman rotated her head. "Oh, I thought you—" she said, and didn't finish. "I'm Jasmine."

Morty came back down the stairs.

"We got forties today," he said, opening the envelope, and Casch felt a surge of expectation.

Morty went first, then it was her turn. She leaned over the foil and inhaled the white curl of smoke. For a second it was like she stood up too fast, the blood draining from her face.

But just as quick the rush was gone, and her lips opened, the warm feeling cloaking her.

———

"Let me get some for the road," she said later, eyelids closing over tiny pupils.

"How many you want?" Morty said. He cleared his throat and sat up.

"Uh, I got, I got—" her fingers rummaged in her purse.

"These're forty a pill."

"What?" Her eyes came open. "What'd you say?"

"Forty a pill."

"They were thirty before."

"These're forty milligrams."

"Don't know how you guys afford them pills," Jasmine said, shaking her head. "You doing dates behind Bintliff's?"

"What?" said Casch, turning her head. Then she looked at Morty. "Can I get three for a hundred?"

"Did you hear what I said?"

She dispensed four precious twenties. Morty shook his head but opened the envelope. Extracted one pill and held it out to her.

"Uh? Two, that should be two," she said.

"No, you already smoked one," he said.

"I'd like to exchange this comforter for this one."

"No problem, ma'am. Do you have your receipt?"

"No, sorry."

"Okay, no problem."

The kid behind the service counter scanned the first one, then the second one.

"It looks like there's a price difference," he said. "That'll be, twelve dollars."

"Sure." She handed him the money.

"Great, you are all set," he said, tearing off the receipt.

———

"I'd like to return this comforter."

"Sure, no problem, ma'am. Do you have your receipt?"

"Yeah."

Scour the parking lot. Haven't found a receipt? You haven't looked long enough. They're there, tiny white flags caught behind a tire, or blown into the mulched island by the cart return. Got one? Go inside. Find that thing.

"I'd like to return this."

"Sure, no problem. Do you have your receipt?"

"Yep."

The phone vibrated in her hand. Automated call. Electric bill, four weeks past due. Fees accruing, service disruption possible.

Nine a.m. turns out to be a really good time. No one is watching for shoplifting first thing in the morning.

Shrimp, salmon, shrink-wrapped steaks.

Infant formula. Duh. That stuff retails for twenty bucks a cannister.

—

She parked by the loading dock behind Mix & Match, Greenfield's premier discount grocer. She banged on the back door. Nothing. Banged again.

Finally a guy pushed it open. Brown teeth, football jacket.

"Can I help you?"

"Yeah, I have a supply of infant formula, is that something you guys would be interested in?"

"Infant formula," he said.

"Yeah." She gestured toward her van. "I can grab it and show you."

"Uh, I'll come take a look," he said. He followed her out into the sunny lot. She opened the hatch. His eyebrows just barely moved.

"Yeah. Yeah, we can use that."

The next morning was gorgeous, birds chirping as Casch and the kids waited for the carrot-colored bus. When they were gone she took a shower, she washed her hair. Slipped on hoop earrings, her jean jacket, sunglasses. I am on a roll.

She drove south toward a Walmart just across the state line in Massachusetts. Now that could be a good place to look for receipts in the parking lot, she thought. Maybe people aren't so hard up down there.

But when she scoured the parking lot, she didn't find a thing. She wandered into the store and idly took a shopping cart.

An elderly man in a blue vest was setting up a display of

Fourth of July shwag, and for a second she thought he should be sitting on a porch, taking in the day. But no. Grandpa has to be here, working for the man. She shook her head as she pushed farther into the store.

Still, she felt a twinge about what she was doing. You know you got to teach the kids stealing is wrong. That was the worst feeling. Not being who Molly and Dean believed she was.

When she cruised by electronics, she saw there was a giant flat-screen TV on special. Would you look at that. She pretended to examine a bin of DVDs. She glanced around at the other items on display—there were laptops, there were phones. Those smaller items had the anti-theft thing on them, a crisscrossed wire around each box, like ribbon on a Christmas present. But see that, there was no wire on the big TVs. There was one mounted on display and then there were boxes lined up on the floor. Imagine getting out of here with one of those. Ha, it was ridiculous; you could never.

"Excuse me?"

Casch looked up as a woman with gray hair waved a receipt in the direction of a skinny sales associate.

"Yes, ma'am?" he said, rounding the TV display.

"I just bought one of these. They said someone would help me?"

"Yeah, no problem," the kid replied.

Casch continued thumbing the DVDs as she watched from the corner of her eye. He didn't even check; he didn't even look at her receipt. He just lifted the giant TV into her cart. Then they wheeled it away like that, the woman pushing the cart while the sales associate held the box steady.

Casch blinked as she watched them go.

Today is win-a-free-TV day.

Be awesome; win a TV.

She had been holding *Shrek 2*, which she tossed back in the pile. She pushed her cart toward the rear of the store. Her heart was already hammering.

Don't be ridiculous, you're not stealing a TV.

But you see what that woman did? She's on her way to the parking lot right now with her new flat-screen. You know how much you could get for that at the pawn shop? It's still in the box, it's gold.

Her heart was racing. You need to buy one thing, you need a receipt to wave at that kid. Was she really doing this?

How killer. How brilliant. Have the sales associate carry your goods out the door? I am unstoppable.

Her hands were sweaty on the cart's handle as she headed into housewares and back up toward the front of the store. She had to buy something. In grocery she grabbed a thing of ground beef, a bag of buns. Then got in line at checkout.

"You have yourself a nice day," said the lady cashier, handing Casch her plastic bag and tearing off the receipt.

"You too."

"I wish. I'm stuck in here."

Casch dropped the plastic bag into her cart and then pushed it around the checkout area and back into the store. She held the receipt prominently in one hand. Her palms were sweating, her fingers sticky on the paper. Her heart was going crazy now.

Behind her the door alarm sounded and she jumped, turning around to look. A customer with shopping bags was exiting and someone in a blue vest was waving him through. That's right, wave him on through. Those alarms go off all day, don't they?

She continued on toward electronics. Would they check her

at the door? Had they checked that other woman at the door? Stop, she thought. Stop, don't do this. This is dumb. Don't do it.

But she didn't stop. At electronics she had to wait several minutes for the skinny sales associate to appear, and she almost lost her nerve. But then there he was.

"Hey," she said, trying to keep her voice even as she gently waved her receipt, "I got one of these flat screens, they told me you'd help carry it out?"

"Oh, yeah, no problem."

"Thanks, I appreciate it."

"No worries," he said kindly, hoisting the huge box into her cart. "It gives me an excuse to go outside, see the sun shining, you know?"

That night she made burgers and sat watching Molly and Dean wolf them down, the sticky bottle of ketchup sitting out on the table.

"Mom, did you see outside? My snow peas are this tall," said Molly, chewing with her mouth open as she measured out a couple inches with her finger and thumb.

"Really, baby?"

"Yeah. The ones at school are this tall." She showed with her fingers, the school ones were taller. "The teacher says we have to put up a *trellis*, that they'll climb it," she said.

"What do you mean, climb it?" said Dean, using the heel of his hand to wipe the side of his mouth.

"They really climb it. They grow little hands."

"Mom, is that true? Can plants grow hands?" said Dean.

"Well, they're not really hands. It's a vine; it grows up the thing, the trellis."

"What's a trellis?"

"Like a ladder."

"Mom?" said Molly. She said it quiet.

"Yeah, Moll?"

"Can we make a trellis for my garden?"

"Uh. Okay."

"We can?" She lit up, surprised.

"Yeah, sure. We'll find something."

Molly took a bite, chewed. Smiled.

After dinner Molly and Dean got in their pj's and used the new strawberry-bubblegum toothpaste while Casch washed the frying pan. As she dried her hands, she stood looking at a pile of mail on the counter. She grabbed the top envelope and tore it open.

What bill was this? She didn't recognize it. It was pages long. EMERGENCY, DX XRAY, EXAM OTHER, TREATMENT OTHER, PHARMACY, ADJUSTMENTS. On the last page it said TOTAL CHARGES $4,036.

She laughed. This is why you can never go to the doctor.

"Cartoons, Mom," said Dean as Casch flipped the channels. She had climbed into her bed wearing all her clothes, hair tied up in a bun, one kid on either side of her.

"Oh, I thought you wanted to watch the news?" she said.

"MOM."

She left it on the news while Dean tried swatting for the remote.

—leaked from Olson-Abrams Pharmaceutical, maker of a painkiller that industry experts say is the most profitable prescription drug in US history.

"MOM," said Dean.

—company recently halted distribution of the medicine and is now the target of a spate of lawsuits alleging it caused rampant addiction.

It went to commercial and Casch, skin prickling, began slowly to flip the channels. That was the problem, she thought, her cheeks flushing. You can give people meds, but don't just take them away.

"That one, Mom, go back," said Dean.

She flipped to the last channel and set the remote on top of the covers. He snuggled against her shoulder.

"Mom, does the shark know he's bad?" Dean asked.

"What?" she said, looking down at him. Then she looked at the TV. On the screen a cartoon shark was tracking behind a swimmer. The music quickened as the shark grew closer.

"The shark isn't bad," said Molly. "He's just hungry."

The shark closed in on the swimmer. Dean looked up at Casch.

"What if the bad guys think they're good guys?" he asked.

11

In a move so decisive she surprised herself, Casch put the kids on the bus and went straight to the YMCA, cruising through the main entrance before nine a.m. Look who has her shit together. She signed out a pair of boxing gloves. You can't think how many people's sweat is in these things, just take them and say thank you to the very caffeinated woman who works the front.

She passed the vending machines and found that the building was quiet, nearly empty. How about that, look at this early bird with the worm. In the second-floor stairwell, where the heavy bag hung, she wrapped her hands and pulled on the gloves. Wished there was music playing. You need a soundtrack. Can someone turn on GNR? "Welcome to the Jungle."

She bounced a little. Jabbed with her left. Another jab. A punch from her right. Once she got going, each swing brought an exhale that sprayed spit from her lips, which landed in dots on the bag and the black floormats underfoot. Anyone got a problem with my spit? Didn't think so.

She bounced and swung and her hair loosened from her ponytail. She went on like that and no one came up the stairs. She always hated it when people came by and saw her.

Which was funny, she thought, as her right fist hit the black leather bag and the chain creaked. Funny because she was kicking ass. Look at me kicking ass. You don't want no one seeing you kick ass?

Then someone did come up the stairwell, an older guy. Normally she would stop, she would casually bob around until the person was gone. This time she forced herself not to, she kept swinging. Because who cares. Somehow she'd believed that she shouldn't be seen, like she had to hide to be safe.

There was a time you needed to hide, she thought, weaving around the bag, throwing a jab. There was that time. But not anymore. Because you can handle yourself now.

And didn't that hit the spot, she thought, when she pulled off her gloves and grabbed her water. Time for a cigarette.

She was in the car on the way home when her phone chimed and she saw it was Topher. Immediate zing down her chest to her pussy. He was driving south this morning; he wanted to come by. Yes, please.

The number of pairs of panties she had creamed through thinking about him. The other day she was grabbing dirty clothes off the floor, tossing them toward the hamper, and she'd paused at the panties with the marbled green pattern. She'd been wearing them while lying on the couch replaying in her mind the last time they fucked, when she'd been on her stomach, Topher on top of her, his forearms holding hers. Who knows how long she spent on the couch replaying that one fuck. When she picked those green panties off the floor she ran her thumb over the crotch, expecting to find them white and crusty, like any soiled drawers.

But instead the crotch was iridescent. She had double-taked at it and stared at the wide sparkly smear. Then she grinned. Because there was glitter between her legs.

In bed she got on her hands and knees, and he started doing her.

"You feel okay?" he asked.

"Mmm," she said. She turned her head to look back at him, on his knees, inside her. "You feel okay?" she asked.

"Oh, yeah," he said, nodding and looking toward her ass in his hands, and his face and shoulders melted in pleasure.

She turned back toward the pillows smiling.

Afterward the late-morning sun came in the window and warmed the backs of her bare legs as Casch lay across the bed with her chin resting in her hands. Topher had put his boxers on and was sitting with a children's book across his lap as he rolled a joint.

"Did you ever make up games when you were little?" he asked, glancing at her as he pinched weed from the grinder. He spread it along the rolling paper then capped the grinder and set it in the bedsheets.

"That's a funny question," she said.

"Well no, it's because I used to build these castles in our backyard, I had these whole scenarios. I was just wondering if you did anything like that?"

"My mom used to clean houses," said Casch slowly, "and I had to go with her all the time. And I'd pretend whatever house we were in was ours."

She stared off as she thought about it.

"And actually, there was this one big yellow farmhouse that was so gorgeous, like ridiculous. And check this out. In the backyard was this treehouse that was a miniature of the real house. I was so jealous. The treehouse had windows with little shutters, the siding was painted the same yellow as the actual house, it was so sharp."

"Lucky kids," he said.

"Right? But my mom wouldn't let me go up there. She was all, don't you dare touch a thing. And for the longest time I was dying to check it out. So one day, you know, Mom was upstairs, I sneak outside. I go out back, I run across the yard, I'm like, this is my big moment!"

He grinned.

"And I don't really know what I expected. Maybe I thought"—her voice got soft—"maybe there was a part of me that thought it really was magic up there? Like maybe fairies lived there or something? I don't know. Anyways, I climb up into it, and of course, it's just a friggin' plywood box."

His expression changed.

"And there was mouse shit all over the floor, and I'm like, this is what I've been wanting? A plywood box full of mouse shit?"

"It's funny you say that," he said.

"What?"

"About a plywood box."

"What do you mean?"

"My Gram and I used to have this saying. When she first said it, I was about to break the thing that held our firewood. But then it became our saying. 'Are you smarter than the box?'"

"Are you smarter than the box," said Casch.

"Yeah."

"I like that."

He smiled, looking down at his hands as he lifted the joint the way he always did, gently, and ran his tongue along the edge of the paper. Then, with a fingertip, he sealed it closed.

"How often are you going to New York?" she asked, checking the time on her phone. She'd been thinking she would maybe hit another Walmart today, if she had time.

"Couple times a week. If I'm on the road by noon today I'm good. I usually make deliveries late afternoon. Grab something to eat, then back on the road."

"How do you even know people down there?"

"Through this guy I served with."

"Served with?"

"Oh, I was in the army," he said, and lit the joint. He tugged with his lips until it was going.

She watched his face.

"Did you, were you, overseas?" she said.

"Yeah. Afghanistan."

For a while they were quiet, their fingertips touching as they pinched the joint back and forth. Casch, still on her stomach, watched her own smoky exhale open in the light and disappear.

"What was it like over there?" she said.

"Where?"

"In the war."

"I don't really like talking about it."

"Oh. Okay, no worries."

"You all set?"

"Yeah."

He pressed the joint into the plastic dish on the bedside table.

"When I first got home, everyone was always, thank you for your service, thank you for your service. I couldn't stand it."

"Why? What's wrong with that?"

He lay backward beside her and interlaced his fingers over his stomach. "I never really talked about this before," he said, and was quiet for a second before he went on. "The funny thing is, you go over it a million times in your head, but you never talk about it. I feel like I could tell you, though," he said, and rotated his head toward her. Their eyes met.

"You sure you want to hear this?" he said.

"Yeah," she said, watching his face.

"I'm all cottonmouth," he said. He sat up and drank from the glass on the little table. Then lay back down.

"I mean, if you ask two different people, they'll tell you two different things. I'm just one guy who was there, I only know what it was like for me, you know? But, I mean, I guess, the best way to describe it is to tell you the lies."

"What?"

"The lies. I never told this to anyone before. It's good that I'm high." He stared at the ceiling and was quiet. Then he said, "The war started because of 9/11, right? So, you know, we know what they did to us. And over there people don't have, like, basic rights. So it seems simple. You have to go over there and take them down. You have to kill in the name of good. That's lie number one. You kill in the name of good, lie number one.

"Because, soon as you get there, oh, wait a second. You're in this tiny village, you've been briefed, you know your mission, you know the coordinates, you know what you're doing. But wait, do you? Because you get out there and, and, who the fuck is who? Any insurgent who thinks he's about to get hit will drop his weapon and grab a shovel, try to look like a farmer. Or is that actually a real farmer, some innocent guy trying to feed his family? Plus a known fucking Taliban strategy is they get you to hit civilians, because they don't give a fuck, and it will just make people hate you. So you get out there, and, and who the fuck is who? And the first time you hit the wrong target, the first time you realize you—"

He stopped.

"Officially, you know, that's a really big deal. Officially you have to get, like, major permission up the chain of command if you think you need to hit a target where it's suspected civilians reside. This is a major serious deal. And it's like, we do everything to avoid killing civilians. We're building schools, we're building hospitals. But when you're out there scared as fuck and you don't know which ones are who, the actual truth is that every single one of you—"

"You can't think about that," he said, not looking at her. "You can't think about that or you will fucking lose your mind. Like when you learn these people used to have a religion where every river and tree and everything had a spirit, had a soul, that's who you're killing."

She held her breath as she watched him.

"Anyways. Lie number two. Lie number two is that we're all in this together. Nope. The whole fucking country forgot we're even at war. Actually, you get home, you look around, and honestly sometimes it's like, this is what I was fighting for? Everyone's so materialistic. Apparently we forgot to teach kids that serving is what matters. That's what's beautiful about being over there, no one forgets that for one second. But, so, no. We're not all in this together. That's lie number two."

He was quiet for a minute.

"Lie number three, now we're getting into it, lie number three is that some deaths count more than others. The whole time you're there, right, there's this tally of US soldiers killed in

Afghanistan. Everyone knows the number, that's a sacred number.

"It gets reported back here, too," he went on, "if anyone's paying attention. But while we're keeping this count on the number killed, this whole time, people are getting killed left and right. Like you'll hear that day's report and oh, another thirty Afghan police were killed. That's a normal day. And women are dying, children are dying. You could be out on patrol, you could see a kid out herding some goats. Maybe there's a mama goat and a couple baby goats, cutest little things, and you could be right there on patrol and this kid and his goats get blown away. It's so fucking loud you feel it inside your skull. You drop to the ground, you can't breathe cause of the smoke, and whenever it is you finally try to get up, you realize the kid's arm is there in front of you. You're looking at his bloody severed arm. Then if it's your lucky day you'll see the mom come out of her house, you'll see her wailing, screaming, waving her arms at the sky. Now, does any of that change the tally? Nope, sure doesn't. Tally stays the same. He's not a US soldier, he's a hajji kid, he goes on some other list. But you saw his mother and you know his death doesn't count any less, you saw what it meant that she lost her kid. It's a fucking lie, those deaths don't count any less. That's a fucking lie."

His eyes were glassy as he shook his head.

"I'm not saying I'm innocent," he said, swiveling to look at her. "You hear me? I'm not saying it's someone else's fault, that's not what I'm saying at all. Anyways. The fourth lie. You ready?"

Casch, mouth open, chest thumping, nodded just barely.

"You get sort of accustomed to seeing bodies. Maybe you see a body and, hey, you knew that kid. Maybe you knew he had this plan to go home and marry his girlfriend. But there goes his body. And it's like, you get bitter. He's just another body. And you kind of, you want to not care, you know? Because you can't care about every single one, you'll go fucking crazy. And if you go crazy, then you'll go home in a body bag, too. So you sort of try to just, not think about it. Forget about it, you know? It doesn't matter, it's just one more. And that's the lie that the war tries to make you believe, that it's okay, that he didn't matter. But if that's true, it means you don't matter either. If his life didn't matter, then your life doesn't matter. So there it is, the fourth lie. The fourth lie is that your life doesn't matter."

He stared at the ceiling.

"And I'm not saying that your life, or my life, I'm not saying our lives matter in the *American* way. The American way is like, life is a movie, you're the star. Fuck that, not true. Life is not a movie, you are not the star, okay? But your life matters. In the same way the fox's life matters."

"What?" she said. She looked at his eyes. A throb had started in her chest.

"The fox," he said, and he stared back at her. "The fox has its place in the ecosystem, right? It eats rodents and stuff. It keeps like mice or whatever from getting out of control. Like maybe if there were no foxes then that treehouse you went up into would've been crawling with mice, like mice running all over your feet. A fox could maybe get all the way into that tree— you know they have retractable claws? That's how they're the only canine that can climb trees. Actually, you ever seen a fox cub? I saw a den one time. It was random, in the cemetery where my Gram's buried. The mama fox made her den there and she must've been out hunting, and I just came across these three little pups. So ridiculously cute. I didn't mess with them, obviously. Foxes are actually incredibly caring of their young. I read one time about a baby fox that got caught in a trap, probably snapped its leg, but then survived for weeks—you know how? Because the mama fox brought food to it while it was trapped. I mean, are you kidding me?" he said, swallowing, and Casch thought he was going to cry. He squirmed his shoulders against the bed.

"And foxes also eat whatever they can find, so if there's some fruit or berries or whatever, they'll chow it. And if they've got extra food, they'll store it in a little hole. Isn't that cool? Another thing that's crazy is they can live in pretty much any habitat. They'll be in the center of town, in someone's trash, or way out in the wild, whatever, they'll figure it out. And they travel big distances, and of course they shit along the way, right? They're shitting out rodent fur but also the seeds of whatever fruit they ate, so what they end up doing is they're planting new seeds. Nature's gardeners. You get me? Not to mention that the fox will eat dead flesh if it finds something in the woods or wherever, it doesn't let anything go to waste. Okay? So you see the fox *matters*, the fox is important. And I just happen to think foxes are cool, but you could pick any animal, and they've got some role to play.

"And the thing that gets me," he said, sitting up, reaching for the cup of water, "is that Indians knew this shit a thousand years before the arrival of the white man. Like, life is a movie, you're the star? Ha, no. You are part of a bigger system. All of nature supports you, and in return you have some role to play. You see? Like the fox. Your life matters."

Casch gazed at him without blinking as the throbbing pushed against her ribs. She watched him drink from the cup, tilting it back as he finished. It was the feeling she'd only ever had for her children, that she was splitting open.

He set the empty cup on the stand, and she scooted toward him, looping her arms around his waist, her bare skin against his.

"Jesus, I went off on this whole thing," he murmured. But he let his face come forward so that his lips were in her hair, and she felt his breath on the crown of her head.

The next afternoon, when she knocked at the Amity Street duplex, Morty opened the door and shook his head.

"I'm out," he said.

"What?"

"I'm out of them pills."

"What do you mean, out?"

"They're hard to get and I'm out."

"Uh—" she started to say, but he pulled his head back inside and the door clicked shut.

She stood there for a second, blinking, staring at the door's vinyl ridges. Slowly she turned and went down the steps.

She crossed Amity and climbed back in her van. And sat there.

You know what? It's fine.

It's fine.

You don't need those overpriced pills anyways.

She started the engine.

I'm done. I don't need those pills.

She pulled away from the curb.

Thank you, Morty, for being an incompetent drug dealer.

And she turned on the radio as she drove away.

12

The June morning seemed huge and empty as soon as she put the kids on the bus. She came back in the apartment, pulled the door closed. Last night, after bringing him home from his dad's house, Dean had wanted her to lie down with him at bedtime. "Sure, baby," she'd said, and she had the idea to find a book in the pile under Molly's bed.

"Let's read *Corduroy*," said Molly, cross-legged, watching Casch sift through the pile.

"Ooh, that's a good one."

So all three of them squeezed into Dean's twin bed, Molly's wavy hair soft against her neck as Casch read and the kids studied each picture.

And she would have pressed pause right then if she could have. Don't grow up, you guys, she wanted to say. Let's please just stay like this.

When they got to the end of the book, Molly said, "The girl didn't mind that he was missing a button."

"That's right," said Casch, adjusting her shoulder so she could look at her daughter.

"I like that," Molly said.

"Me too," said Casch.

"Let's read another one," said Dean.

But now it was morning and they were at school. She would go out and grab a coffee, get an iced coffee. She went in her room to get her shoes. And she would text Topher. She stopped and pulled her phone from her hoodie pocket, fired off a message. The thing about the pills is they made you feel so good you keep thinking about it. Realistically, you don't just forget. She lifted her purse from the couch.

Coffee, coffee. But she hadn't gotten her shoes. She went in the bedroom and stood at the open double doors of the closet—the doors were always open, because one of the hinges was broken. A few shirts drooped from hangers and everything else in a heap on the floor. Look, Topher already wrote back. Yes, going to the city, he was asking if she wanted to go for a walk. Perfect, a walk. She replied and put the phone away.

She stared at the hamper as she slid her feet into her flip-flops. The thing was overflowing, on top were her nasty gym clothes. Bingo. She should do laundry.

And if she was really on top of it, she'd put the load in right now, then go get coffee. By the time she came back she could put it in the dryer. Boom, look at that, she thought, stuffing the clothes down into the hamper. From the back corner of the closet, she grabbed the orange jug of detergent, its plastic mouth slimy and stuck with cat hair. Look, there was her red hoodie. She pulled it out. How long had that been missing. She tossed it on the bed. Went to the dresser and sorted five quarters from the chipped YMCA mug.

What you can't do is let yourself think about maybe wanting a pill. She dropped the coins into her sweatshirt pocket, where they sagged against her hip. Because that's just going to mess with your head. She grabbed the hamper and detergent. In the kids' room she collected clothes off the floor, then shuffled through the kitchen and out back. Keep yourself busy. Wait, keys. She went back in the house and grabbed her keys.

The screen door slammed behind her as she walked around the rear of the building. The heavy door to the laundry room had a jiggly lock. She dropped her stuff. You have to fiddle with the key, twist, then pull. She held it open with her foot as she grabbed the hamper and flipped on the light with the side of the hand holding the detergent. She descended cement steps, whiffing the mildew then stepping around people's bikes.

At the washers she set down her laundry, and with her foot, slid aside someone's empty SpongeBob hamper. Just to the left was a table where people left their detergents and boxes of dryer sheets—she always thought, You're going to trust people like that? She always went over, just curious, and lifted the jugs to see how full they were. If hers was really low and there was a full one sitting right there, you know. It's not going to kill someone if you use a little. She'd only done that a couple of times. Everyone's poor, don't take their shit. It's different with stores; they're not going out of business because you lifted a few steaks. But you can't think about the stuff you lifted. If you start thinking about that, you'll feel like trash. And see, that just makes you want a pill.

She was shaking the ice melt in the bottom of the Dunkin' cup when she heard Topher knock. Her phone buzzed at the same time. She pulled open the door as she looked down at her phone.

"Oh, it's the kids' school," she said, frowning as he leaned in and kissed her. "Hello?"

A woman's voice started talking fast. There was a field trip today, kids were supposed to have swimsuits and towels.

"We sent out a notice, in the mail?" the woman said.

"Oh," said Casch, glancing at Topher, her cheeks warming, "well I can just run them over right now, can't I? I'll be there in five minutes."

"Okay," said the woman, and Casch hung up and dashed into their room.

"You need help?" Topher called.

In their bedroom she found Molly's suit at the back of the mostly empty underwear drawer. But then couldn't find Dean's. She grabbed a pair of shorts instead and ran to the bathroom. She didn't take the thick striped one. She grabbed two thinner towels underneath. Out in the living room, she grabbed her purse off the couch.

"I've gotta run over to their school, you wanna come with?"

"I'll drive you," he said, sliding away his phone.

So they were hopping in the Ranger, and she was telling him where to go—up Silver and then a left, through a quiet neighborhood, to enter the back side of the school parking lot. The Ranger hadn't even come to a full stop before Casch was swinging open her door and jumping out and running up to the entrance, towels tucked in her armpit and the suits waving in her hand like flags. Inside she handed them off to a secretary in a soft pink sweater. She was back outside in a second.

"All set," she said.

He was looking at her, smiling.

"What."

"You're just, you're a great mom."

Her eyes darted away. Tell that to DCF, she didn't say. "If I were a great mom I would've remembered in the first place," she said.

"Not true, everyone forgets stuff. And you're doing this all by yourself." He glanced in the side mirror as he pulled away. "I mean, where are their dads to remember their swimsuits?"

Her head lifted. She had thought maybe he would judge her for having two baby daddies—and Molly's dad gone to northern New Hampshire, out of touch for years now. But Topher didn't seem to think it was her fault at all.

"My parents sure never brought me anything at school, I can tell you that," he murmured. "They left me with Gram and never came back, like I wasn't even worth their time."

When they got home and her clothes were off, she went back to her old habit. Her mind went somewhere else and returned when he finished.

They lay for a while in the quiet, his face buried in her shoulder.

"You're like the perfect human," he said, muffled.

Why did he have to say that. She pulled away a little.

Gently he reached to gather her back to him. But she stayed tense.

"What's wrong?"

She didn't say anything.

"Casch?"

"Maybe I worry," she said, swallowing, "maybe I worry, that you'll think the same things about me that I think about myself."

He looked up.

"Bad things?"

She nodded.

"That's not the stuff I'm thinking about."

"What's the stuff you're thinking about?" she asked softly.

For a long time he didn't answer. She thought he wasn't going to, and she was about to pull away and get up, when he said, so quiet it was almost a whisper, "Maybe I'm thinking, why would she like me?"

It was almost two that night when she reached for her phone on the pillow beside her and checked the time again. She couldn't fall asleep, her throat was itchy, she kept coughing. She released the phone and touched a hand to her breastbone. Sweat was beading there. Her eyelids wouldn't stay closed.

And her mind wouldn't stop circling. She wiped away the sweat. She needed something to knock her out, shut her mind off. She remembered Russ playing Nintendo with her, laughing at her jokes.

And at night, he would crack a few beers, and they would watch the Red Sox. Of course Flora didn't give two shits about baseball, which was why Casch got into it. She would sit next to Russ on the couch. José Canseco was the only player whose name she knew. So whenever the Sox were at bat she was always gunning for *a homer like Canseco*. One day Russ brought home a child-sized Sox hat from the sporting goods store that used to be on Main Street, and after that she always wore it while they watched on TV. Then he won two tickets in an Easter raffle, and he said that he would bring *her*.

The weird thing was, he'd never been to a game. A Sox fan his whole life, he'd never gone to Fenway. He was going now, though, and he was taking her. When they got into Boston, Casch remembered he became suddenly nervous, there was so much traffic, cars were honking, and when he got scared, she got scared, too. But eventually he piloted them to Fenway. They passed through the turnstiles and the crowds were thick and powerful, a crush of people all trying to get to their seats. Casch had been struck by all the things to buy. T-shirts and hot dogs and popcorn and pretzels and programs and cotton candy, she wanted all the things in this hall of booths that appeared endless in both directions. Russ had glanced at her and taken her hand. "Don't let go," he'd said. This must be what it's like to have a father. But the Sox lost.

She reached a hand under her and wiped sweat from the small of her back.

When she got a little older, it was Russ who chauffeured her and her friends around. It was Russ who didn't mind taking them to the mall that had the arcade. Look at us, an actual family. It went on like that, right up until a night when she was fourteen. They were watching TV on the couch; he was crushing beers. She fell asleep and woke to him unzipping her jeans.

It had been two days on the toilet moaning, arms wrapped around her naked clammy shoulders. In bed, every inch of her ached, just rolling over was excruciating. She thought about the $200 from Marylouise. Under the sheets, her legs kicked.

"Mom?" said a small voice, backlit in the doorway.

"Yeah, baby."

"Mom, are you okay?"

"Mommy's sick, baby."

Silence.

"You still there, Moll?"

"Yeah."

"What do you need, baby?"

For a second Molly didn't say anything. Then, "Can I do anything, Mom? Can I help?"

Casch raised her head off the pillow. Molly came tiptoeing in.

"You're the best," she said, hoarse, looking at her daughter. Molly smiled a tiny smile just as Casch's phone, on the bed beside her, buzzed. She looked at it.

New supply, said Morty's text. And her energy surged to a hundred.

"Hey, baby?" she said, sitting up. "I'm gonna go get some medicine. Can you watch your brother for me?"

Molly nodded.

And Casch went out the door in Santa-patterned pajama pants.

With a sweaty finger, she flipped on the windshield wipers. She could see herself clicking the lighter under the foil; she tasted burnt marshmallows. When she got to Amity Street, she threw it into park and ran up to the door.

"Oh, hey, Casch, listen," said Morty, when he let her inside, her hair damp with rain, "what I'm hearing is that last batch was it."

"What."

"The last pills, you got a few of them, that was it."

"You kidding?" she said, the craving clawing up her throat. "Why'd you say you had more?"

"Right, yeah. So what I have for you, I can give you something else. Same high, but cheaper. Plus, I know I can get it."

"No-o," she said. She took a half step back.

"You been getting sick?" he said.

For a second she was frozen. Then she nodded.

"Yeah, that's what I figured. Just have a seat," he said, waving a hand toward the couch. Her eyes pooled with tears. "Let me go upstairs and grab it."

Then she was alone. She heard his footsteps overhead. She looked at the door. She could leave now. She could slip out the door.

But do you want to feel better? She lowered herself onto the couch.

She heard a door close upstairs and Morty came padding down, the pit bull at his heels.

"You ever meet Oscar?" he said.

She nodded as the dog came over and nosed his head into Casch's lap. She stroked his thick collarless neck, and he licked her fingers. She blinked tears as Morty plopped onto the couch beside her.

"He's a real good boy, isn't he," he said, unknotting a tiny baggie. He pulled something from his pocket.

You have to be kidding me, she whispered, or maybe she didn't say it, maybe she only thought it. He held the open baggie in his palm for her to see. The powder was brownish, like infant formula.

"I'm not gonna—" she said, hoarse, shaking her head. She just wanted the yellow pill. The lighter clicking underneath.

From his pocket Morty had taken a small knife that he now unfolded, dipping the blade's tip into the bag. He brought up a tiny hill of powder. The dog turned a circle and slumped against her leg.

"You're feeling sick, all you do is a dip like this," he said.

She stared at it.

"That's it?"

"Yeah." He looked at her. "You thought I meant shoot this? Fuck no, you don't need that."

"Fucking right I don't."

"Here," he said. Carefully he brought the tip of the knife up toward her. She leaned in, pressed two fingers to one nostril and sniffed with the other. A warm feeling came down her head.

And she felt—okay. She was okay. She wasn't sick. She was fine.

She looked at the baggie.

"How much is that?" she said.

"This? Fifteen."

"Fifteen dollars?"

"Yeah."

Everything was going to be okay.

When she got home she went into the kids' room. They had pushed Dean's toys out of the way and were sitting on the floor, a deck of cards spread out around them.

"Guys want to watch a movie?"

A minute later, the three of them were snuggled in her bed.

The following afternoon she marched into her room and got the big pile of mail. She brought it to the kitchen and grabbed the newer mail off the counter and stacked it all together on the table. Otis jumped up and walked delicately across the envelopes before she shooed him away and started tearing stuff open. Her phone buzzed with a message, and she glanced at it. Shit, Gabi. Casch knew she'd blown her off. But she couldn't deal with that right now, look at all this.

Here was the notice about bringing swimsuits for the field trip; she tossed that one in the trash pile. She uncovered a letter from DCF—how had she missed that? Hurriedly she scanned it. Under review, it said. Her *case* was *under review*. Did that mean they were done—no more surprise visits?

But it didn't say, and she put it aside.

She sorted everything until only bills remained. She was going to figure this out.

She still hadn't paid the light bill, she probably owed a couple months on that—where was it? She shuffled the papers. Here. It was bolded at the top. She owed $51.29. She stared at it. She almost got the lights shut off over $51.29. Her mind hummed.

13

He stood over the stained toilet and looked at the ancient linoleum that was curling up from the floor. Must be some kind of leak, he realized, staring into the corner, must be water leaking and pooling up under the flooring, for who knows how long. Look at the drywall, you could see it, moist rust-colored filth coming up from the floor and staining the wall. He should get someone in here to look at that.

Russ pressed the wobbly handle to flush and came out of the bathroom. The phone was ringing. Why wasn't anyone answering the phone? He hurried over and grabbed the manila receiver.

"Kramer's, this is Russ."

"Russ, it's Ronnie."

For a hair of a second Russ was blank. In forty years of being best friends, Ronnie had never once phoned him at work.

"Hey, Ronnie, everything okay?"

"No, everything's not okay. Aaron overdosed, we're at the hospital."

"I'm leaving right now. I'm coming over there," he said, and started to hang up.

"Wait a second. I've gotta get out of here. I've been here all night. Cindy's staying, she's not leaving his side."

"You want to get some lunch?" said Russ.

"I don't think I can eat. Listen, I'm going home to take a shower. And tonight I'm going to my meeting."

"Meeting?"

"Al-Anon, you remember?"

"Oh, yeah. Course."

"Cindy and me been going together. But I thought maybe you'd come with me tonight."

Russ stood blinking, the phone pressed to his face.

"Sure, bud. Of course I'll go."

The church function room was cold.

Ronnie fixed them coffees in small Styrofoam cups, and they settled in folding chairs around a table that was several smaller tables pushed together. As other people filed in and the chill of the metal spread over his rear, Russ saw that they were the only men. He shifted on the hard chair. In his periphery he looked at his friend, peering down at his cup. How do you help a guy in that situation? The whole thing pissed Russ off. That's right, he was pissed off. He stared straight ahead.

"Newcomer?"

Russ glanced up.

"Newcomer?" a lady in a baseball cap said again, looking at him.

"What?"

"We have literature for newcomers," she said, and slid a blue pamphlet across the table. He was about to say no but two other women were looking at him. The pamphlet sat there.

At the top of the hour the baseball cap lady cleared her throat and started reading from a binder whose pages were encased in plastic.

"Many who come to Al-Anon feel completely hopeless," she read, and Russ, taking a hot sip, glanced at Ronnie. He set down the coffee and folded his arms over his chest. The church's old plumbing gurgled as the woman read on. In the center of the table, a tented piece of cardboard said, "Think."

Then everyone was turning in their seats and Russ looked where everyone else was looking. There was a girl with close-cropped dark hair at the other end of the table.

"I'm Nachalah," she said.

"HI, NACHALAH."

"Yeah, thanks. You know sometimes I think the single biggest piece of wisdom I've—"

Russ didn't know how long the meeting went. It couldn't be more than an hour. Could it? Again he glanced at Ronnie.

Ronnie had told him the kid had come home just two days before, asking for money.

Russ had been hearing these updates all along, Ronnie telling him when Aaron was sober, telling him that he'd started lifting weights at the YMCA. Then Russ wouldn't hear anything for a while, and the next thing he heard the kid would be on drugs again. Ronnie's temples had gone completely gray. Every time he heard the latest news, Russ wanted to throttle that kid. He couldn't have asked for better parents, and this is how he repaid them? But Ronnie told him you learn to blame the disease not the person.

"The disease?" Russ had said, squinting.

"Yeah."

"What do you mean?"

"The addiction," Ronnie said.

Russ glanced at the girl talking.

"—sixth step, right? But I kind of want to back up for a second, to just this whole idea of a higher power—"

Russ sniffed. Higher power, listen to this.

"—realized my higher power didn't have to be god-with-a-capital-G. My higher power could be, for instance, the knowledge in this room."

She had a nose piercing, he saw. Russ did not care for piercings. She was still talking; how long did this go?

"—under my belt and realized I am part of that knowledge, you know? I have some of that knowledge within me. And at that point I start to look at this whole kettle of fish a little differently. At the same time, this is important, I was having this health issue, is this weird to talk about? Because I had, I shit you not, a seven-year yeast infection."

Russ glanced around. But everyone was all poker face.

"Shoot, am I over my time? I just need another second. Anyways, doctors and everybody, no one could figure it out, no one knew what the hell was wrong with me. But finally, eventually, I figure it out myself. What I discover is I was eating too much sugar, and it was throwing my whole system off. And when I stopped eating so much sugar, not only did the problem disappear, but I felt a million percent better. And I think I look a lot better too, like it's released this *glow*. But how did that happen? No doctor knew the answer. This was my body basically sending up smoke signals. And here comes my big epiphany, because, you know, we've all got shit hanging over us. But I feel like if I just get quiet for a second, and I don't rush it, I probably actually have the answer. And, bingo, that's what we're doing when we pray. So, yeah, that's it. Pass."

"THANKS, NACHALAH."

Everyone was quiet for a second. Russ watched as the girl took out a package of gum and unwrapped a piece. She saw him looking and he looked away.

—

"Thanks, Russ, thanks for coming with me," Ronnie said afterward as they stood in the parking lot, and his head came forward as he started to cry. Ronnie's son was unconscious in a hospital bed and neither man said what they both knew, that the kid wasn't going to make it.

"You don't have to thank me," said Russ, his throat hoarse. "You know I got your back here." He grabbed Ronnie and hugged him.

Over his friend's shoulder, Russ looked out at the church playground.

14

opher's foot was heavy on the gas as his eyes drifted to the woods along the highway, the trees a wall of green. He had gaped at all the green when he first came back to Vermont; he would always remember that. It had been like he'd never seen this place before. And maybe he sort of hadn't; he'd taken it for granted. But when he got back here, he finally did see. That this place was like a thousand years of rains had just finished, and then the sun popped out.

Casch had told him that her mom had the kids today, their first day of summer vacation. He glanced at the speedometer. Eighty was too fast. He eased off. He hadn't been planning to, but yesterday he'd told Connor and Tory about her. They had finished in the field and had gone down to Shea's for a pitcher. Topher had taken a long sip and set the glass on the sticky bar top. There were MLB highlights flashing overhead and none of them said anything. They drank and half watched the TV. Finally Topher had topped off their glasses and said, "I been seeing this girl."

Connor's head swiveled. "What did you say?"

"I been seeing this girl."

"No shit."

"Who?" said Tory.

"You don't know her. She's down in Greenfield."

"Greenfield's a hole," Tory said.

"Who cares?" said Connor.

"She has two kids," said Topher, taking a sip.

"Whoa."

"Yeah, but I don't mind."

Connor was smiling. "Look at you, you like this chick."

"I do, actually. First time we hung out I was like, let's go for a hike, or a walk, whatever, she said sure. Turns out she had a broken foot. Didn't give a fuck, she's a warrior. Then you should see her with her kids, how dedicated she is. Plus she boxes—she could kick Tory's ass."

"What? Shut up."

When he got to Greenfield, he went east at the rotary, made the left, and swung into Greenfield Terrace. When Casch opened the door, she was barefoot and wearing a red sweatshirt, smiling and receiving his kiss.

"Let me take you to lunch," he said.

They went to a spot just across the Connecticut River. They ordered sandwiches from the walk-up window and sat, with a view down to the water, on chairs made from tree stumps. He took a bite of his Reuben.

"See these rounds of wood?" he said, chewing, tapping the stump beneath him.

She wiped her mouth and nodded.

"When I was a kid, my Gram would split all our wood herself. Until I was big enough to do it, she'd do all of it. I'm talking like she'd be out there with the maul, which has to weigh ten pounds, splitting rounds like this one."

"You're joking."

"Nope."

"You know I'm starting to think, is this Gram a made-up character?" said Casch, grinning. "Did she really exist?"

"Dude," he said. His chin rotated to one side as he gave her a look.

Casch licked sauce from her fingers.

"Next thing I know, you're going to be telling me she was solving town mysteries. Was Gram by any chance an amateur detective? Was she played by Angela Lansbury?"

"You would have loved her," he said.

Her face softened and they looked at one another and went back to eating their sandwiches.

"You, actually, you remind me of her," Topher said after swallowing a bite. "You would've split the wood too. You do whatever it takes, I seen you."

Casch looked away smiling. "Thanks," she said, and for a second they sat in comfortable silence.

"The shittiest thing was that after Gram died, the bank re-possessed the cabin," Topher said, wiping his hands on a paper napkin. "There was debt and stuff. But it's still there, there's people living in it. This is the place my Gram and grandpa built with their own hands. So what I've always wanted to do is buy it back."

She had been peering down into the black flow of the river, but now she looked up at him.

"You should. You should do that," she said.

"The problem is, even if I have the money, I don't have income on the books. So how am I going to get a mortgage?"

"That's my whole idea with nursing school," she said, sitting forward, "because if you're a nurse you get salary and benefits and everything. So that's, actually, that's exactly what I was thinking. That if I was a nurse, I could maybe buy a house. For the kids and me."

"What do you mean, if you were a nurse? You're going to be a nurse. You're going to nursing school."

She shifted on the stump-chair. She had not finished her sandwich. She wrapped it back in the paper and set it aside.

They drove through downtown and he pulled into the plaza with the liquor store. The parking spots in front were taken and he pulled up, instead, in front of the check-cashing place next door.

"You want anything?"

She half smiled.

"One pack of gold Parliaments coming up," he said, climbing out and passing the front window of the check place, where hand-painted bubble letters said We Buy Gift Cards. He saw that someone had gone to the trouble of drawing imitation logos for Home Depot and Best Buy.

When they got back to Greenfield Terrace, they sat on her sunny back steps with their shoulders touching, each of them sipping a cold Red Stripe.

"That's Molly's garden," said Casch, wiping her mouth and pointing.

"Really."

"Yeah. That's cool, right?"

"Very cool," he said, looking at her. He set his beer on the step and got up to examine the patch. "Her snow peas are starting to come in," he said.

He saw that the peas had climbed a little piece of plastic fencing and were now growing over it. On the stalks below, pods were emerging from soft white flowers.

He glanced and saw that Casch was watching him. Their eyes met and neither of them looked away. Somewhere behind him, a mourning dove cooed. Then there was a different noise. Voices, from inside the apartment.

"Fuck," said Casch, standing up, "they weren't supposed to be back till five."

"Mom."

"MOM!"

Suddenly her kids were spilling out the door. Topher, his mouth open, stood completely still.

Here was her son, smaller than Topher had pictured. He had sandy hair, he was reaching for Casch's hand, he was saying, "Mom, guess what I got?"

And here was her daughter, tall and lanky, a sweatshirt tied around her waist, looking right at him.

"Who are you?" she said. His heart punched in his chest.

Their grandma had come outside behind them. She had deep creases around her mouth, frizzy hair. She was looking at him. So were both kids. He looked at Molly.

"I'm Topher," he said. He stepped forward and reached out his hand. "It's nice to meet you, Molly."

She looked at the offered hand.

"Molly, I was just looking at your garden," he said, his hand hanging there, "and I'm impressed."

"You are?"

"Yeah. Your snow peas are doing great. But I was wondering, do you want, I could add some more fencing"—he stepped back; he pointed—"right here? So they can keep growing up?"

She studied him. Then looked toward the peas. Finally she nodded.

"Okay," she said.

The next time he and the guys went to the field it was like the plants had shot up six inches.

"Holy fuck," said Connor.

"How much you think we're gonna make off this?" said Tory. "We're talking a hundred and fifty grand, right?"

That was about what Topher had been thinking, too, but he hadn't said it out loud. He pulled an energy bar from his pocket, tore open the foil, and broke off a piece. Connor started unpacking supplies. No one said anything else.

They went to get water and returned slowly to the field, each of them straining with a jug in either hand. Yesterday, before he left Greenfield, Topher had run to Home Depot and gotten chicken wire to build up the trellis in Molly's garden. She had stood there, her arms folded, directing him. He smiled thinking about it. Dean was shy but you could see he would follow whatever his sister did. Topher set down the jugs and wiped his forehead. He had texted Casch last night, soon as he got home, and suggested taking them all for ice cream.

When he'd emptied the jugs, he joined Connor and Tory, who were standing in the shade of an old apple tree drinking from a plastic gallon.

"You heard about that one that got busted," Connor was saying to Tory.

"What, where?" said Tory.

"South. Southern V-T, you heard about this," said Connor.

"I didn't hear, and apparently you guys didn't tell me." Tory looked at Topher. "You knew about this?"

"Yeah."

"Some big weed operation gets busted and you guys don't even mention it to me?"

"It wasn't big, and it doesn't concern us," Topher said.

"Doesn't concern us?"

"It doesn't. There are people growing weed everywhere. And some of them are morons who have no clue what they're doing."

"If cops are going around busting weed farms, I'd say it concerns us."

"Just don't worry about it," said Topher. "We're fine."

After he knocked on the door, he could hear her voice inside the apartment.

"He's here, you guys, he's here, grab your shoes."

He was smiling when the door swung open.

They couldn't all fit in the Ranger, so they piled into Casch's van. Crumpled straw wrappers and a Dunkin' cup festooned the floor by Topher's sneakers as they rolled out of the parking lot and started north.

"Topher, what's your favorite bird?" said Molly from the wayback.

His eyebrows lifted and he turned around to look at her. She was leaning into the center, peering at him.

"That is a great question. And I would have to say, the great blue heron."

"Do you know that one?" said Casch, glancing at Molly in the rearview.

"Course I do, Mom."

"Oh, sorry," said Casch, and she grinned at Topher from the side of her mouth.

"Do you like the great blue heron?" he asked, looking back at Molly.

"I—think so. Why do you like it?"

"Well. When I was growing up, we lived by this swamp. It was beautiful, all cattails and red-winged blackbirds nesting there. And sometimes I'd see this heron standing in the water. Thing was huge. But also, you know, totally silent and, and graceful. You know what I mean? That's why I like 'em."

"That's why I like 'em too," said Molly, nodding.

"Me too," said Dean.

"No, you don't," said Molly.

The creamee at the edge of the cornfield was low-slung with a pitched roof. They ordered soft serve and settled at a picnic table, Dean beside Topher, facing a view so perfect it bordered on the absurd, the twinkling of the field merging into the deeper green of the hills and the cloudless sky unfolding overhead.

"Do you like Spider-Man?" said Dean.

"Yeah," said Topher, licking his vanilla.

That evening she walked him out to his truck, the air humid and her rubber flip-flops slapping the pavement as the sky turned fruit-punch pink.

She had not invited him to spend the night. He had thought: Maybe. Maybe now that the kids knew him, maybe. But she didn't say anything about it, and when he suggested that it was getting to be time for him to go, she had nodded and stood up.

"Hey, I hate to do this," she said as they got to the Ranger and stopped.

Dread opened in his stomach. "Do what," he said.

"Could I borrow some money?"

"Oh, sure," he said as relief flooded him, and he reached into his pocket.

Alone at the kitchen table the next morning, Casch pressed her cigarette into the dish. The first of July had crept up on her. Last month's rent was due right after she offloaded the infant formula, and so she had scraped together just enough. But she didn't have it for this month.

Her phone buzzed. Gabi, she couldn't talk to Gabi.

Time went so fast was the thing. It seemed like she had just gotten that infant formula. How could that have been a month ago. Although that probably meant they'd sold all that inventory.

Meaning, they would be ready for more?

She got up and got her purse.

"Molly, watch your brother," she said.

Out of the blue the manager at The 99 called and said he had one shift a week she could have. *One* shift a week. It pissed her off. But still, it was better than nothing.

Was it really better than nothing, though? When she finally got back in there for her first shift in months—and Gabi pulled her into a hug—she felt humiliated.

Dipped van key into baggie and sniffed. Dipped again, sniffed again.

———

On July 17, Molly's eleventh birthday, she and Topher and the kids climbed in the van, Topher at the wheel. Casch watched him checking the side mirror as he merged onto the highway. She smiled just barely. You could get used to this.

"What?" he said, glancing at her.

But she just shrugged and smiled out the passenger window.

"What?" said Molly from the back.

When Topher got off the highway twenty minutes later, there was a gas station and then nothing, a road that went east away from the interstate and turned to dirt.

"Guys, watch for a sign that says trail parking," said Topher, glancing in the rearview at the kids.

"Okay."

"Okay."

"I see it!" said Molly, pointing.

"Perfect, thank you," he said, hitting the blinker. There was a scraping sound under the car as he pulled into the rutted dirt lot.

"Sorry," he said, glancing at Casch.

"She's seen worse."

There was only one other car in the parking lot, which was bordered on one side by grass dotted with dandelions, and then a huge pond. They all hopped out—Molly opened the slider from the back—and Topher went over to an information board that had a big map sheltered by a tiny roof covered in faded wood shingles. Molly followed him.

"We're going to take the pond loop trail," he said, pointing so she could see. "You guys ready?" he asked, turning around to look at Casch and Dean.

"Ready," said Casch softly, folding her arms over her baggy T-shirt.

There was a breeze rustling the trees as they started walking the hard-packed trail. It was too narrow to go side by side, tall grasses on either side, so Topher led, followed by Molly, then Dean, and Casch in the rear. Molly and Dean immediately started asking Topher questions, and at first Casch listened. Then she fell behind and watched. She watched Topher turn every few steps to point at something. She was back just far enough that she couldn't make out what he was saying. Instead she heard a bird sing two pretty notes over and over again.

The trail curved into the woods. Now it was shady, and Casch swatted at the bugs. They went along for a while like that. It had been maybe ten minutes when the three of them suddenly stopped in the trail up ahead of her. Topher was squatting down when Casch came up to them.

"What is it?" she said.

"Mom, shhh," said Molly, and Topher pointed at a tree a few feet away. At first Casch couldn't see what they were looking at.

"It's a porcupine," Topher whispered. Casch stared where he was pointing, at the base of the tree where the bark had split. Now her eyes got it—there was a hollow in the tree, and an animal hiding inside. From where she was standing, Casch could only see a patch of fur.

Actually, she realized, you could kind of see it was quills—the ends of the quills were white, as if the porcupine were turning gray. And the quills were just barely rising and falling: the animal's breath.

"THAT WAS SO COOL!" said Molly when they started walking again. She skipped and ran past Topher up the trail.

"Topher, what do porcupines eat?" said Dean.

"I don't know. That's a really good question."

Casch looked at Dean and watched him take in this idea,

that he had asked a good question. He blinked, then smiled privately as he turned and kept walking.

When the trail curved again and came out of the woods, they were on the far side of the pond, the parking lot just visible across the water.

"Look," said Molly, pointing at some geese in the grass. There were two large geese and four smaller ones, and goose poop all over the ground.

"That's a whole family," said Topher. "Those are the parents and the babies."

"But they're not like cute little babies," Molly objected.

"No, they're teenagers; they hatched in the spring. They're learning how to go out on their own."

Casch watched Topher stare at the birds, hands in his pockets. One of the adult geese was cleaning her feathers while the smaller ones pecked around in the grass.

Casch looked at Molly, then Dean.

And she had a strange feeling.

Which was: She was happy.

She scratched a mosquito bite on her arm.

It was scary to be happy. You know you can lose everything.

Topher stepped forward and pulled something from the tall grass. When he stood up she saw it was a Miller Lite can.

"What are you doing with that?" asked Molly.

"Throwing it away."

When the four of them sat down at the little kitchen table that night, Casch put the first steak in front of the birthday girl. But Molly said, "I'm a vegetarian."

"What?"

"I'm a vegetarian now."

"Since when?"

"I decided."

"What, why?"

"Because the animals, Mom."

"But you knew I was getting steaks. Why didn't you ask for something else?" said Casch, sliding the paper plate in front of Dean.

"I did. I asked for ice cream cake."

Casch looked at her. Then she glanced at Topher. Then back at Molly.

Then they all started laughing. Dean giggled too. All four of them were laughing. Casch, shaking her head, got up and went to the freezer and pulled out the white box. She cut a fat slice of blue ice cream cake and plopped it on a fresh paper plate.

"Girl, it's your birthday," she said, shaking her head.

After they had started eating, Topher put down his fork.

"Wait a second, you guys," he said, wiping his mouth. "Molly, don't you have peas in your garden?"

"Yeah."

"And cukes? Cucumbers?"

"Yeah."

"Well let's go pick 'em. Shouldn't we have 'em for your birthday?"

"Yeah," said Molly, nodding slowly, "yeah, we should."

She pushed out her chair. Dean did the same, and Topher followed them outside.

When they came back in, each of them had a handful, a jumble of snow peas and little cucumbers. They dumped it all in the center of the table. The cucumbers were curved and prickly and some of them had wilted yellow flowers on their ends. Topher grabbed one and rubbed away the spines with his thumbs, then took a loud bite.

"That's how you eat a cucumber?" said Dean.

"Why not?" said Topher.

Casch and Topher sat at the kitchen table talking softly after dinner, while out in the living room, the kids watched TV. At last Topher stood and, without saying anything, stepped into the living room.

"Hey guys, I have an idea."

"What?"

"What?"

"Come outside with me."

"Why?" said Molly.

"Just c'mon."

They both got up, leaving the TV on.

"Want to come too?" he said to Casch as they came through the kitchen. She looked at him curiously and pushed out her chair.

Outside, he led them down the embankment. It was loud with the sound of cars rushing on the interstate below.

"Look," he said.

For a second they were all peering into the green-black of the trees and listening to the highway. It didn't seem like there was anything else. Then there was one yellow flash.

"Oh," said Molly, pointing.

A firefly made a tiny luminous streak by Dean's face, and he inhaled. They all stood and watched the bugs that lit up and went dark as high as the tops of the trees. After a while it was like the lights made a wave, flashing from left to right and right to left, a rolling wave of blinking lights.

After the long silence, Dean looked up and said, "Are fire-flies the proof of magic?"

And all three of them looked at him.

15

I t was raining by the time Topher had inched through the bottleneck on the Saw Mill River Parkway, past the three-car pileup, to the exit. Down on the streets the sidewalks were empty. He went by a fried chicken place where a couple souls had taken shelter under the orange awning and stood peering out at the drizzle.

He turned at the light and went two more blocks until he cruised by the train station. It looked old-fashioned, made of brick with a huge clock in the arch above the entrance. Whenever he came to this one, he always thought, That could be Vermont. Bellow's Falls, maybe, where they had a brick clock tower. New York, he knew, used to be like Vermont—old town centers, not so many people. It wasn't always traffic jams.

Not that you'd know it today. There was a line of taxis, and someone honking behind him, and a truck with its hazards on, trying to make a delivery. He could never live here. He couldn't even find a place to pull over. He would have to drive around.

The radio had gone to commercial, and he switched it off as he made a right, his wipers squeaking. He went under the tracks and turned to take the street along the back side of the station. There were cars waiting on this side, too, to pick up people who came down the long staircase from the platform. And boom, there you go. Someone had jumped into the passenger side of an SUV and the driver was pulling out. There was one car ahead of him. Were they going to take the spot? Nope, it was his. He nosed the Ranger in. Then switched off the engine and texted his location.

He liked making deliveries to Cal, who'd been buying his weed since some of his first trips to the city. Besides sending him customers, he'd shown Topher a couple good watering holes. Made New York a little more familiar.

"Topher, your shit is like the gourmet," he had said one time, rolling a spliff as they sat in the Ranger. "It's like going to a fancy restaurant. Little pickup truck comes down from the farm upstate, drops off the finest product. That's you."

Topher had grinned. It was because of Cal saying that that Topher started seeing himself that way. I'm driving fine produce to the city.

His phone buzzed with a text from Cal.

10 min

Topher settled back in the seat.

Plus Cal had been raised by his grandma. Topher found that out when he'd asked where to get food in the neighborhood. Cal said this little Greek place, said there was a grandma in the back who did all the cooking, that's why it was so good. Said she reminded him of his own gram. That got them talking. Unlike Topher, though, Cal knew his siblings—kids his mom had raised.

"I was the lucky one," Cal had said. "The best thing that could've happened to me was getting out of there and being brought up by my grandma."

That had taken Topher by surprise. *I was the lucky one.*

Cal was carrying a gym bag and a broken umbrella when he came hurrying up the sidewalk and jumped in the truck.

"What up, my man, sorry I'm late. Got caught up at the gym."

"No problem."

"Funniest thing happened, I gotta tell you this. I was lifting, right, but you can see the cardio machines, they're on the other side of the free weights. And this cat I've never seen before comes in and gets on the treadmill and jacks it way up, clearly thinks he's the man. And he's been on there, I don't know, ten minutes, actually probably not even, and check this out. He trips, and the treadmill throws him straight back onto the floor."

"Shut up."

"No, no, and that's not even the good part. This cat *starts doing sit-ups on the floor*, trying to pretend his ass meant to fall off that treadmill. The whole gym was laughing at him."

Topher's forehead angled toward the steering wheel as he laughed.

"I love the gym, you go to the gym? One thing I always thought I wouldn't be down with is the gay guys kind of checking you out, you know what I mean? But you know what? It's kind of flattering. One time this guy was all complimenting me, and I'm like, listen, I don't swing that way—but thanks for noticing, because I *have* been working on my calves!"

Cal pulled out his wallet. After he'd paid and zipped his purchase into the duffel, he said, "Yo, tell me something, Topher man, what's with this truck?"

"What do you mean?"

"What is this, an '89?"

"It's a '99."

"You ever think about upgrading?"

"Nah man, this is my style."

Cal looked skeptical. "Did you forget to pay yourself, is that the issue?"

Topher laughed. "It's not an *issue*," he said.

"All right, well, you let me know when you want to go car shopping. I got a friend with some nice inventory."

"Thanks, I'll keep that in mind. Hey, I'm starving, you wanna grab some food?"

"Nah, I can't today. But I got a question for you."

"Shoot."

"I got a buddy who's been driving some stuff up north. It's kind of the reverse of what you do. He moves stuff from the city up to a couple spots. And he's looking for some more guys to do transport."

"Oh yeah?"

"Yeah, I guess business is good. He needs more drivers. I was like, you should ask Topher, he's going up there anyways—assuming your truck doesn't break down. Are you close to Canada?"

"Uh, not really."

"What, a couple hours?"

"Yeah."

"Close enough. I mean, he's got guys from the city going all the way up to the border. I'm like, shit, you should ask Topher. This is small packages I'm talking about. You could make a couple grand just for driving home."

"A couple grand for transport?" said Topher.

"Something like that."

"You want me to move some blow is what you're saying."

"Not exactly."

Topher looked at him.

"Anyways," said Cal, glancing out the window, "you can think it over or whatever."

When he got back to White River that night, he drank a Red Stripe in the shower. Then lay on top of the sheets in his boxers, scrolling the chat forums.

"You got me curious now," he murmured, sipping a fresh Stripe. He scrolled through a couple threads but couldn't find what he was looking for. He had an idea of what Cal was talking about. Although Cal might be full of shit.

At the bottom of one thread there was a link to an older one. And then, there it was.

not gonna kid u. its the perfect cut

had 1 customer found w/ needle still in her arm. Bad batch 2 much fentanyl

its the perfect cut til ur sister over doses n dies by her storage unit

Biggest problem is Police problem not drug problem.Had to do 2 1/2 years in jail ,got caught selling to undercover and got 5 years on the top.Prison just a waste of time.Never stopped me selling or using

B-town H is about to get a new shipment, Im getting early. A little while back when the white came i think like 10 ppl died-it was all fentanyl.

I have found new low in the pharmaceutical. Give away a month supply of high grade fentanyl for free. This allow more than enough time to create addicts. Mind you Im not complaining. But tell me why Im dirty dealer but they make bank. Hypocrites Im saying.

sound like u r complaining

I am from a place north of Boston (& NO I DO NOT KNOW JARED!) Long enough (almost) history off/on & 10 yrs methadone. Dont be idiots. Cutting H use coffee grinder & not even a quarter fentanyl, the rest H.

This had to be what Cal was talking about. Only something so potent would move in small volumes for that much money.

Toward the bottom of the thread his eye caught on something.

u cocksuckers dont get it. fentanyl come from china, it's war

There were always conspiracy theories on the forums, dipshits claiming insider info about the DEA or the CIA. Even if fentanyl did come in from China, what did it matter?

But maybe it was the soldier in him that double-taked. The guy had dropped a link, and Topher's finger hovered. He tapped it and drained the last sip of his beer.

It went to a page that said Special Operations Command—that was US Army, Fort Bragg, unless it was a fake. The report was long and full of jargon, and acronyms, which did sound like Army. And it didn't have any real info. Of course Army isn't in the business of publishing sensitive information in unclassified reports. But there was one cryptic reference to what it called China's drug warfare.

16

On the last day of summer vacation, the four of them went to the river. Casch parked in the spot by the covered bridge, and they went in a little parade, arms full of towels and snacks, on the path down the grassy embankment. The water was low—summer had mostly been dry—but there was one pool still deep enough to swim. Molly was the first in the water, kicking off her too-small sandals and tossing aside her shorts as she waded in. Dean was right behind her. He didn't need floaties anymore; he was a tank now. Tomorrow he would start the second grade.

Casch and Topher sat on the rocks with their feet in the water. Sunlight twinkled. She shielded her eyes as she watched the kids dunking.

"Aren't you guys getting in the water?" said Molly, tucking wet strands of hair behind her ears. Her swimsuit was black with sunflowers—Flora had bought it for her.

"In a minute."

"Yeah, come swimming. Topher, swim with me," said Dean, his arms pumping in the water.

Topher, grinning, peeled off his T-shirt and wobbled barefoot across the shallow part.

"Mom, you too," said Molly.

Casch was going to protest. The sun felt good, she didn't want to get up. But she smiled at Molly, got slowly to her feet, and they all swam together.

Afterward they came out to shore and Casch pulled out the snacks she'd brought. Chips and dip and a cold bottle of cherry punch, which Dean guzzled until he had a clown-red circle around his lips. They were all quiet after that, Molly and Dean standing wrapped in towels, Casch and Topher sitting, all of them just looking out at the day.

They had been silent a minute when a bird went diving into the water just upriver from them. They all watched as the thing fluttered out and disappeared into the trees.

"What was that!" said Molly.

"I think a kingfisher," said Topher.

"A what?"

"A kingfisher. They dive like that and catch little fish. I don't think that one caught anything, though."

They all kept looking but nothing else happened. The kids got bored, shed their towels, and went back in the water. Topher settled against a rock.

"Two nights a week at the restaurant is enough for you?" he said, interlacing his fingers over his stomach.

"What?" she said, head jerking.

"I mean, you're getting by on that?"

"Why are you asking?"

"Because, you know. When they gave you that second shift you said two nights was still only half what you had before."

She didn't look at him.

"I was just wondering," he said.

There was a long pause and at last he said, "Actually, honestly I've noticed you haven't really been yourself."

"What?"

"You look, I don't know—"

"What do I look like?"

"Just, stressed, I guess."

"Oh, thanks a lot," she said, shaking her head, looking away.

"No, I just mean—" he said, but didn't finish.

She didn't say anything, and they kept their eyes on the kids in the water.

"And I was thinking," he went on, "I know you don't want me to spend the night because of the kids. But would it be different if, if we moved in together?"

For a second she froze.

"You know, then you wouldn't have to pay the bills by yourself."

But she was frozen. She didn't know for how long. The kids splashed and the sun descended and Topher kept talking. And finally he stopped and looked at her. And waited. The words that came from her mouth were, "I know how to take care of myself."

He squinted. "Of course you do," he said.

She stared down toward the rocks, her chest thudding.

"If we move in together," she said, "what am I supposed to tell the kids when you get popped for dealing?"

He flinched.

The sun dipped behind the tops of the trees. Dean, standing on a rock, his trunks dripping, called, "Mom, watch this!"

"Okay, baby," she said.

"Just one question," said Topher quietly. "When were you going to tell me you're not going to nursing school?"

"Excuse me?" came a voice from behind. "Ma'am, excuse me?"

Casch's face was hot as she continued pushing the cart toward the exit.

"Excuse me, ma'am."

She pushed the cart through the automatic door into the vestibule.

"Ma'am."

She kept going through the vestibule as she slid her hand into her purse and brought her phone to her ear. She pressed it against her shoulder as she said, "Yes, this is . . . What? Oh my god."

"MA'AM."

She turned around. A kid in a black apron had followed her out. She gestured at her phone.

"I'm sorry, ma'am, but—"

"Yes, I will, I'm on my way," she said into the phone. Then she held it away from her face and looked at the kid.

"Ma'am, do you have your—"

"It's my daughter's school," she said. "There's some kind of emergency." Then back to the phone, "I'll be there as soon as I can. God, I hope she's okay."

In one movement Casch lowered the phone from her ear and rushed away, the cart's wheels rattling across the asphalt, as the kid stood, his mouth open, by the exit.

She drove back to Vermont before pulling over. Strands of hair stuck to her damp neck as she got out the baggie—which was empty, basically. She sniffed up the bit that was left. It didn't do hardly anything. She licked her finger and ran it along the inside of the plastic and rubbed her gums.

Even after she offloaded the steaks at the back of Sevens, her pulse kept thudding. She had sweat through her shirt. There were circles under her arms as she tucked the warm bills in the cup holder and drove on to Amity Street.

It seemed like she had been here every day, she thought, as she parked by the fire hydrant across the street. All summer she'd had to make excuses to the kids about where she was going. Now, at least, they were back in school. She didn't have to explain herself.

Inside the door she waved to Jasmine as Morty passed her the baggies and took her money. Then she was back out in the car. Sniffing. Feeling better.

She sat there for a second, touching her nose, watching a guy in a newsboy hat push a baby stroller up the uneven sidewalk.

It wasn't like before. It wasn't like thirty milligrams on a piece of tinfoil. She closed her eyes. You felt like a goddess. This? She looked at the baggie. This was maintenance.

By three thirty she was in the door of The 99. At the server station she clocked in—two and change dollars per hour, how about that, she always thought to herself, the lavish minimum wage for tipped workers. She went to the kitchen to grab the silverware and then sat down and started doing roll-ups with Gabi, who chatted while Casch zoned out. Soon Gabi had finished a whole pile.

"Hey girl, you okay?" she asked.

"Yeah, I'm fine."

But Gabi was studying her face.

The whole night went on like that. She was slow at everything. She forgot to put in one table's entire order, which meant she had to beg the kitchen to do it fast. By then it had been forty minutes, though, and the table—two older couples, who frowned at her—left no tip at all.

———

"They get *fired* if they harass you, bro," said one of the kids standing in line in front of her. He had a handful of frozen burritos.

She was at the Price Chopper across from The 99—the place she always used to shop, before—with her cans of tomato soup and a thing of cheese. It felt strange going to checkout.

"Why, though?" said the other kid.

"I don't know. But my sister's boyfriend lifted, like, almost a thousand bucks of stuff."

"Shut up."

"I swear to god."

"And nobody stops you?"

"It's company policy."

"How would you even carry out that much shit."

"You don't know the trick; the trick is the copper wire. It's like a couple hundred bucks a roll."

Casch pretended to thumb a magazine. She had heard this before, that Home Depot had a policy of not intercepting shoplifters. She'd never believed it. But maybe it was worth looking into.

The Greenfield Home Depot was in a strip mall just past McDonald's. Casch could not remember ever coming here. She always pictured guys pulling up in new trucks and going inside for washer-dryers, or patio furniture. Must be nice, she thought, looking up at the American flag waving overhead. She passed through the enormous automatic doors.

Just inside the entrance was what looked like a mile of glossy red and black snowblowers. She grabbed an orange shopping basket and marched toward the back, like she was getting something real specific. You don't want to look like a newbie.

There was no need to worry about that, though, as it turned out. She didn't see anyone who worked there until after she had gotten clear to the other side of the store and there was a guy in an orange apron helping one customer. Another customer was waiting impatiently, shifting his weight from one foot to the other.

Nice, she thought. They're short-staffed.

When she entered the aisle for electrical, a bell chimed and Casch felt a shot of nerves. The empty basket hung off her arm as she looked around slowly until her eyes caught a You're On Camera sign. And below it, Jesus. There was a screen, a small screen broadcasting her own face looking into a camera.

But, see, that's the point, she thought, turning away. Right? That's their whole plan, because they don't stop you on your way out. Right?

Anyways, she thought, this was just recon.

The whole aisle was different kinds of wire. She squinted at the bolded prices that ran along the bottom of each shelf and couldn't find anything like what those kids had said. There was nothing so expensive.

Then she saw it. On the top shelf, much bigger than she'd pictured, rolls of wire that were like giant movie reels. And those kids weren't wrong. These suckers were $200 a pop.

She didn't touch them. She walked up the aisle, opposite direction from the camera, and returned her shopping basket to the stack by the entrance. She zigzagged past the key-making station in the direction of the checkout. And what they had, she saw, was a huge self-checkout zone. Which would seem like a good thing except they had one employee, bored AF, posted there with her arms folded, watching.

Although.

Casch kept walking, like she was heading back toward building supplies. Then she swiveled around. See, who's going to stop you if you come sailing from the other direction and out the door?

And what you want, she thought, watching a guy in white socks and cargo shorts tote his goods out the exit, is a couple of those sand-colored plastic bags. With a long fresh receipt hanging out the top.

She made one more loop, scanning price labels as she went. Finally, from the paint section, she selected two plastic brushes that were seventy-nine cents apiece. At self-checkout she inserted two crumpled dollar bills in the machine and placed each brush in its own bag. As she collected her receipt and strolled toward the exit, she heard the disinterested employee say to an inquiring customer, "Store credit only, if you don't have your receipt."

She was smoking a joint by herself on Friday afternoon when there was a knock on the door. Her body went stiff. Are you kidding me? She glanced around then ashed the joint into yesterday's lunch plate. She had thought DCF was done. They couldn't come in now, the whole place smelled like weed.

She had to hide.

There was more knocking and she sunk into the couch. The window was mostly covered by the shade. But if someone really wanted to, they could probably see in.

Get down on the floor, crawl to the bedroom.

Slowly she slinked off the couch and started across the carpet.

"Casch?" said a voice, muffled, from outside.

She stopped.

"Casch?"

She got up and opened the door. It was Topher on the step, two bags of groceries in his hands.

"Oh," she said. "Hi."

"I thought I'd cook dinner," he said. He seemed to be searching her eyes. "It's this thing my Gram used to make, macaroni with peas—no meat, so Molly can eat it?"

She stared at him. He was nervous, waiting on her answer.

"Uh, okay," she said, "that would be great, actually."

His shoulders eased.

She followed behind as he carried the stuff to the kitchen. When he'd set the bags on the counter, he turned and they looked at each other.

She didn't think, she stepped forward and kissed him. He was surprised for a second, then kissed her back. Then he was pulling her into her room.

On the bed he gathered her into him and slid his hand inside the elastic of her leggings. He was reaching and touching. She felt a zing and her hips squirmed.

Then it seemed like they had been there for a long time. She could feel the weed in her forehead. She was sweating. His touch was gentle but fast.

Warmth was pouring into her. Still he was touching. Her heart was speeding. How long had they been lying here. He kept touching, soft but fast. Soft but fast. And all the feeling gathered and rose in her chest.

But before it could open, bright, in her throat, she pushed his hand away.

"The kids will be getting off the bus," she murmured, and pulled herself up.

After Molly and Dean chowed the macaroni and curled up on the couch, Casch rinsed the dishes and Topher cleaned crumbs from the table. The sound of cartoons floated in from the living room.

"So what do you think if I just spend the night?" he said from behind her. "Instead of driving all the way back to White River?"

She was still for a second. Then flipped off the water. She wiped her hands on the dish towel and turned to look at him. "Okay," she said, nodding.

Later he waited at the kitchen table while she tucked the kids in. And she wasn't unhappy, after switching out their light and closing their door, that Topher was still here.

"Watch a movie?" she asked, folding her arms in the kitchen doorway.

"Sure."

In her bedroom she fiddled with the DVD player while he kicked off his sneakers and lay down. After the movie had been going awhile, he scooted closer, and held her hand.

When she woke—early for a Saturday—he was asleep beside her, his face pressed into the pillow. Around his neck was the chain he wore, the kind for dog tags. But no tags. Just the chain.

She watched his freckled shoulder rising and falling. He was so sturdy. An asteroid could hit the earth and you'd be okay. You'd be the last humans safe and fed.

But see, she needed a morning dose, and here he was. So now she had to sneak off to the bathroom like this wasn't her own home.

Which she did, slipping out of bed and grabbing her purse off the floor and going into the bathroom to sniff.

When he woke he kissed her and put on his pants and said, "I'll get coffees."

And he came back with the coffees plus donuts for the kids.

"Donuts for breakfast!" said Dean, bringing his to the couch. Molly grabbed hers and came back to the couch too.

"Guys, what do you say?"

"Thank you."

"Thank you."

"No prob," said Topher, grinning at them. Then he followed Casch out to the back step.

It was cool but sunny, and soon the kids came outside and went poking into the woods. Dean found an ancient, rusted Budweiser can, older than any of them, filled with black soil. He held it up for them to see.

"That is awesome," said Topher.

"Great find," said Casch.

Eventually Topher got up and went in the house. She knew he would be getting on the road; it had to be noon by now. Maybe he was going to the city. She stood and went inside.

But he wasn't anywhere. The apartment silent, the bathroom door open. She looked in the bedroom.

She found him bent over on the far side of the bed, like he was looking at something on the floor.

And then she saw—he was in her purse.

He was holding her baggie.

"WHAT THE FUCK," she said, running over, grabbing the purse away. But he had the baggie in his hand.

"WHAT THE FUCK, GET OUT OF MY SHIT."

His mouth was open. He didn't say anything.

"I can't believe this. I cannot fucking believe you," she gasped, and then she was reaching, quick, and, *there*, snatched the baggie from his hand.

She had thought Topher was different. She thought he would never, that he would never—but she was wrong. She was wrong about everyone.

"You—?" he said.

The shame lit her face.

"Get out," she said, "get the fuck out."

He was staring at her.

"Did you hear what I said?"

"I was putting this in your purse," he said, opening his other hand. In it was a wad of bills.

She looked at the money. For a second she hesitated. Then she shook her head.

"Get out."

17

At the yard he kept screwing up. He forgot things, he wrote things down wrong. Kevin with the gelled hair had to come in with the clipboard, and said, "Russ, you sure about this?"

Russ looked down at the penciled order and saw that Kevin was right. What dumbass wrote this? But the dumbass was him, it was his scrawl. He made some excuse.

"Oh, you see, it should've been—" he stammered.

"No worries, boss," said Kevin. Taking the pencil from behind his ear, Russ struck a line through the old spec and scribbled the correction.

He worked late because they were busy and his own fuckups set them back. When he finally got home and opened the door from the garage into the kitchen, dinner was on the table. Flora was leaning up against the counter, drink in her hand, watching the little TV.

"You hear about this?" she said, gesturing at the screen as he dumped his keys.

Russ nodded.

"And Greenfield's suing? Suing a big drug company?" she said.

"Yeah."

"Seems crazy," she said, jiggling the ice in her glass. She sipped and set it by her place at the table. "I hope you're hungry. I went to the Polish farm stand."

On the table there was yellow corn on the cob and a platter of grilled chicken—Flor didn't need him to operate the grill, she just fired it up, did it herself—and tomato slices fanned out on a plate. The TV was still going on the countertop when they sat down. He watched until it went to commercial.

"Ronnie wants to go down to that company's headquarters in Connecticut," he said, taking a drumstick.

"What for?"

"I guess he's been talking to these other parents. They're planning some kind of protest."

"Protest?"

"Yeah."

"This lawsuit, doesn't it seem ridiculous?" Flora asked, sipping her drink. "Greenfield suing some big pharmaceutical company—have people gone delusional? This town doesn't have a snowball's chance in hell."

Russ got up and got a Pepsi from the fridge.

"I would have to say I agree with you," he said, popping the tab, sitting back down. "Although in the paper the mayor said she knows this whole thing'll go on after her term is up. Said she doesn't give two shits, said the town is going to slug it out as long as it takes."

He set down the soda and started on the drumstick.

"You know what else Ronnie told me?" he said, chewing.

Flora sipped her drink, didn't say anything.

"Ronnie said he got to talking to a cop at Home Depot. Actually he says the good thing about working retail is you get to talk to everyone, isn't that Ronnie for you. Anyways, he was talking to this cop, and the guy lets it slip that there're going to be raids."

"Raids?"

"On heroin dens. Right here in Greenfield."

The following Wednesday after the meeting, Ronnie volunteered to help put away literature, as it was called. Russ waited across from the restroom by the rear exit, hands in his pockets, shaking his head—another hour of god this, god that—while Ronnie gathered up pamphlets and stacked them in plastic tubs. If Ronnie wasn't his best friend, if his kid hadn't died, if he hadn't explicitly asked Russ to come to this garbage with him. Russ was shaking his head when the bathroom door swung open.

It was the short-haired girl, her right thumb hooked under the thin strap of her purse. She glanced at him and smiled.

"Keep coming," she said.

"What?"

"Keep coming. To meetings."

"Oh. Thanks."

"I'm Nachalah," she said, extending her hand.

"Russ," he said, reaching to shake her hand. "What kind of name is that?"

"Hebrew."

"Oh," he said, "my boss is Jewish."

She looked at him.

"At the scrapyard, Kramer Scrap."

She cocked her head.

"You been coming to these meetings a long time?" he said, pulling his other hand from his pocket, straightening himself.

"Oh, yeah," she said, nodding, "forever. This is sanity right here. Although, I mean, you're new, right? I probably didn't really start feeling it until I had a sponsor and did my fifth step. Well, fourth and fifth. That's why we say keep coming. How many meetings you been to?"

"I'm just here for my friend," he said, gesturing.

She smiled, her cheeks dimpling. "Oh, sure," she said, and pushed out the door.

18

He drove halfway back to White River. He turned on the radio. He turned off the radio. He sprayed the windshield with washer fluid, turned on the wipers, turned off the wipers. Are you fucking kidding me. How did he not know. Your girlfriend's using and you don't even know? You have to be fucking kidding. That is special stupid.

Or had he known.

Why was she looking so stressed all the time? Maybe he had known. Maybe he knew all along. Maybe he knew and didn't want to admit it.

Of *course* she was using—you could see it. She'd been looking like shit. He'd tried to ignore it. He tried to pretend it was something else. She's just stressed, she's a single mom, she's stressed, help her out and everything will be fine. Ha, yeah, everything will be fine.

He passed the sign for Route 103. What the fuck am I doing? She's going to kill herself. She doesn't understand. She has no idea. She can't be fucking with that stuff. Are you kidding me? The kids. She doesn't even know. She could fucking die.

He sped off the exit. Crossed under the highway and got back on going south.

He had to talk to her. This wasn't even, this wasn't like—it was so messed up. It's not *just* heroin, is that what you're going to say?

But he had to go talk to her. Baby, you can't be messing with that; it's way more dangerous than you think. You can't just be, you can't be doing that shit and thinking you'll be okay. Fentanyl is different, fentanyl will kill you in one second, one wrong batch.

His foot pressed the gas. He held the wheel with both hands for he didn't know how long.

Then he laughed.

You think you're going to just *explain* it to her? You're going to say, what? Babe, this isn't the good old days, when the heroin was pure?

He laughed. He laughed loud. I'm sure that'll go over real well. Isn't that what everyone wants, someone telling them to quit.

He looked at the signs. He was on the southbound side; it was miles until the next exit. When it finally came, he got off and got back on heading north. He turned on the radio. The farther north you go, the sparser the stations. There was nothing to listen to.

What the fuck was wrong with her. She could *die*. Are you fucking stupid? You got two kids, are you fucking crazy?

And what was he going to do, *let* her die?

He stared straight ahead.

Then he took the next exit and this time drove all the way back to Greenfield.

When he pulled into Greenfield Terrace, he saw that her van was still there. Just go talk to her, talk to her until she hears it, that's the only option. He knocked but there was no answer.

He leaned into the door and heard the TV. Knocked again.

Finally it opened a crack. It was Molly.

"Hi," she said, peering at him, her wavy hair framing her face.

"Hey, Molly. Where's your mom?"

"In her room."

"Could you grab her for me?"

"Okay," she said.

When Casch appeared, her eyes were narrow. She didn't say anything. Dean was on the couch, both kids watching her.

She stepped outside so that for a second she was right next to him and he could smell cigarettes. She pulled the door closed and kept walking. She went all the way down to his truck before she turned and looked at him.

"Let me make this real clear," she said.

"Casch, I know—"

"You don't know. Because I already told you once to get the fuck out and now here you are."

"Just give me one second, okay? I happen to know this, this, shit, I happen to know. Casch, this is fucking real, you can't be messing with that. You could fucking die."

"I'm not some junkie, you dick."

"No, no, no, I'm not saying—"

"Get the fuck out of here."

"I'm trying to help you! Do you know how stubborn you're being?"

"I'm being stubborn? I fucking broke up with you. What are you even doing here? Get. Out."

She tried to charge past him, but he reached for her wrist. Immediately she snapped herself free.

"Don't you ever—" she said, looking him in the eye. Then she rushed up the step and slammed the door.

———

There was a rattling sound, a banging and a rattling. The room was bright, his pillow wet, and there was a banging sound.

Topher came out of his bedroom in his boxers. Connor was peering in through the cloudy glass pane on the kitchen door.

"What the hell?" said Topher, unlocking it, rubbing his face.

"You were supposed to meet us an hour ago," Connor said. "What's wrong with you? Where's your phone?"

"Uh," said Topher, and he looked back toward his room.

"You get banged up last night?" Connor peered past him to the Red Stripe bottles on the counter.

"I'm fine."

Connor studied him.

"I'll grab you a coffee. Get dressed, I'll be right back."

He tried calling. He left her messages. He tried to explain.

He missed knowing a little more about her every day. One time he had seen her sifting through the bills on the dresser. He'd watched her for a second before she realized he was in the doorway. He always knew she wasn't trying to show any weakness. But she was doing everything by herself. He wanted to say, No one's made of titanium.

He thought about Dean wearing a Spider-Man T-shirt and trying to follow the questions his sister asked. How his expression changed when he understood; he'd go from serious to satisfied. You could actually see him learning.

He thought about Molly, the way she would ask something and look at you and you're totally disarmed.

"Topher, are there enough homes for all the animals?"

"Uh, no."

"Why not?"

What are you supposed to say. Do you tell the truth? We keep cutting down forests and building stuff for people. Or do you lie? But you can't lie, she's watching you, completely alert. What you need is for the truth to be different. You need the world to be better, for her.

He went back to Greenfield Terrace. He knocked on her door, but Casch wouldn't answer. He saw her van; he knew she was there. He tried sitting and waiting for her to come out. Like a stalker. But she didn't come out, and finally he drove away.

He texted but she never replied. After a couple weeks, he didn't text anymore.

He went to the city, made three deliveries in one trip. The last one was Cal. It was dark out, the glow of a streetlight reflecting off an empty stretch of sidewalk, by the time Topher pulled up to meet him.

"You think about that offer?" Cal asked when he had paid and zipped away his bud. The smell of his cologne had filled the cab. "About helping with a little transport?"

"Oh, yeah," said Topher, "thanks man, I appreciate it. But I'm all set, I got my routine and everything."

Cal looked unmoved. "You want to grab a beer?"

"Nah man, I got another drop-off."

When Cal had climbed out and disappeared around the corner, Topher drove up the avenue until he saw a package store. He grabbed a couple singles, cracked one when he was back in the truck, and got on the highway.

He listened to Hot 97 as he sipped the beer and drove. The station disappeared up in Connecticut. He usually kept it on until it got staticky. He nodded his head; he glanced in the rearview mirror. And saw the cop behind him.

"Fuck," he said, setting the beer into the cup holder. How long had the cop been there. His eyes darted from the mirror to the speedometer. He hadn't been speeding, or only a little. He eased off the gas so he was going exactly the speed limit. The cop's lights came on. Fuck. Fuck. He hit his blinker and eased to the side.

The cop swerved into the left lane and went roaring past him.

He was shirtless the next night on a folded towel on his bedroom floor, doing crunches. He could hear the TV in the downstairs apartment. A fly had gotten trapped in the spiderweb by the closet door. He looked at it each time his head came forward. In the middle of his third set, he stopped and grabbed his phone. Hesitated. Called her.

Please pick up. Please pick up.

It rang and rang, but she didn't answer. He tossed it on the bed and switched to push-ups.

Then it buzzed. His heartbeat spiked. He leapt and grabbed it.

But it was a number he didn't recognize. Area code 973, New Jersey.

"Hello?"

"Topher? Hey man, it's Alex."

For a second, Topher was blank. Though he and Alex had spoken all the time in the first year after they'd come home, he didn't know when he'd last heard his voice.

"Hey man, what's up?"

"Long time, right?" said Alex, sort of laughing. "How you been?"

"Uh"—Topher glanced around the room—"uh, okay. Same old, you know."

"You still in Vermont and everything?"

"Yeah, yep. Still up in V-T," he said, and started pacing the room.

"Growing bud?"

"You know it."

"I miss that shit."

"You quit?"

"Had to. I'm going back."

Topher stopped moving. "Going back—reenlisted?"

"No. FDG is sending me."

Topher stared at the cracked white paint on his closet door. "You're going back as a contractor?"

"Yeah. There are actually more contractors than troops now. That's weird, right?"

"That is weird," said Topher, squinting as he tried to picture it. "Did you finish college and everything?"

"Yep. And, and I'm engaged," he said, and Topher could tell that his friend was smiling as he said it.

"What! Congratulations! What's her name?"

"Cara."

"Good for you," said Topher, his eyes closing for a second. "Good for you, how long you guys been together?"

"Almost two years. We're going to wait to get married; you'll get the invitation. Right now I'm about to ship out and everything."

"How long you got to be over there?"

"Nine months this time. After that I'll be able to do shorter terms."

"They paying you good?"

"Yeah. Actually, get this, it's four times what we were making."

"Shut up."

"I'm serious."

Topher sat on the edge of the bed. "Well, it sounds like, sounds like you got your shit together. When do you leave?"

"Next week. It took forever to get my security clearance, then finally it comes through, and everything has to be done yesterday, you know how it is. I've got my physicals the next couple days and then I'm out. But I, uh, wanted to let you know. That it won't be the same without you."

Topher felt that in the center of his chest. "Thanks," he said, "thank you."

For a second they didn't say anything, and he got up and started pacing again.

"Hey, Alex, can I ask you something?"

"Sure, of course."

"Do you know about this drug fentanyl?"

There was a beat of silence.

"I hope it's nothing you're messing with."

"No, no. But do you think—this is kind of random. Is it actually, the fentanyl, is it coming from China? Like, is China doing it on purpose?"

"Oh, that's what you're asking?" said Alex. "Well, you know about the Opium Wars, right?"

"What?"

"The Opium Wars. Nineteenth century I'm talking about."

"Uh. No."

"Okay, well back then China was kind of a kingpin in exports. They were making all the stuff the rest of the world wanted. So kind of like today, actually. But back then it was like tea and silk and stuff. Anyways the British were basically like, we're paying too much money to China. And at that time Britain had India by the balls, right, so one thing they do is the British start growing opium in India. Then they bring it over to China and they're like, any of you guys want this? And people are obviously, you know, happy to have some fine narcotics. Which was a huge win for the British—plus Americans, too, because you know we didn't miss the chance to get in on some lucrative drug dealing. But over in China, the emperor is like, fuck no. And he goes and declares war on drugs. So, yeah, a lot like today. But back then it was the reverse, China was declaring the war on drugs. And that didn't go over so well, because Britain had all this opium to sell. So what do you think the British Navy went and did?"

"Uh. War?"

"Good guess. Yeah the British went in and blew the shit out them. Basically forced China to allow opium so people could smoke all the dope they wanted. Actually, if I have my dates right, this is kind of the beginning of what's called the years of humiliation for China. So, there you go."

"Oh," said Topher, and there was a long pause.

"You get what I'm saying?" said Alex.

"Not really, actually."

"China hasn't forgotten is what I'm saying."

"You mean—?"

"Fentanyl is China beating the white man at his own game."

When he and Alex hung up, Topher stared at the phone.

You got to stop thinking about her. You got no other choice. Stop thinking about her.

19

The morning after she kicked Topher out, she found her pack of Parliaments empty.

"Let's get donuts for breakfast," she said, grabbing her purse. Molly and Dean were on the couch.

"Donuts again?" said Molly, looking from the TV.

"Do you want 'em or not?"

They got their shoes on. And of course after she had gotten the donuts, they were peaceful cherubs in the back of the van, chewing doughy mouthfuls, while she jammed the straw in the lid of her iced coffee and drove a couple blocks to the store. She ran inside to get smokes and came back.

For a while they just sat there. In the rearview she could see Molly and Dean licking sugar glaze from their fingers. Casch pinched the candy-striped straw in her fingers.

She knew what she really needed. Pill on the foil, click of the lighter. In the car seat she leaned back and tasted burnt marshmallow. Why couldn't she feel like that. That was what she needed. Not everyone judging her. Not the whole world messing with her. What she would give for one of those pills. She closed her eyes.

And when she opened them, she found herself looking at the bubble letters in the window of the check-cashing place. We Buy Gift Cards it said, with a Home Depot logo drawn in by hand. She stared at the big orange lettering.

"Mom, what are we doing?" said Molly.

"Nothing," said Casch, and fired the engine.

She went on Monday morning, soon as the kids were on the bus. This time she didn't take an orange shopping basket.

She went marching past the snowblowers toward the back of the store. She walked through appliances and then made a loop up toward electrical. When she entered the aisle and heard the bell chime, she kept her back to the camera. For a second she stood pretending to consider the options. There was no one around, but she did it anyway. She put one finger to the price label on an eye-level shelf, like she was maybe doing the math, considering real hard which one to get. Then, decisively, she reached up and grabbed one, then two, giant spools of copper wire.

Her back was still to the camera. She kept it that way as she exited the aisle the same way she'd come and went back to appliances. Walked along the far wall of the store and into an empty aisle in building supplies. Facing a stack of aluminum roofing, she pulled two plastic bags from her hoodie, like no big deal, and dropped one spool into each bag. Positioned a receipt so it waved conspicuously. Then she was walking, expressionless, up toward the front of the store.

But there.

There, to the right. An orange apron.

He was looking at her.

Her heart started galloping. Keep your face blank. You're a customer heading for the exit, everything's fine.

No, he's looking, he won't stop looking, he is coming your way. Fuck. FUCK.

"You're, Casch?"

When he said it she was trembling.

"Uh. Yeah."

"Hey, I'm Ronnie. Russ's friend, Ronnie. You probably don't remember me."

"Oh. Hi."

"How are you?"

"Oh, okay. Getting by."

"How are your kids?"

"Good. Molly's like an adult, it's crazy."

"It's amazing how fast—" he said, looking at her face, looking at her like he could see straight to her insides.

Then he glanced down at the shopping bags. The plastic had begun to strain under the weight of the spools, the handles carving red half-moons into her fingers.

"I've gotta run," she said, and for a second she made herself look right at him. She looked straight in his eyes, because screw Russ and anyone he's ever been friends with. Then she kept walking, right past self-checkout.

She was out the door. She was outside, everything was fine.

But she was never going back there.

So now she was driving around with four hundred dollars of copper wire that she couldn't swap for store credit, meaning no gift card that could be swapped for cash.

176

Meaning, the stuff was worthless. Couldn't anything go her way? Couldn't a single friggin thing go her way?

She drove around the rotary. What was she even doing? She had nowhere to be.

And the baggie she just got was already out. She touched her nose. It goes quicker than you think. You think a little will go a long way, but it doesn't. You need a little more than last time every time.

She went around the rotary again. There was the big honking sign for The 99, so big you could see it from the highway.

And then she realized who to ask about the copper.

"You can get like two bucks a pound for copper at the scrapyard," said Rick, taking a drag on his cigarette.

It was afternoon and the two of them stood over the picnic table behind the restaurant. Casch had been relieved that Gabi wasn't working lunch today—she just needed to talk to Rick, needed to take care of business.

"The scrapyard," she repeated.

"Yeah. That's why people rip pipes out of foreclosed homes. You never heard of that? Copper's valuable."

"I can't go to the scrapyard," she said, shaking her head. "My mom's husband is manager there."

For a second they didn't say anything. The only sound was a truck rattling along the highway.

"I can go with you tomorrow if you want," he said, flicking his cigarette. "You can just wait in the car."

When she went to Morty's the next morning, Jasmine was on the couch and Casch sat down beside her with a fresh baggie. She picked at the knot with a fingernail, then dipped the van key and sniffed. Dipped again, sniffed again. And again. Her nose was raw but she felt okay.

"You know you're wasting it like that," said Jasmine, tapping a cigarette from a smushed pack.

"What."

"Sniffing it like that, you're wasting it. You don't use all that when you're shooting it. When you shoot it, you feel it, you know what I mean?"

Casch swallowed the drip in her throat and didn't say anything.

She left Morty's and picked up Rick and they drove east across town. She had never been alone with Rick. The radio was on low, and for a minute they didn't say anything. His skin looked almost yellow in the morning light.

"Did you really know the guy who killed that woman?" she said, glancing at him. Back in the spring a woman had been murdered in Greenfield, and Gabi had told her that Rick knew who did it way before the police figured it out.

"He dated my sister's friend—it was sad. Wicked sad."

She looked over at him. On his neck just below his ear was a small cross tattooed in blue ink.

When she got to the chain-link fence that marked the start of the scrapyard, she pulled over and turned off the car. Reaching behind her seat, she gathered up the unspooled copper and handed it to him.

Then she watched from behind her sunglasses as he walked through the yard's main gate. There was a semi parked there and she saw a couple guys walking back and forth. She could hear the beep of another truck backing up. Rick disappeared. She clicked the car keys between her fingers and remembered coming here as a girl. There had been a heap of scrap metal, tall as a building, and she recalled the crazy jumble of objects in the heap. Bicycle frames bent and twisted, old sinks ripped from countertops, sections of piping like big metal pasta. The place was so messy, so electric.

She had a blurry recollection of Russ standing in the sunshine, talking about the yard. She hadn't paid attention to what he said, but there was a piece of a story that stood out in her mind. Some guy had built the scrapyard out of nothing, and people were glad to get rid of stuff they thought was junk. But it wasn't trash, that was the thing. None of it was trash, it was all treasure. It was all waiting to become something new. For a hazy second Casch saw her young self, arms folded over her bony chest, grinning against the deafening noise of a car getting crushed.

Sitting in the van now, she watched a thickset figure cross her sightline. She was too far away to see his face. But she knew who it was. Russ was pointing; he was looking down at a clipboard; he was pointing and shouting. Her eyes narrowed. Then Rick popped out of nowhere, crossed right behind Russ and came striding out toward the gate, his hands in the pockets of his sagging jeans.

"It was over two bucks a pound, so you got sixty bucks," he said, climbing into the passenger seat and handing her three twenties and a few warm coins. Her fingers closed over the money.

"You're not taking a cut?" she said.

"Nah, it's cool," he said, shrugging. His eyes fell to her body.

—

"In school we learned about the Indians," said Molly.

"Oh, yeah?" said Casch. She emptied the box of pasta into the pot and rubbed her forehead with two fingers. Dean was at the table coloring.

"Did you know there's a tribe in Greenfield? Did you know they're called the Abenaki?" said Molly. She said it slow, Ah-ben-aki.

"Uh, no. I didn't know that."

"A woman visited our class, and she said there used to be so many fish in the river that you looked in the water and all you saw was them all moving together, that's how many fish there were."

"Is that true, Mom?" said Dean. "Is that possible?"

"I guess so, if she said it," said Casch, rubbing her forehead. She turned around and stirred the pasta with a fork.

"The woman said the Abenaki are still here," Molly went on, "and the teacher said we're going to learn about wild plants in the spring. She said you can go in the woods and find plants you can eat. Why don't we do that, Mom?"

For a second Casch didn't say anything. Molly stood waiting for an answer.

"I know one of them," said Casch suddenly. "I know one of the plants."

"You do?" Molly's eyebrows lifted in surprise.

"Yeah, it's called, shoot, what's it called?"

"Maybe Topher knows the plants," Molly said.

Casch went back to stirring the pasta.

"Maybe Topher knows how to make a canoe," said Dean.

"What if we didn't get food at the store?" said Molly. "What if we went looking for it in the woods?"

Casch stirred.

"Maybe then we wouldn't have to eat spaghetti every night," said Molly.

"You got a problem with dinner?" said Casch, turning back around.

Molly looked at the floor.

"Ramp," said Casch. "That's what it's called. Wild ramp."

There was a bright orange note stuck to the front door when she came back from taking out the trash the next morning. "Late," it said, with smaller words underneath.

She tore it off and stared at it. What day was it.

It was September, of course it was September. The first of the month had come and gone.

And she didn't have it. She didn't have the money.

She could maybe figure it out if her mind wasn't such a fog, she thought, pushing inside and turning the deadbolt behind her. If she could clear her head and feel better, then she could figure out how to pull together the money.

"Seven dollars?" she repeated.

In the glass case in front of her, there was a row of ugly watches beside a tray of diamond rings.

"And that's generous, I can't get more than twenty for it," said the man behind the counter. Just over his shoulder was a row of TVs, most of them nicer than the one from her bedroom that was sitting in front of him on the glass countertop, its cord hanging limp.

"You want to do it or not?" he said.

She filled out the slip and took the five and two singles.

Then she drove back across the river that was the line between New Hampshire and Vermont and went direct to Amity Street. She sunk into the couch beside Jasmine. Oscar licked her hand.

"Hey, girl," said Jasmine. Morty disappeared up the stairs.

"Hey."

When Morty came back down, he dropped the baggie on the table. "Fifteen," he said.

She didn't look at him.

"I have seven bucks."

"You're kidding."

For a second she didn't say anything.

"If you just take the seven, I'll have more later today. I just need this for now," she said. She could feel him looking at her, but she didn't look up.

"Oh, just give her a break," said Jasmine.

"You stay out of this," he said. But then he said, "Okay, give me the seven, but you make sure to get me the rest today."

She still didn't look at him. She passed him the folded bills just as someone else was knocking. Morty grabbed the money and went to answer it. Casch picked at the knot. Dipped the key and sniffed.

"I used to be like you," said Jasmine.

Casch looked up at her. "What?"

"I used to be like you. Scared of needles. But trust me, girl. You get over it."

Casch looked at the baggie. "How do you even—" she said, mucus in her throat, but she didn't finish.

"Know how to do it?"

"Yeah."

"At first you got to have someone do it for you."

There was a pounding in Casch's ears as she stared at the baggie in her palm.

"But once you know what it feels like, I mean. You never go back to that."

"Hey? Jasmine?"

"What."

"Uh?"

"You want me to do it for you?"

Casch swallowed.

"I don't like doing it for other people," Jasmine said, shaking her head.

"Oh. Sure," said Casch, nodding. The pounding kept on in her ears. The only other sound was Morty talking to a guy at the door. Then he went upstairs and left the guy standing there.

He looked familiar, Casch thought, staring at him from the couch. He had a pinched nose. He tapped his foot as he stood there. She watched him. Where did she know him from?

Morty came back down. And she realized, that was him. That was the guy who drove over her foot. Morty was handing him product.

They'd arrested him, she remembered—but that was months ago now. He must have gotten out.

Her mouth opened. Her head was pounding; she was sweating.

What was she going to say. He was giving Morty money. This was her chance. She should go take a swing at his face, that's what she should do.

But he was turning and leaving and the door clicked behind him.

"Casch," said Morty, putting the bills in the pocket of his sweatpants, "how you doing on getting that money?"

"Oh, leave her alone," said Jasmine. She had popped a fresh cigarette in her mouth and was holding it there, unlit. When Morty walked away she rolled her eyes. "Don't let him bother you," she said.

Casch's face was frozen. Why hadn't she said anything? What was wrong with her?

Jasmine was looking at her. "You been getting sick?" she asked.

Casch's eyes went to Jasmine. She nodded one nod.

"Fuck it, whatever, I'll do it," said Jasmine. "Come upstairs."

Casch's face flushed.

"You want to or not?"

For a second she didn't move. But then she nodded.

Oscar trotted up the carpeted stairs between them. This is who you are now? She pressed that thought away. This is how you're going to feel better.

She hadn't been in the upstairs before. There was shag carpet in the hallway and a musty smell, and the only light came in around the frayed edges of a vinyl shade. There were three shut doors.

Jasmine opened one of them and plopped onto a bare mattress. "Gimme that," she said, reaching her hand for the baggie. Then she plucked something off the floor.

The pounding was going in her ears. You're really doing this?

Jasmine spooned out a little brownish powder and squirted it with water. She clicked a lighter underneath and in a second it bubbled. With her mouth Jasmine pulled the orange cap off a needle and used the tip to stir.

"Here," said Jasmine, gesturing at the spot beside her, cap still in her mouth, and Casch sat down. Her heart was going a thousand a minute.

She looked the other way when she stuck out her arm. She felt a yank above her elbow, and something knotted there. Jasmine was tapping the crook of her arm. Casch was wincing, bracing for the needle. And *shit*, there it was. She inhaled. And then

One orgasmic instant and her head rang and the warmth cloaked her.

"There you go," said Jasmine softly, untying the thing.

20

That Wednesday when the meeting finished, Russ and Ronnie walked out to the church parking lot in silence. It was seven o'clock, the sun already down. Ronnie sunk into his battered Celica and pulled away as Russ went slowly on to his car.

"You have a good night now, Russ," said someone behind him, and he turned to look.

"Oh hey, you too, Na, Na-cha-lah."

He shook his head at himself; he sounded like a moron.

She had stopped and was peering at him in the dark.

"You want to get a coffee?" she said.

His stomach waved. The girl was asking him to coffee.

"Now?" he said.

She smiled, nodded.

That was how he came to be sitting behind a paper cup, in a chair bolted to the McDonald's floor, looking across the laminate table at the stud sparkling from the girl's left nostril. Russ was not normally a fan of piercings, but this suited her. With both hands wrapped around the coffee like she was warming herself, Nachalah raised the cup to her lips and sipped. She had rings on every finger, even her thumbs.

What was he supposed to say? He never knew how to do this. What do you say to a girl? But she saved them, she just started talking.

"—drinks a night was pretty normal in my house, and every few weeks Dad would move out, have a new girlfriend. Mom would send my brother looking for him. Eventually, though, you know, I got older, I started calling them on their shit. Do you want to hear this?"

"Sure," he said, shifting in the hard chair, looking at her.

"Okay," she nodded. She peered at him and he had a swallow of coffee.

"So I got older and realized people don't have to operate that way, like there are other options, you know? By that time they're divorced, Dad moved to Jersey with his new wife, my mom's still in Queens, I really did start calling them on their shit. But what happened, especially with my mom, what happened was I might as well have been the devil, the way she treated me. The moment I stopped accepting her dysfunctional shit, she's like, you ungrateful cunt. And there's this part of me that was like, maybe I am the problem, you know?"

She looked at him with very large eyes. Never, he had never, met anyone who talked like her.

"It doesn't sound like you did anything wrong," he said. The words came out slow.

"You know, there's this complicated muck of shit that other people did to us and what we did to other people. And what I've learned, see this is the program talking, what I've learned is you can't be honest about what other people did to you without being honest about what you did to others. That's after the fifth step."

He fiddled with the coffee lid. This right here was the problem with the psychobabble. She didn't get it. Shit, could she see his hand shaking? As if *the twelve steps* are going to make things disappear. Grow up.

"So, Russ," she said, leaning back in the chair, "you're an interesting character."

"Oh-h?"

"Yeah. Al-Anon is mostly women. More dudes have been coming lately, actually. But not"—she looked at him—"well. If you don't mind my asking, what really brings you in?"

"My friend asked me to come along with him."

"Al-Anon's not the sort of thing you usually do with a friend. Do you think there was a reason your friend thought, maybe, that you—"

Again their eyes met. That was how she was so pretty, those eyes. He looked down at his coffee.

"I mean, sometimes we come in thinking it's for one thing, then find out it's another. I guess I'm just saying, I hope your friend keeps you coming long enough that you, you know, get something out of it."

"Uh-huh," he nodded, and sipped the coffee.

"Like tonight's meeting, we're on the ninth step, right? There was this, like, legendary Al-Anon story, true story, that kind of set off a lightbulb for me. Starts off typical, newcomer can't imagine doing the ninth step. She's all, I'm not making amends, shit's not *my* fault—we've all been there, right? Anyway, she gets remarried and her new husband gets a promotion that moves them right near her parents. So it turns out, all along, she had some shit with her parents that was hanging over her. You get me? And now that she's basically neighbors with them, it's like, are you going to pony up? So finally she does. I mean, she does her eighth step first, she gets all ready, she makes her list of people she's harmed, et cetera, and finally she goes and makes amends with her mom. I don't know what went down between them. There was just some shit, and she knew she had to clear it up. So she went and did it, right, she went and really talked to her mom, and then after that, she and her husband go off on vacation. And while they're on vacation she gets a call from Dad. Mom had a heart attack. You follow? That was the very last conversation she ever had with her mother."

Nachalah stretched her back against the chair.

"And that was this major kick in the ass for me. You know, get your house in order, life's crazy, people die. Take care of your shit. I mean, easy does it, obviously. You've got to do each step. But you get my drift."

She lifted her coffee. Russ, squinting, pressed his lips together. She really believed this garbage.

"I know, you're skeptical," she nodded, "but I promise you, you keep coming to meetings, at some point you realize this program works, that whatever's troubling you, the steps work. There's a reason so many people follow it."

She smiled at him across the table.

He sniffed a laugh. She had no clue, there are some things that can't ever be forgiven. You think your steps work? Let me tell you this, how about this? And suddenly he had the urge to tell her what happened to him.

In his neck his pulse spiked. What was wrong with him? Why would he tell her? He'd never told anyone.

She was looking at him curiously. He should go. He should just get up and go.

"You okay?" she said.

"Yeah, thanks," he said, standing up, off balance for a second, "I got to get home. Nice talking to you."

———

At the scrapyard in the morning, he stood by his desk squinting at the clipboard, rubbing his forehead. He had a headache. Right—here. He pressed with his fingers.

"Russ?"

He looked up. Kevin was standing in the doorway.

"Yeah, hey?"

"Russ, that order's all set. We're gonna start Delaware."

"Really," he said, "ahead of schedule?"

"Yeah, how about that for a change?" Kevin smiled.

Russ looked at him. He was a good kid. "Okay then," said Russ, "get to it."

"Sure thing. But hey, Russ, can I ask you something?"

———

It was warm that morning when Casch came outside with an idea. She climbed in her van and slipped on her sunglasses.

It had been years since she'd been to Flora and Russ's ranch. Not that that was long enough, she thought, as she cruised into their neighborhood. If she came back in a hundred years, it would still be too soon. But she parked around the block and shuffled up the sidewalk toward their place.

When she got to the driveway, she glanced around to check if anyone was watching, then cut across the grass and around the back of the garage. Both of them would be at work, but she peeped in the garage window anyway just to make sure both cars were gone. Then she went striding across the backyard and pulled open the shed door. It creaked on its hinges. The shed was dark inside and smelled like rotting grass. But in the corner, behind the lawn mower, she could see a green ball cap hanging from a nail. She leaned and lifted the hat, and there was the key. Of course the key was there, nothing changed at this house. That key had been hanging from that nail since José Canseco played for the Red Sox.

Quietly she unlocked the door into the garage and let herself inside.

The smell of coffee hung in the kitchen, and there was the pansy wall clock. She stared at it, its ticking the only sound. Then she glanced around. The place was so clean. The counters and sink and everything were all wiped down, with one plaid dish towel neatly folded. It was so clean it pissed her off. Okay, Mom. You win.

She was silent as she crossed the living room. They'd gotten a new TV, she saw, this one much bigger than the old one. In the hall on the far side of the living room, she felt a wave of sick as she passed what used to be her room. It looked hollow now, just an empty desk. She kept on down the hall.

Of course Flora had made their bed, and there were decorative pillows that matched the heinous teal swirly pattern of the comforter. For half a second Casch stood frowning at it.

Then she turned and opened the closet. She knew just where it was, on Russ's side, up on the top shelf. An old mayonnaise jar—glass, that's how old it was. Filled to the top with change. She could just barely reach it, and when she nudged it off the shelf, it almost dropped. Almost dropped right on her bad foot, because it was way heavier than she expected. Had to be over a hundred dollars in here, she thought. With the jar in her hands, she started out.

—

"Ask me something?" Russ repeated.

"Yeah," said Kevin, edging into the office, "I need some advice."

"Advice."

"Yeah. And, you know, I look up to you."

Russ blinked at him.

"My real dad's never been around," said Kevin.

"Oh?"

"Yeah, so. So, my girlfriend wants to move to Boston."

Russ rubbed his forehead.

"I mean, not, like immediately, I'm not saying I'm leaving my job," he said quickly.

"Okay."

"But she's looking for work in Boston. She wants to maybe get into real estate."

"Real estate?"

"Yeah."

"Huh."

"And so, I just, kind of need some advice, you know? Like, if she gets a job, should I move with her? Tag along, basically? And just hope I find something in Boston? You know what I mean?"

"How old are you?"

"Twenty-four."

Russ had thought the kid was eighteen. "What do you, uh, like about this girl?"

Kevin brightened. "She's fun, she's ambitious. She's really cool, Russ."

"Well, Kevin. There's really only one thing I can say to that," he said, clearing his throat.

The kid, so earnest, waited for Russ to go on.

"Which is, have you considered what *you* actually want? You get my meaning there? Do *you* actually want to go to Boston?"

Kevin stared at him. "I think I might," he said.

"Oh. Well, so. You can go to Boston. You don't have to marry her."

They were both quiet.

"Okay," said Kevin at last, nodding. "Cool, thanks, Russ."

"Anytime."

He turned to go.

"Oh, hey, Kevin?"

"Hm?"

"Listen, I think I'm coming down with something. Sounds like you guys are all set, ahead of schedule and everything, so I'm going to go ahead and take off."

Kevin hesitated. "I hope it was okay I asked you that?" he said.

"Oh, sure. No problem at all. I'm just a little, under the weather. Let the other guys know, will you?"

"Sure, Russ, you got it."

When he left the yard late morning, Russ forgot his lunchbox. He slipped quietly out the side door. He gripped the 4Runner's steering wheel as he rolled out onto River Street. Went up the hill, past the turnoff to Poet's Seat, and downhill toward home.

———

Casch stepped into the garage and closed the door softly behind her. It was cool and dark in here, and for a second, felt nice. She had a headache—she'd had a headache all morning, she realized.

The jar, weighty in her hands, would turn into a hundred bucks in one second in the coin machine at the Price Chopper. That would make her feel better. It wouldn't pay the rent, but it was something. She crossed the empty garage toward the door out back.

But all at once there was a thundering rattle and her head jerked up and the garage door was lifting. Her pulse zoomed, she rushed for the door.

If she had left it wide open, she could have maybe slipped out. But it was closed, and she had to reach for the knob. And as she reached with her right hand, the heavy jar, unsteady in her left, slipped and dropped. Glass shards and a thousand coins sprayed across the moist cement floor.

And she and Russ were looking at one another.

———

He flipped off the engine and got out.

"Wha—?" he said, his mouth open. It had been years since he'd seen Casch. She looked a lifetime older. His eyes fell to the coins and followed them around the floor, then back up to her. She was staring at the ground. He took a step in her direction, and she looked up.

"What—?" he started to say.

"Don't try to say anything," she said, shaking her head, voice cracking. "Don't try to tell me anything; you don't know me."

"Listen, Casch—" he said, shaking his head, taking another step toward her. But his head ached and he didn't even know what he was trying to say. Again his eyes fell to the broken glass.

Which was why he didn't see her body pivot from her right

hip and then her right fist shoot forward and connect, powerful—surprisingly powerful—with his cheekbone.

"FUCK," he said, grabbing his face.

And she was gone.

———

She sat in the van gasping, rubbing her fist. She'd run all the way
back to the car—not that he'd followed her. She checked her
mirrors again. No. He was back there licking his wounds. She
half smiled.

Because that was a goddamn perfect move. A perfect shot.
The way she'd pivoted and swung and connected, that was beautiful. One side of her mouth lifted into a smile as she replayed it
in her mind. A strange feeling melted over her.

She was—proud.

Yeah, she was.

"You. Are. A kick-ass bitch," she said, and then she said it
again. She said it louder. She said, "YOU, CASCH ABBEY, ARE A
KICK-ASS BITCH."

She laughed. She was a crazy person shouting in her car.

"BABY, YOU ARE A KICK-ASS BITCH."

It was true! Nobody was going to tell her otherwise. Nobody
was going to fuck with her. Look at her, taking care of herself.
You know what this calls for? Music. She turned on the car and
punched through the stations. She heard the Rihanna song,
nodded her head. Only girl in the world. From her purse she
fished her last cigarette and lit it.

She was still broke and she still needed the rent. But she
would make that trade any day, a hundred bucks in a coin jar for
a clean shot at Russ's face. She would make that trade every day

of her life. She bobbed her head. She exhaled a bone-colored puff of smoke.

After a while, sitting there, the problem of the rent floated back and settled over her. What she needed was someone who had real money. Who has real money? She sat there, smoking down the cigarette, thinking.

———

"Oh my god, what happened to you?"

"Just a . . . accident . . . at the yard," he said.

"Jesus, Russ, you look like hell. You want ice?" said Flora, fluttering around the couch.

"No, no. I'm fine."

It was a little after seven the next morning when the phone rang. Of course he would normally be at the yard, but he wasn't going in with the shiner. He had already called one of the guys to open for him.

From the couch he heard Flora answer the phone in the kitchen.

"Oh my god, calm down," she said, "calm down."

Silence.

"*What*?"

Silence.

"What coffee can?"

Silence.

"Me and Russ are coming over now. You shouldn't be alone. We'll be over in a minute."

He heard her slam down the phone.

"You will not believe this," she said, hurrying into the living room.

"What?"

"Marylouise got home, you know, after her night shift?"

"Yeah?"

"And her house was robbed."

21

"Casch, can you come talk to me, please?"

The manager was sitting at a high-top with papers spread out around him. She had only just come in the door. She was on time and everything, her black apron tucked in her armpit. It was three thirty on the nose.

"Uh, sure," she said, stomach waving as she punched her number into the computer at the server station. What did he know? No, he couldn't know. Was he going to fire her? First you cut my shifts, now you fire me? Her hands were cold as she weaved over to his table.

"Listen, Casch," said Chris, setting down his pen, "one of the new girls quit. And I'm wondering, would you be able to pick up two more shifts?"

She stared at him.

"Two more shifts?"

"Yeah. I was thinking, since you went down from four, maybe you'd be able to go back up to four? Then I don't have to hire anyone else."

"Uh, yeah, sure," she said, gathering all her weight on her right foot, "I can do that."

"Great, thanks."

She looked at him and nodded. Then turned and went to get the silverware from the kitchen. Those two shifts put her back to her old schedule. Back to normal.

"Hey, girl," said Rick, wiping his hands on a dish towel, "how you doin?"

"Okay?" she said. And maybe she really was okay. She lifted her head and nodded slowly. That made him smile. But she was already turning and heading back to the dining room.

It was a Saturday and it turned out to be one of their busiest nights ever. People kept pouring in. It had to be tourists. They must be heading north. Was it already fall? That was a thing about Vermont: People came to look at the trees change color. But whatever it was, the place was so busy they were on a wait, customers collecting in the doorway and listening for their names to be called.

"I am completely slammed," said Casch, grinning as she carried three pints in a triangle between her hands and passed Gabi on the floor.

"Thank you, Jesus," said Gabi.

Casch was still grinning as she went to deliver the beers. She set them down and with the side of her wrist, brushed a strand of hair from her face as she said, "So what can we get you folks tonight?"

By the time the shift was over she had messed up one table's order. But it didn't matter. When she counted her earnings, she had the most ever, three hundred dollars. Standing by the bar, she undid her apron.

"Boy, I needed tonight," said Gabi, coming up behind her.

"Me too," Casch whispered.

"I put these winter coats on layaway for my girls, cute ones with fur hoods. Now I can go pick those suckers up."

Casch blinked at her. "Hey, Gabi?" she said.

"Hm?"

"You think you could do me a favor?"

"Sure, girl, what's up?"

From the money in front of her, Casch counted out two hundred dollars.

"When you're at school next, you think you could give them this?"

She tried to hand Gabi the money.

"What's this?" her friend asked, studying Casch's face. Weeks ago Gabi had peppered her with questions: Are you signed up for classes? What's your schedule? But Casch had only shrugged, and finally Gabi stopped asking.

"Say it's the deposit for Casch Abbey, nursing school," said Casch now.

Gabi stared at her. Then she seemed to get it.

"Okay, I got you," she said softly, and Casch pressed the bills into her palm.

"Guys, I'm going out for a while," she said in the morning, poking her head into the kids' room.

"Where?"

"Just out."

"You said we would do something special this weekend," said Molly.

"Did I say that?"

"Yeah."

"Well, later. We'll do it later."

"Where are you going?"

"None of your business."

"Mom, don't."

"I'll be back."

Morty, shirtless, let her in.

"Oh good, it's Casch. She'll agree with me," said Jasmine from the couch. "Look, Casch, come here. Look at these pimples on his back, see?"

"Shut up," said Morty.

"Just let me ask her. See, look at those. All I'm saying is, let me pop them, right? Obviously they need popping."

"It hurts when you do it," he said.

"Uh?" said Casch, looking at Morty then Jasmine, who started laughing.

"Fuck you both," said Morty, and went upstairs.

"Poor baby, he got no pain tolerance," said Jasmine, lighting a cigarette. "You want a smoke?"

"Sure, if you can spare one."

"I went to New Hampshire yesterday. I got a carton. Actually, you know what?"

Jasmine got up and grabbed a pack out of the box on the kitchen counter.

"Here you go, hon."

"Really?"

"Sure. I got a whole carton."

"Hey, thank you," said Casch, accepting the pack from Jasmine's outstretched hand.

When Morty came back and she had paid for the baggie, she rolled it between her fingertips, watching Jasmine smoke down her cigarette. Then she said, "Hey, would you, uh—"

"Girl, you gotta learn how to do it yourself."

"I feel like I'll screw it up. But I know you'll do it right."

For a long pause neither of them said anything.

"Okay," said Jasmine, hoarse, nodding. She took a drag on the cigarette and put it out. "I got you. I know how it is."

Jasmine did know how it was, Casch thought as she followed her up the stairs, her eyes level with the loose tank top that hung from her friend's skinny shoulders.

Jasmine tied her off, slid in the needle, pushed the plunger just barely, and pulled it back to check for blood. She pressed it slowly until the whole barrel had emptied.

"There you go," she said softly.

Casch shuddered as the warmth melted down her head. Then she was just happy. Cozy happiness. The thing she never got to feel. That everything was all right.

That Friday she didn't have to work. She came back from Morty's and was sitting on the front step when Molly got off the bus. Dean's dad had picked him up from school.

"Where are we going?" said Molly, frowning, after Casch stood and gestured toward the van.

"You'll see," she said, brushing off the rear of her leggings.

Ten minutes later they pulled into the parking lot at Poet's Seat. Molly peered out the window at the trees.

"I walked in here one time," said Casch. "There are trails and stuff. I think you'll like it."

"Okay," said Molly, turning to look at her mother, surprised. "But let's go up the tower first." She jumped out and slammed the door.

Casch followed Molly across the dirt lot and glanced at a bronze plaque while Molly started up the iron staircase, her footfalls echoing. "For Those Who Seek Solace in Nature," the plaque said. Someone had spray-painted *ICE* beside it.

The tower was four stories of jagged brown stones mortared together with cement, a steel spiral staircase running up the middle, and arched lookout windows at every level. When she got to the top, Casch stood beside Molly, the breeze swirling their hair.

The trees had begun to turn orange and apple red, and the whole town spread below them like a picture map. Straight ahead was the hospital, a huge flat building with antennas on top, surrounded by a parking lot, the empty spaces marked off with white lines. A couple blocks beyond the hospital, you could see the old silver factory, and the yellow arches of McDonald's. To the west you could see the jail.

"It's funny," said Molly.

"What?"

"When you look at it like this, it's so simple."

Casch, blinking, followed Molly back down to the parking lot.

Just beyond her van there was a blaze of paint on a tree marking a trail heading downhill. Casch thought it was the way she and Topher had gone. For a while the two of them walked along in silence. The trail grew steep, which Casch didn't remember. Was this the right way? She glanced behind her.

She remembered Topher stopping and showing her a flower, then picking a leaf for her to taste. There was so much green on both sides of the trail, how would you ever know which plant was which?

"I want to know what all the plants are," said Molly, reading her mind.

"Wouldn't that be cool?"

"You know what we learned at school? That you can make medicine from pine trees. The teacher said when it's flu season you should make tea from pine trees and then you'll stay healthy when everyone else gets sick."

"Wow, that's handy," said Casch.

"How do you make tea from pine trees?"

"I have no idea."

"Well maybe when you're a nurse, you'll know the plants, and you can help people get their medicines that way."

"Uh," said Casch, squinting into the trees, "I'm not sure they teach that."

"Why wouldn't they teach that? In school I said my mom's going to be a nurse and she's going to heal people. And we learned that you can eat dandelion leaves."

"Oh, yeah?" said Casch, brushing away a tear.

"Yeah. Like instead of lettuce, you can eat leaves from dandelions. And dandelions grow everywhere, they even grow at our house."

"That's true, they grow in cracks in the sidewalk," said Casch, clearing her throat.

"Yeah. It seems better that way."

"What way?"

"Going to the woods for food. Because when we go to the store you can't afford hardly anything. If I knew the plants I could get food for us."

An ache split down Casch's chest.

"Well, I doubt you and Dean would want dandelion for dinner," she said, phlegmy.

Molly didn't say anything.

"And what would we do all winter?"

"I'll ask the teacher."

"And there's no ice cream cake out here," said Casch, trying to smile.

"There's raspberries though, and we never get to have raspberries. You always say they cost too much."

Casch frowned. That was true, those little things cost five bucks, and the kids destroyed them before they even got home from the store.

"Bears eat berries and they don't have any money," Molly said.

"Yeah, well. You'll understand when you're an adult."

"Being an adult seems dumb," said Molly. Then she stopped and looked at something. "I know those ones; you can eat those," she said. She was pointing toward something growing low on the ground.

"Really?" said Casch.

"Yeah, they're called winterberries."

"I don't think you should, maybe it's better to—"

"No, I'm sure," Molly said, and squatted by a plant that looked like holly. She picked a miniscule red berry between her thumb and pointer finger and ate it.

"Minty," she said. She plucked another and handed it to Casch. It was smaller than a Tic Tac.

"You sure?"

"Yeah, Mom, I'm sure."

Casch popped it in her mouth. It did taste minty. Subtle but minty. She watched Molly pick a few more, then wade farther off the trail.

For a while Casch stood waiting as the sun lowered into the trees. Everything was still. In the quiet she could hear the sound of water moving somewhere down the hill. The thought floated across her mind that it was going to get dark, that she should hurry Molly along. But that thought slipped away. And again she was just standing there, listening to the water.

Then there was something on the trail. Twenty feet in front of her, something was on the trail. Casch felt a flick of fear. Something was there, something was looking at her.

For one single beat, Casch was looking at a fox. And it was looking back at her. They both froze. The animal was small, with rust-colored fur that glowed orange in the late-afternoon light. It seemed unreal, its gaze so deliberate as they stared at one another.

Just off the trail, Molly stood up. Casch blinked. And the fox, noiseless, disappeared. Casch tried to hold the image in her head. But it had been so quick that, a second later, she already doubted what she'd seen.

Molly stepped back on the trail.

"Time to head back?" said Casch, hoarse.

It grew dark as they started up the hill, and fear crept up Casch's back. She shouldn't have brought Molly here—to get lost in the woods at dark. She heard a noise in the trees and jerked her head. Any creep could be in these woods, waiting for a girl to walk by.

But Molly kept striding ahead, and soon they were cresting at the parking lot.

When Casch got home from the restaurant on Monday night, Flora was asleep on the couch, her legs crossed at the ankles. She snorted and opened her eyes at the sound of the door. Casch watched as her mother lifted herself from the couch. Neither of them said a word.

Ever since she'd decked Russ, Casch had been waiting. She

had thought she'd hear it from Flora, maybe that same day. Would Flora show up at her door screaming? Would she say, "YOU COME TO MY HOUSE AND PUNCH MY HUSBAND? THAT'S HOW YOU REPAY ME?"

Yeah, Mom, that's how I repay you.

Casch kept waiting, but nothing happened. After slugging Russ, the first time she saw Flora was a night like this, coming home from the restaurant. Flora acted all normal. "You're out of milk," she had said, getting her jacket. And Casch had stood completely still.

So Russ had kept it from her. He must have swept away all the coins before Flora got home, must have cleaned up the whole mess. Wouldn't she have liked to be a fly on the wall for that, spectating Russ's face puffing up purple while he crouched and plucked a thousand coins off the garage floor.

"How were the kids tonight?" she said as Flora looked around for her purse.

"Nonstop, you know."

Casch bristled. Why did she bother to ask? Of course her mother was going to criticize, of course she would say the kids were too much, or the kitchen was filthy, or they were out of milk, whatever it was.

"They were trying to build a birdhouse from a cardboard box."

"Oh, yeah?"

"Yeah." Flora grabbed her sand-colored purse from under the coffee table. Then she was still for a second, looking at Casch. "You know, you really done a good job with them," she said.

"What?"

"I'm just saying, you done a good job. Molly's the smartest thing I ever met. Both of them, they're good kids."

Casch stood blinking.

"But I been worried about you," Flora continued, clearing her throat, not meeting Casch's eyes.

"What?"

"You don't look like yourself."

She should've known. Anything nice Flora said was going to be followed by this.

"I'm fine," she said.

They looked at each other for a second. Then Flora went around her and out the door.

Gently Casch lowered herself onto the couch. Her jacket was still on, purse over her shoulder. The door clicked shut.

I am a good mom. But she had thought Flora would never notice.

She sat there for a while. I *am* a good mom.

She clutched her purse. She wasn't sleepy. She didn't want to go to bed.

She could go to Morty's, she realized. Right now, she could go to Morty's. She felt the anticipation. She had the money from her shift. She looked at her phone. It was ten thirty; they wouldn't mind. Of course they wouldn't mind. She stood up.

She had never left the kids like that, though, and she looked toward their shut door. But they weren't babies, and they were sound asleep.

Quietly she ducked out of the apartment.

She climbed back in the van and pulled out of Greenfield Terrace. She passed the jail and turned right. The anticipation filled her throat. To have a minute where everything feels good, that's all. A minute where nothing hurts. She went up Silver and made a right on Amity.

That was when she saw the lights. Blue lights.

Just be like anybody, she thought. You're minding your own business. You're driving your own street.

But it wasn't just one cop car, she saw, squinting at the next block. There had to be ten cop cars up there. The van idled slowly forward as she craned to see.

And then she did see. That the cops were at Morty's.

22

Ronnie came out his front door toting a windbreaker and a plastic travel mug. He shuffled down the front walk, opened the passenger door, and climbed inside.

"Morning, bud," said Russ.

"What happened to you?" Ronnie said, pulling his head back to look.

"Just a little accident at the yard. I'm fine. All set? Hit the road?"

"All set," said Ronnie. He slid his mug into the cup holder and clicked his safety belt.

Russ pulled away from the curb. He drove out to Main Street, and at the rotary, merged onto the interstate heading southbound. It was a Friday, late September, all blue sky and puffy clouds. He was missing work and didn't care. After thirty years, they could get on without him.

Not that he wanted to drive to Connecticut, he thought, glancing at his friend. But Ronnie had asked him to come, and anyway, there was no turning around now. He switched on the radio, the morning weather. Ronnie had taken a protein bar from his pocket and was tearing open the foil.

"You want some of this?" he asked.

Russ glanced over. "What is it?"

Ronnie smoothed out the wrapper and read the labeling. "Says twelve grams of protein. We've got boxes of this stuff. Aaron would buy it when he was sober." Ronnie took a bite and chewed. "Tastes terrible," he said.

"I should've stopped and gotten you some breakfast," Russ said, looking at him.

"Nah, I'm not really hungry anyways." He crinkled the wrapper over the brown lump and dropped it on the floor by his feet.

For a while they didn't say anything.

"So what's the, uh, plan for today?" Russ asked.

"We're meeting everyone right at the building. This one couple that's been doing all the research thinks Richard Olson himself will be there today. That's the guy who owns the company."

"Oh?" said Russ, adjusting his hands on the steering wheel.

"Yeah. Plan is, I guess we stand out there. We have to be a certain setback from the building, apparently, so they can't call the cops. And we just kind of wait. Kind of camp out, wait for Olson."

"Are you going to, to try talking to him?"

Ronnie jerked his head.

"That bastard better talk to us! Our kids, our kids dead, and imagine if he won't even talk to us?"

Russ held the steering wheel with both hands, and they were quiet again. Finally Ronnie said, "There's more stuff that's come out about him."

"Oh?"

"Yeah. You know I told you employees were leaking stuff to reporters?"

"Okay."

"Well, someone leaked a bunch of emails. From years ago, from when the drug was new. When they first started to know they had a problem. People were getting addicted and Richard Olson"—Ronnie released a nasal exhale as he said the name—"sent these emails, because employees were getting worried. You can't make this up."

"What? What'd he say?"

"Olson said people get *themselves* addicted. He said they are *criminals* and they do it *with full criminal intent.*"

Russ blinked as the words sunk in. They passed a Home Depot semi in the right lane.

"But that's not even the worst part," said Ronnie. "The worst part is that Olson called drug addicts *the scum of the earth.*"

"The scum of the earth," Russ repeated.

"Yeah."

"These are the people who take his medicine?"

"That's right. And there's one more thing. After all that, as if that weren't enough, right? After all that, apparently the company now has some kind of plan to get into the addiction treatment business."

"You're kidding," said Russ, glancing at him.

"Not kidding. Apparently the company is now calling addiction treatment *an attractive market.*"

They crossed through Massachusetts in an hour and hit traffic around Hartford. Then the road was quiet again. The sun was out and the 4Runner's thermostat said sixty-six degrees. This isn't so bad, Russ thought, it was no big deal driving to Connecticut. He settled back into the leather seat, just a couple fingers on the wheel. They were going to a place called Springdale, north of New York City. Ronnie had the directions.

At New Haven they split off from the interstate and took the Merritt Parkway. Traffic got thicker, the cars nicer. Russ went back to holding the wheel with both hands.

"We're looking for Tresser Boulevard," said Ronnie, reading from a scrap of paper when they had taken the exit. Russ found the streets confusing; he accidentally took a one-way.

"Dammit," he said, sitting forward, and they had to drive in a loop.

"That's it," said Ronnie. "Look."

Russ looked where Ronnie was pointing and saw the name across the mirrored glass building. Olson-Abrams, it said in giant slanted lettering. They rolled to a stop at a light, and both of them craned their necks to peer up at it. The building was like an upside-down cake, each floor a layer. But every layer was bigger than the one below it so that it was strangely top-heavy, the uppermost floor jutting out and overshadowing the ones underneath.

The light turned green.

"Where should I park?"

"Uh?"

They found a garage a couple blocks away. "Fifteen dollars?" Russ huffed, reading the sign.

"I'll pay," said Ronnie.

"No, no."

When they came out to the sidewalk, Russ was starving and needed to take a piss. They passed a guy selling hot dogs from a silver cart, and Russ inhaled the scent of cooked meat. He was about to suggest grabbing a couple when Ronnie, turning the corner, said, "That's them."

Russ followed him and saw that it was only a handful of people, a few of them holding signs under their arms. If you were just driving by, you wouldn't even notice. Ronnie quickened his step, but Russ slowed down.

"Hey, buddy, I'm going to grab one of those dogs, you want one?"

"Sure," said Ronnie, without looking back.

He used the bathroom at a Dunkin', then ate a bratwurst smothered in kraut and brown mustard while standing a few feet back from the cart. He finished and ordered two more.

When he came around the block, he saw that Ronnie had joined the circle of people. For a minute Russ stood off Ronnie's shoulder, a red-checkered hot dog tray in either hand, shifting his weight while the people talked. He saw why they had chosen this spot. Just beyond where they were standing was the entrance to the building's underground garage.

"Is that—?" a woman in the circle finally said, pointing behind Ronnie, who turned.

"Oh, thanks, bud. Hey guys, this is my friend Russ."

"Thanks for coming," someone said, and they all nodded their heads. Ronnie relieved Russ of one checkered tray, and they ate without saying anything.

"My goodness, what happened to your eye?" a woman asked, adjusting the sign under her arm when Ronnie went to throw away the trash.

"Just, uh, accident," he said. The woman was pretty. She wore deep-red lipstick and diamond earrings. She had dark skin and some kind of accent, Russ guessed India.

"Where are you from?" he said.

"New Jersey."

The man beside her—her husband, Russ guessed—was saying something, and everyone else fell silent to listen. The man said he had a friend who was a *financial investigator* and there was reason to think that, since the lawsuits had started getting attention, Olson had been pulling money out of the company.

"It means he's getting scared," the guy said.

"That's why we have to keep up the pressure," said someone else.

"You know it's billions of dollars they're pulling out," said the first guy. He wore a starched blue shirt and wire-rim glasses. He gestured up at the building with his chin and said, "They're trying to make sure that no matter what happens with the lawsuits, they'll spend the rest of their lives on a yacht."

"While our kids are dead." The woman who'd spoken to Russ raised her sign. Pasted on the poster board was an enlarged photo of a girl with an enormous toothy smile and the words: To Olson: Tomorrow Would Be My Twenty-Fifth Birthday but You Got Me Hooked on Drugs and Now I'm Dead.

Russ took half a step back.

It was nearly dusk when someone said, "That's him, *that's him.*"

Russ, who had been sitting on a retaining wall in front of some bushes, lifted his head. Ronnie and the others snapped to attention, got up, raised their signs, and lined the curb. Russ couldn't see anything. He leaned around, trying to get a look.

A long white Suburban had emerged from the underground garage and was pulling up to the street. That was Olson? The group raised their signs and shouted. Russ's forehead creased as he watched. How did they even know it was him?

But it hardly mattered. The driver, who wore a chauffeur's black cap, didn't even glance at them. The rear windows were tinted. Maybe Richard Olson really was there in the back seat. Maybe he was just behind that darkened window. Maybe he was only a few feet away, looking out at them. But there was no way to tell.

They shouted and waved their signs as the driver made a leisurely turn and the candy-white SUV glided past them, out onto the boulevard. Everyone shouted and watched as it continued down the block and disappeared from view.

They were quiet on the way home. At a rest stop on the Merritt Parkway, they got sandwiches, then kept on north. It had been dark for hours when they crossed out of Massachusetts and were almost back to Greenfield.

"I guess Olson has a place in Vermont," Ronnie said, breaking the long silence. "I heard he has a second home, or a third home, whatever."

"That so?" said Russ, glancing at his buddy as the headlights from a southbound car washed over them. Ronnie better not want to go there too. Today was enough for Russ.

But all Ronnie said was, "I bet it's real nice."

23

She was pale Monday morning as the kids got ready for school. Dean couldn't find his jacket, and she walked blindly around the apartment because she knew she should look for it. Finally she took his hand and put him on the bus without it. When she came back inside, she went to the kitchen and lowered herself into a chair. Otis crossed under her legs and hopped up on the table.

Jasmine and Morty would be in the jail by now. They would be in county lockup, she figured. Then they'd get put somewhere else. Somewhere long-term. Maybe Jasmine would get something shorter, but Morty wouldn't see daylight. You get caught dealing heroin, you don't stay in county. You go to prison.

Hell, you get caught dealing pot, you go to prison.

For a second she saw Topher like he was standing right there. "Are you smarter than the box?" he said, smiling at her.

Her mind dragged over everything that had happened. The broken foot, not being able to work. Everything snowballing— she had almost gotten busted, like a dumbass, for stealing steaks at the Price Chopper.

And Marylouise. Marylouise, who out of pure kindness gave

her $200 for nursing school. And what had Casch done? She pressed her eyes closed hard. She took Marylouise's coffee can of cash—and she took her TVs, too. She had to make it look like a real burglary, couldn't have Marylouise suspecting it was her. The shame sucked air from her throat. She'd pawned the TVs. You are trash. You are a piece of trash.

But that thought just made her want one thing only. To feel good. For one second. To feel warm. Safe.

A cigarette, she needed a cigarette. She got the pack from her purse. Jasmine had given her this pack. She slid one out and lit it.

That stuff was all behind her now, she thought, taking a long trembly drag. Morty and Jasmine were gone. Topher was gone. Somehow she had her job back. She'd even paid the deposit for nursing school; she'd given Gabi the money.

It was time to go back to the way everything had been. She knew it. She knew that's what she had to do.

When she'd finished the cigarette, she pressed the butt into the dish and stood up. There was a mound of mail sitting on the counter. How was she going to do everything? Somehow she had to figure it out. She stared at the mail. Then her gaze fixed on the return address of the envelope on top.

How had she not noticed?

She snatched the letter from DCF and tore it open. Her eyes ran down the page.

After thorough assessment, this agency has determined the complaint of neglect to be <u>*unsupported*</u>.

She stared at the words.

They were done. It was finished.

She had her kids, and it was over.

A day and a half later, yawning at the start of her shift, her throat felt itchy and she needed to cough. You can't cough by the silverware, though. She tried to hold it in. The first customers came in. You can't cough when you have tables. She needed to cough; it was trying to come up her throat.

She forgot people's orders and didn't care. The minutes crawled by. Grabbing a pitcher of water at the server station, she heard Gabi and another waitress talking about someone's weed field. A helicopter had flown over and taken pictures, busted up the whole thing.

"You don't know what you're talking about," Casch scoffed, and she charged off with the pitcher. But not before she saw the way Gabi was looking at her.

A woman holding a big leather purse in her lap sent back her water because she didn't want ice. I'll give you ice, Casch thought.

Two guys at a bar table had the nerve to ask what she was doing later.

"Why don't you go fuck yourselves," she said. They left no tip, but it was worth it.

Finally her last table closed out. She grabbed the credit card slip. Then she was out coughing by the bathrooms. She coughed and her stomach churned. She grabbed her belly. It was in the handicap stall of the women's room at The 99 that the shitting began.

The next day, in her own bathroom, keening back and forth on the toilet, she started puking. When she dragged herself back to bed, the sheets scratched up against her skin. It hurt to move. It hurt to lie still. Time slowed to a drip.

One thing blazed in her mind. She thought of Jasmine in the upstairs room. The tank top that hung loose from Jasmine's shoulders. There you go, Jasmine would say, her voice gentle, after she emptied the barrel into Casch's vein. And she groaned.

She heard the kids come home from school. They were on the couch watching TV when she went to the bathroom.

"Mom?" said Molly, looking up. They'd thought she was at work.

"Mommy's sick," said Casch, and shut the bathroom door.

She trudged back to bed. She was thirsty. She was thirsty but she knew she'd throw up anything she swallowed. Have a cigarette.

There was a buzzing noise. It made her face twitch. She swatted around in the covers with a clammy hand. Where was her stupid phone? When she found it, the buzzing had stopped. She looked at the screen.

Topher.

She stared at it. Then chucked the phone to the floor.

On the morning of the third day, it was like her bones began slowly to separate from her flesh. Her skeleton twisting and ripping. She moaned. No. Please no.

At some point Gabi was there. Casch heard her voice in the living room, talking to the kids. Then she came in the bedroom. She put her hand on Casch's forehead. She left the room, was gone for a while, and when she reappeared she had a thing of soup. Casch sipped some of the broth.

But she knew what she really needed. If she could get just a little bit. God, just a little bit. That's all she needed. She writhed and, at last, pushed away the tangled covers. She got down on her hands and knees and searched the floor for her phone. But when she found it, it was dead.

By afternoon that day, hours after she'd plugged it into the wall, the cracked phone flickered to life. She let out a grateful breath. There were all these messages. But she texted the only person who could help.

Rick replied right away, saying people had been asking about her. She stared at the message. She had never called out of work, she realized. She never told them she was sick. Can't think about that now. She typed her message.

> u know anyone besides morty?

he got busted

> i know. do u know anyone else

maybe. what u lookin 4?

Her chest pounded.

> h

Rick didn't write back.

―――

And then, finally, he did. She had been slumped on the couch with the kids, their hot arms and legs pressing into her.

"Guys, I don't feel good," she said, squirming away. When their bedtime came, Dean wanted her to tuck him in. "I'm turning off the light now, okay?" she gasped, standing at the door and finally pulling it closed. She let out a breath. And went to check her phone.

There was Rick's message.

he meet u in price chopper lot

She felt a burst of anticipation.

when

For a while he didn't answer, and she stood there, clutching the phone.

30min

She waited in her van on the edge of the parking lot just as Rick instructed. Her body ached with anticipation. She fiddled with her keys. Her foot tapped, headlights streaking across her eyes, the keys clicking between her fingers, and she thought of Jasmine.

"Girl, you gotta learn how to do it yourself," Jasmine had said. Why didn't she listen? Why would she leave this to someone else? If there was one thing she knew, it was that she had to take care of herself.

"I'll figure it out," she rasped aloud to no one.

Just then an ice-blue Honda Civic pulled in.

———

Afterward she gunned it to Federal, to the twenty-four-hour pharmacy. She recoiled under the lights. Get what you need; get what you need and get out. In the pocket of her hoodie, her fingers were wrapped around the tiny package. It was different from Morty's, a waxy baggie instead of the knotted plastic.

She hadn't been to the pharmacy since they cut off her meds, she realized. She approached the counter. She explained what she needed.

"You know, for insulin," she said.

"They're in the aisle," the woman replied, her mouth a straight dry line across her face.

Casch blinked at her. "What aisle?"

"Four."

In the car, quaking with anticipation, she tore the package open with her teeth. She was going to feel better. She was about to feel better. There was some water in her rubber water bottle. But she didn't have a spoon. Her eyes searched. There, she had a bottle cap. From the passenger floor she grabbed an old lemonade bottle and unscrewed the cap. Reached in her purse for the lighter.

But she needed something to tie her arm. Fuck. Fuck, fuck, fuck. She looked around the car.

And there, on the floor of the backseat, were Molly's old Reeboks, the laces undone.

24

I t was still dark out as Topher stood in the bed of the Ranger, double-checking supplies. Saws, clippers, piles of tarps. Tie-downs. He'd checked everything last night. Then he had barely slept, he just lay there going over the details in his head. Don't forget heavy plastic bags. You need a bunch of bags to collect stray branches—don't you leave them out in the field.

Behind him, the lights in the first-floor apartment went on. Topher felt a wave in his stomach; it was time to go. The neighbors were up. The sun was about to rise. He hopped down and slammed the tailgate. Showtime.

At the gas station he splashed coffee into a Styrofoam cup. Then the sky was eggshell pink as he drove west out of town. He drank the coffee too quick and thought that he should've had some water. The radio was all talk shows. He reached to switch it off, but it went to weather. Mostly sunny, high of sixty-five. Perfect, he thought, leaning back. He drained the coffee and squeezed the cup until it cracked.

It was full daylight as he rolled down the gravel to their meeting spot. That was when he saw the clean white sedan parked by the old gate.

His face dropped. What was that.

Connor and Tory pulled up a second later and all of them got out.

"What. The fuck. Is that?" said Connor. For a second all three of them stood staring at it.

It was wrong. The car was completely wrong. They did sometimes see vehicles parked along this road. There were cars that belonged to hikers, and trucks when hunters were out scouting. The sedan was different.

Topher went up and cupped his hands at the window and peered inside. It was so clean it could have been a rental car.

"What do you want to do?" said Tory when Topher stepped back.

The three of them were quiet. Maybe we're just being paranoid, Topher thought. But today was not a day for a fuckup. Stay smart. Are you smarter than the box?

"We gotta wait," he said. "We can't harvest today."

"But the plants are way ready," said Tory quietly.

That was true. The plants were perfect. Topher had insisted they not make the mistake of harvesting too early and cheating themselves out of additional poundage. But now the branches had gotten so heavy with bud that Topher started worrying they would snap. Today was the day; they had to get the weed out.

Suddenly there was a sound overhead and all three of them jerked and looked. Topher's heart started knocking in his chest. Was it a helicopter? Where was it? He couldn't see it. Was it a helicopter?

But it was just a two-seater. Some rich guy's toy airplane buzzing overhead.

They all looked back down. Fixed their eyes on the sedan.

"Tonight," he said, "let's go in tonight."

"In the dark?"

"Yeah. Get yourselves some nice headlamps. Let's meet back here at ten."

The wooden staircase up to his apartment was a little uneven. You had to look where you were stepping or you could bust an ankle. On the landing he pulled open the screen and unlocked the door, pushed into the kitchen, and stepped around the trash bags that were slumped there.

He had the whole day now. He didn't want these hours; he wanted to be in the field. He should try to sleep. They would have to work all night, and he was already exhausted.

He thought about taking out the trash but went into his room instead. It wasn't just last night; lately he hadn't been sleeping at all. Every night he tried to tire himself out. He'd be on the floor doing push-ups, sit-ups; he'd watch movies. Finally it would be three in the morning and he thought he would definitely pass out now. But then he'd just lie there and think about Casch. After a long time he would turn on his side and think about Molly and Dean. Did they think he just disappeared on them? That was a fist in his stomach. What are you supposed to do when you love her for the same reason she dumped you, that she's stubborn as hell?

In the bedroom now, the sallow vinyl shades were drawn over the windows. It was dim but not dark enough. The shades didn't block out all the light. He needed those blackout curtains. He would never buy curtains. He undressed to boxers, dropping his clothes in a pile on the old hardwood floor, and got into bed.

That sedan was probably nothing. The cops aren't as smart as you think. Just a couple weeks ago there was a story in the papers about a weed bust on state land. Someone had put fifty plants into land that was part of the state park system. Environmental police broke up the whole thing, called in every kind of reinforcement. They brought in state troopers, helicopters, K-9 units. It was all in the paper, pictures of cops with buzz cuts, wearing bulletproof vests, pulling out sleds full of weed like it was god's work. Whoever had planted the stuff was never found.

The part that wasn't in the paper was that the authorities didn't find the whole operation. There was another smaller field just a little ways from the bigger one. The police never found it. Topher had heard through the grapevine that a couple park employees discovered it afterward and divvied up the harvest for themselves.

See, the cops had their heads up their asses. They went in with drug-sniffing dogs and still missed an entire field.

Everything was going to be fine.

When they returned that night, the sedan was gone. They threw on their backpacks, heavy with supplies, and set out in the dark. They would be lucky to finish by morning.

But they'd only been hiking a few minutes—wordless, trying to make every footstep silent in the leaves—when Topher noticed some flagging. There was a piece of orange plastic ribbon tied to a low branch. Fear spread in his stomach.

He flipped on his headlamp. "Look," he whispered.

Connor and Tory came up behind him. For a second they shined all three lamps on the orange tape.

"What if they're waiting for us," said Tory quietly.

"Or maybe they set up game cameras?" Connor said, and he glanced around.

"What do you want to do?" said Tory slowly.

"What do you mean?" said Topher. "The only thing to do is get in and get out."

He had never been to the field at night. It would have been beautiful under a moon, but tonight was overcast. They shed their packs and pulled out their saws and started working. Every plant was a tree now, each one had the sturdy trunk of a sapling. Which had to be sawed at the base and dragged to the mouth of the field.

Topher spread tarps and they stacked the first trees and went back to cut more. They had the black plastic bags, too, for bagging up stray branches. But it was dark and they were in a rush and they left the smaller stuff on the ground.

While he worked Topher kept hearing noises. Every sound made his heart rush, made him look up and check all around him. He knew that if they had the right equipment—and the feds did—they could take pictures at night from hundreds of feet overhead. Don't think about that.

In his head the sound of choppers wailed as they cut and dragged, cut and dragged and stacked. He kept hearing what it would sound like when a chopper came around that mountain.

And then he did hear something. It wasn't in his head. He heard something. He jerked up. He scanned the clouds.

But apparently it was nothing.

At last they had cut every plant. They had dragged every last one toward the trail. The harvest was done. They had to carry it out.

They started relaying. They practically ran along the trail, ferrying the cut trees to one another, one load after another after another. Topher's legs were heavy, his arms burned, he was barely picking up his feet. He tripped on a root and almost went flying. It was just before six in the morning, the sky changing to its predawn glow, that they had all the plants out to the gate.

Now they would have to make trips, each vehicle would have to make several runs—the harvest strapped down and covered with tarps—to move everything out. Connor and Tory were already loading.

By the time they had packed up the final cargo it was broad daylight. Tory slammed the hatch of his Subaru, Topher had strapped down the pile in the bed of the Ranger, and Connor was waiting in his S-10. And they all pulled away.

25

"Gram's chair was there," said Topher, pointing to a spot in front of the ancient stove, which was a strange tall thing covered in dust. But even under the dust, you could see its ornate pattern, a pattern of curlicues. Curlicues around the top and bottom, curlicues all the way down to its clawed feet. And curlicues across the trapdoor. Dean's hand popped into view as he took the coiled handle in his fingers and opened the stove.

Behind Casch the front door was open. Light was glowing in through hazy windows. And now the doorway was a framed keyhole. Through it she could see a long deep shot to the outside. There was the sound of birds.

Topher was smiling, standing in the middle of the room, his feet in the cloudy floor. He reached out to her.

"Are you smarter than the box?"

The words came from the next room, a big empty space. And here was Gram, short silver hair. She was talking but Casch couldn't hear. Gram waved her hands and Casch saw them in close-up, fingernails clipped to sunken half-moons. Where were the kids? Didn't they want to meet Gram?

To the left was a big window, outside she could see a long row of Christmas trees. They grew in ascending order, smallest to largest.

She couldn't hear but she knew what the old lady had said.

Do you love him?

I didn't come here to be interrogated, she thought, and she wanted to turn and go. But she was still standing there.

"Green light," said Molly.

? thought Casch.

Topher was nodding.

"You can't own the land," he said. "The land owns you."

Molly was looking so serious, the light shining in behind her, the birds chirping. Beep. Beep.

Beep.

"Well look at that."

Casch looked at the woman who was peering at her.

"Well look at that," said the woman again. She moved out of Casch's view. Then reappeared. "Weren't sure you were going to make it."

Casch blinked.

The woman pointed. "Your mother just left. Two days she was sitting here. Then she gets up and leaves, and you wake up. Isn't that how it goes."

Casch watched the nurse check something by the bed, then leave the room.

She felt something weird in her legs. What was that? And prickly in her arms. And her neck.

Then, all of it. All the feeling came pouring back into her body.

Her eyes darted. Everything was clear. Completely clear. A milky shade over the window, an old TV mounted from the ceiling, its screen blank. A whiteboard gridded into boxes that said:

I LIKE TO BE CALLED:

YOUR PLAN FOR TODAY:

Her skin grew sweaty. Then cold. She swallowed. She was swollen and stiff. She began to ache. Her stomach burned. The ache grew. More and more feeling, like her body was a naked nerve. Like iron weights were pressing into her from above. She knew what she needed. Her skin was damp. She knew exactly what she needed.

First she had to get out of here. Now. Before the nurse came back. Before anyone came back.

She was itchy, her body itchy, her whole entire body a big raw itch. Her hand jerked up to scratch her face and pulled on a tube—there was a tube in her arm.

She heard voices in the hall outside the room, and she froze. The voices faded past.

She looked at her bloated pasty arm, at the tape across the needle in the crook of her elbow. With her other arm she reached and, fingers wobbly, managed to pull off the tape. Slid out the needle. She bled and didn't care. Get up. Get up now.

She started to turn, to swing her aching legs to the side of the bed. Fuck. FUCK. There was another tube. In my twat?

This tube was draining brown piss into a bag. She gave it an exploratory pull that sent a white zing of pain up her middle. Now she was in an in-between position, half up, half down, and she thought she would cry from the pain. But she couldn't cry, she had to get out.

She reached between her legs and wrapped her fist around the tube. Took a big breath. And yanked.

The pain came up her throat, her shoulders thrusting forward in the about-to-puke position. But she didn't puke. She did leak piss into the sheets.

Go. GO.

She swung her feet to the floor. She had nothing. No clothes, no phone.

She looked around. Had to be here. Had to be.

There, by the window. A thick white plastic bag. She pushed herself to her feet and felt a burst as the pain shot up the sides of her legs. But she managed to reach the plastic bag. Inside were the last clothes she'd worn.

Leaving a hospital is no different than stealing a steak. Walk like you belong.

Which way? Left, she went left. She passed the nurses' station. There was a woman in pink scrubs looking at her phone. She glanced up.

But Casch was already past. Casch was down the hall, looking at the signs.

Outside the air was cold and damp, and there was the flat glare of an overcast day. She squinted at the parking lot. One row down, a woman was getting into a red Prius.

"Excuse me?" said Casch. The words came out cracked, phlegmy. She started toward her. "Excuse me? Excuse me?"

The gray-haired woman in the seat of the car looked up.

"Excuse me, I'm sorry, could you give me a ride?"

Classical music played softly on the radio as the woman glanced at Casch in the passenger seat, and Casch looked straight ahead, and the dashboard clock changed to 4:03, and the electric vehicle whizzed up to Main Street and turned west.

———

Around the rotary to The 99.

"Are you sure?" said the woman, looking doubtfully out the Prius's windshield at the restaurant parking lot. "Are you sure you want me to leave you here?"

Casch barely heard the question.

"I really hate to do this," she heard herself say, "but could you spare ten dollars? I'm in a real tough spot."

"Oh, honey," said the woman sadly, cocking her head.

But she must have had dough to spare. Because she reached into the black leather fanny pack around her waist and, just like that, pulled out a crisp twenty.

It was quiet inside the restaurant, the bar full but the dining room empty, and she made it halfway up the floor before a younger waitress caught sight of her and came hurrying over.

"Casch, oh my god."

"Oh, hey, I'm just—" she said, and gestured toward the back.

"Are you okay?"

She bristled; she didn't need this girl in her business. But now Gabi was hurrying over too.

"Casch," said Gabi, her voice a whisper, and from Gabi's expression Casch realized what she must look like. She tried to swallow the shame.

"I been so worried about you," Gabi said.

"Listen, I just gotta talk to Rick," she said, avoiding Gabi's eyes, pushing past her.

"Rick," Gabi repeated, her voice hard and flat.

But right then the manager came out of the kitchen.

"Casch," he said, stopping, looking her up and down. "You know, we replaced you."

"You'll never replace me," she heard herself say.

"Have you gotten medical help? Have you seen a doctor?"

"The doctor's the one that got me like this," she said. And she ducked past him into the kitchen.

Rick told her to wait out back. And so she sat, shivering, on top of the picnic table, scratching her arms, looking into the giant aluminum can where cigarettes floated in rainwater. She looked up when she heard the back door open—but it was Gabi.

"Girl, let me take you home," she said, coming over to her.

Casch shook her head.

"I just gotta talk to Rick."

"I'm not stupid," said Gabi softly, "I know what's going on."

Casch sniffed. "You have no idea," she said. "Just leave me alone."

But Gabi wouldn't move. As if this is what I need, Casch thought. "I know how I look to you," she said, her voice hoarse.

"I'm not judging you."

"Of course you're judging me."

"C'mon, let me take you home," Gabi said, and reached for her hand.

"I know you think you're so perfect."

Gabi froze. And right then the door opened, and Rick came out.

"Okay. Fine," said Gabi. "It's your choice."

"You know people been worried about you," Rick said as he

came over. Gabi was shaking her head, looking back at Casch before she slipped inside, the door slamming behind her.

"No one's gotta worry about me," said Casch.

Rick shook his head and drew a package of cigarettes from his pocket. He lit hers first, then his own.

"Can you text that guy?" she said. "See if he can meet me?"

For a second Rick didn't say anything.

"You know you look like shit," he said.

"Why does everyone think they need to tell me how I look? You think you're helping me by saying that?"

"Maybe I am helping you by saying that."

"You can help me by texting that guy."

They smoked down their cigarettes. At last Rick took out his phone.

"He'll meet you across the street," he said, gesturing with a nod toward the grocery store, "same as last time."

"Thanks. Hey, one other thing?" she said.

"What?"

"Can I borrow that lighter?"

He sniffed out one short exhale and handed her the lighter.

"Hey, Casch?" he said.

"What?"

"Don't ever come asking me for anything again."

She waited on the side of the parking lot closest to the road. She watched every car that pulled into the plaza. C'mon, c'mon, c'mon.

She waited a long time like that. Finally she sat down on the curb. She flicked her thumb back and forth against the frayed cuff of her hoodie.

A tiny brown bird flew low above her, and she watched as it went into a dented light post. There was a hole in the post, she saw. There was grass or straw or something spilling out of the hole. The bird had made a home in the light post—it was the sort of thing Molly would notice.

"Mom, look at that," Molly would say. She would ask about the bird. Does the bird like living in a light post? She'd say something like that. Or she'd say, Why does the bird have to live in a parking lot? Why can't the bird live in a tree? Are there enough trees for all the birds?

Or she'd say something she learned in school. She'd stand there, hypnotized, staring at the bird's nest, saying something she learned at school. And eventually Casch would have to hurry her along.

She wiped her eyes with her sleeve. It'll be okay, though. It'll be okay. You're about to feel better, then you can go get the kids. She looked again for the blue Civic.

And there it was. Pulling in and turning her way. She felt a burst of energy.

She paid with the twenty from the Prius lady, and when the stuff was in her pocket, she crossed the parking lot. She went in the grocery store, grabbed a lemonade from the first cooler. She went combing through the pharmacy section. Where are they. Where are they. Here, here.

The package of needles was inside her hoodie, and she was just nobody, walking casually into the restroom.

<hr>

Everything was soft and quiet as she floated out of the store.

When she lifted her head from her lap she was, she seemed to be, back on the curb. By the light post and the bird's nest.

A man was saying something to her. Casch was blinking at him. He was saying something else. This man was telling her what to do.

"I can sit here if I want to," she rasped. "Why don't you get out of my face?"

Behind him, blue lights flashed.

26

Along the interstate the maple trees were the color of fire as Topher barreled south from White River. If he didn't hit traffic, he would get to the city by four. Make his deliveries, and then go see the girl at the Greek place. His right hand held the wheel at twelve o'clock.

A few weeks back he'd noticed her working the counter. Big gold earrings flanking a cute smile. The second time he saw her, they started chatting, and she had smiled and said, "You're not from here, are you?"

He told her Vermont, and she seemed to find it appealing. A real live country boy.

"Wait around, I'm off at nine," she'd said.

"Cool," he replied, like no big deal, like this happens all the time. Then he had hours to kill, nothing to do with himself. He went to a bar he'd gone to once with Cal, sat down and ordered a Stripe. Every time he finished a beer, the bartender was right there asking if he wanted another. He got hammered and the bill was ninety dollars. He was waiting outside when she got off work.

"Country boy goes to the city," she said, or something stupid like that, as she gestured for him to follow her. She had tried to bring him to the subway.

"Let me drive you home," he said, and she did let him, the scent of her shampoo filling the cab of the Ranger.

Her bed was four flights up a dirty stairwell. But her bra was the color of cider, and she had a tattoo, just visible over the elastic of her panties, of a slender crescent moon. And when he fucked her, for a minute he forgot everything. She kept her earrings on, the dim lamplight glinting off two gold discs.

Hopefully she was working today. His first day delivering the outdoor. He checked his phone, then put it in the cup holder.

After they'd gotten everything out of the field, he had thought they were home free. But he hadn't thought about how much space they needed to dry a harvest that size. That almost killed them. The very same day they got everything out, on no sleep, they went and hung branches in their indoor grow rooms —black tents, a closet, an attic—with fans running. Then they were out of space. In a couple hours they were out of space. Which was dangerous. If they didn't get all of it drying, it would get moldy, it would be worthless. They had to hang it anywhere they could. But that was risky, too. You don't want people smelling it; people have big mouths.

Topher had strung it up in his apartment, in his bedroom even, with fans running around the clock. Four days in a row he ran around to every store in forty miles and bought out all the box fans. And still he wasn't sure the bud would dry. After everything, after all that, were they going to lose it now? Once it was all strung up, he went around to all their spots every day. Adjusted every branch, moved around the fans, obsessed. Which was great because he didn't have to think about Casch.

His fingers thrummed the wheel.

Nah, that wasn't true. He thought about her. He had broken down and tried calling her again. It rang but she didn't pick up.

Driving south in the Ranger now, the first sign for Greenfield popped into view.

A few plants had gotten moldy and had to be thrown out. But most of it finished dry and beautiful, ready for clipping. So then he and Connor and Tory had clipped until their fingers cramped, then kept clipping for another week straight. The clippers got jammed with resin. They dipped them in rubbing alcohol, kept clipping. Twelve-hour days like that, sitting in Tory's mom's garage in bucket seats that had been salvaged from wrecked cars, watching movies on the old TV. Sipping beers, clipping. When it was all done and accounted for, they had gotten almost exactly a pound per plant. A hundred and twenty pounds of marijuana. Tory's guess had been right—they were going to clear a hundred grand and then some.

Driving south on the highway now, the second sign for Greenfield appeared. He stared at it until it disappeared behind him. And there was the third sign and the arrow for the exit. The Ranger zoomed by.

It was dark, hours later, when he crossed from Massachusetts back into Vermont, his right hand on the thick fold of money in his pocket.

"Will that be all today?" she'd asked, behind the counter at the Greek place as she rang him up like he was any stranger. It was loud in there, and his hearing wasn't great. He had looked at her, his mouth slightly open. Then he noticed how much makeup she wore. Casch didn't wear any makeup.

He had eaten his dinner standing outside. It was warm in the city, much warmer than Vermont, the heat coming up from a grate in the sidewalk. He leaned against a building as he wolfed down the food, people hurrying along in front of him, their eyes fixed on the ground. He had smushed the Styrofoam container into an overfull trash can and got back on the highway.

The first northbound sign for Greenfield came into view, bright with the shine of his headlights. There were three signs for the Greenfield exit when you went south, then three more signs when you came north. Six signs for Greenfield every trip to New York. There, there went the fifth one.

Then came the sixth one. The arrow, last chance for Greenfield. He was going by, he was almost past, when he jerked the steering wheel and zagged across the divider and went rolling down the off-ramp into the rotary.

He saw her van as soon as he turned into Greenfield Terrace. He backed into a spot diagonal from her door.

Then sat there, his foot tapping. Her windows were dark. He should leave. Just pull back out, get back on the interstate. Go home. Go back to White River before you're too tired to drive another mile.

His hand went to the center console. He took out rolling papers and the grinder. His mind was in the apartment with her—it was warm in there, smelled like dinner, the kids were sleeping. The feeling of being under one roof with the one you love. The ones you love. A family.

He put away the grinder and climbed out of the truck.

He hadn't even gotten up to the door, though, when in the glare of the floodlight he saw the orange paper stuck there. He hurried up the step. Late, it said. He ripped it off. He looked at the darkened windows. He tried the door but it was locked.

He ran around back, past Molly's withered garden, and up

the steps. He pulled back the screen and reached for the door-knob. It turned in his hand.

Inside there was a sour smell, and cat food spilled across the floor.

He called her number but the phone was dead.

He sat out in the Ranger and stared at her door. He slept in the truck. He woke up there. He waited, stupidly, for someone to come or go.

He drove back to White River and gave Connor and Tory their cut of the delivery. He drank two beers in the shower. Rolled a joint and smoked it. Rolled another. Drank six more beers. Slept.

"Hi, there! What can I get you?" said the bartender, throwing down a coaster as Topher grabbed a stool.

"I'm actually just looking for someone."

"Oh, yeah?" the guy said.

Topher had seen him before. This was the bartender who'd served him the first time he came in looking for her.

"Yeah, you know Casch?"

He saw a current of understanding pass over the guy's face.

"She doesn't work here anymore."

"I'm just looking for any way of getting in touch with her."

"I can't give out people's personal information."

"I was just hoping, actually, to maybe get in touch with her mom."

"Her mom?"

"Yeah, I don't know how else to reach her. Did you ever meet her mom? Or maybe someone else did? I'm just—"

"No," the guy said, shaking his head, "and honestly I couldn't tell you even if I did."

"I'm not a friggin stalker," said Topher. "Can I talk to the manager?"

"I am the manager."

After he punched the door of the Ranger in the rear parking lot of The 99, he yelled and grabbed his fist and saw he'd dented the door. "Fuck you," he said.

He got in the truck. Climbed back out. Where did he think he was going. This was the end of the line. Girl's gone. Kids are gone. It's none of your concern. He was holding on to the rim of the truck bed, shaking his head, swallowing back tears, when he heard a door open and slam.

He looked up and saw that someone had come out the back of the restaurant. A guy in baggy jeans was wiping his hands on a towel hanging from his pocket. He pulled out a pack of cigarettes, cupped his hand to shield the breeze as he clicked the lighter.

"Hey," said Topher, stepping back from the truck. "Hey?"

The guy looked up.

"Hey, how's it goin? Listen, I'm trying to find somebody, maybe you could help?"

"Doubt it."

Topher came walking toward him. "You know Casch? Casch Abbey?"

Now the guy looked at him. "Who are you?" he said.

"I'm her friend. You know her?"

"She don't work here no more."

"I know. Her phone's dead and I'm just trying to get in

touch. Like maybe find her mom. You don't know her mom, do you?"

The guy sniffed a laugh. "No, I don't know her mom."

"Or like any other way I could get in touch with her?"

"Nope."

Topher nodded. "Right," he said.

He turned and walked back to the truck.

"Hey, wait a second."

Topher turned around. The guy took another drag, then flicked the cigarette and started toward Topher.

"She did tell me one thing, actually," he said.

"Yeah, what's that?"

"She said her mom's husband works at the scrapyard."

27

T he sun was just about down, though it was only late afternoon, as Russ flipped on his blinker, turned into the
Grab-N-Go, and pulled up to a pump. At the yard today
the owner had come in and had a sit-down with him. Under
normal circumstances, no big deal. They had these meetings
every few months.

But today, last thing on the list, Leonard had said, all serious,
he had said, "Russ, I think it's time we get our operations online."

Russ had blinked at him.

"There's good management software for what we do."

"Management what now?"

"It'll help us reduce, uh, mistakes."

Russ had shifted in his seat.

"It'll make us that much more efficient, you see what I'm
saying?"

Matter of fact, Russ didn't see. They'd been doing it with
clipboards for thirty years. Hell, more than thirty years. It was
thirty years that *Russ* had been doing it with clipboards, but
he'd learned from Leonard's daddy, who'd learned from
Leonard's granddaddy. If there was anyone who should care
about keeping things the old way—if there was anyone who

should have respect for *the way things had always been done*—it was this was guy right here, in the pretty trouser pants. Guy was a prima donna, Russ had always known that. And now he wanted to go and switch the whole operation to *management software*?

The pump clicked. Russ had been leaning against the vehicle. He grabbed the nozzle's handle, swung it around, dribbled gasoline on the concrete as he put the thing back in the cradle.

Then he went striding up to the store's double-wide entrance. He would get himself a coffee, that's what he would do. No frickin way he was going to use any software. You'd have better luck getting a—what was the saying? He pulled open the door. A camel through a needle. You'd have better luck getting a camel through the eye of a needle. He marched over to the coffee. Where do these stupid sayings come from? He grabbed a large Styrofoam cup and started filling it. Who decides something's going to be a saying? Who says, This is a saying now, get a camel through the eye of a needle. It was meaningless, you might as well say, you could say—

Well, he couldn't think of anything. But a camel through a needle was stupid.

He toted the coffee over to the cream dispenser and pushed the red button. A couple drops dribbled out. Of course. Of course, the thing was empty. You know why it's empty? Because this is what people do. They use all the cream, they empty the whole frickin dispenser, and they don't say anything to the clerk.

All you have to do is *say something*, thought Russ, sniffing, looking toward the register. All you have to say is, Excuse me, I finished off the cream. Simple as that. You just *say something*, so the next person doesn't get the shit end of the stick. Is this astrophysics? Is this *management software*? It is not.

"EXCUSE ME?" he said. The checkout counter was on the other side of the chips and magazines. "EXCUSE ME."

There was a lady getting a coffee too, and she glanced at Russ.

"Cream's out," he said, shaking his head at her. "The whole dispenser's out."

She nodded and looked away, like now she was scared of him. Great. And of course he couldn't get any peace and quiet at home, either, because Flor had Molly there. He stood glaring at the woman, who was doing a mix of the coffees, some hazelnut, some French vanilla. Molly was there moping around, sitting on his couch, making him jumpy. You couldn't believe this girl was only twelve, she looked sixteen. She dragged around the house the same way her mother used to, wearing her little jeans, giving one-word answers to things.

"EXCUSE ME," he said, craning his neck to look at the cashier, who was ringing someone up.

"Uh. Yeah?" said the guy—sideburns, red baseball cap—glancing from the register toward Russ.

"CREAM'S OUT," he said, pointing.

"Oh, okay. Give me a second."

"Hm."

Russ stood there holding the cup. He looked at the dispenser, a stainless steel job with a sticker on the front. Cream Machine, it said, with a design of cow spots. You know, he could probably just—

And he set the coffee on the counter and started taking the thing apart.

———

After dinner the three of them watched TV. He had his stockinged feet on the coffee table, Flor in the armchair sipping a drink, Molly slumped at the end of the couch wearing an oversized sweatshirt. After a while Flor dozed off and started snoring.

Russ glanced at Molly. The two of them could laugh about it. Listen to grandma, honking like a three-hundred-pound man. But Molly didn't seem to notice, and anyway, she didn't look at him. His eyes went back to the screen. Ten o'clock news was about to start.

Flor snorted and woke herself up. She looked down at the booklet of word puzzles in her lap, squinting at it for a second, like she was in the middle of a clue. Then closed it.

"I'm turning in," she said, rubbing a wrinkled cheek. She looked at Molly, who didn't look back at her or say anything. "Moll?" she said. "You staying up?"

Molly shrugged. That was all this girl did, shrug and say nothing. Flor lifted herself from the chair and padded off.

Russ could hear the faucet in the bathroom. Then quiet. He looked at Molly.

"You care what we watch?" he said.

She shook her head.

"Okay, well how about we watch the news now, then you pick something after that?"

She didn't say anything; she didn't even move. He palmed the remote and turned up the volume.

—today discovered what appeared to be a large marijuana operation on private land near White River Junction. A surveyor came across the field early this morning and alerted local authorities, who have since turned the investigation over to state police and the federal DEA. Officials estimate that the perpetrators harvested hundreds of pounds of marijuana just days ago from plants they had covertly—

"Great, that's what we need, right?" he said. "More drugs."

—*land belonging to pharmaceutical baron Richard Olson. Olson, who resides in New York City, is a major investor in Vermont ski resorts. Just hours ago, he issued a public statement condemning the trespassing and unlawful use of his property to grow an illicit substance.*

Then the news went to sports, the start of hockey season.

"Sox didn't even make the playoffs," he said, glancing at Molly. "You like the Red Sox?"

Molly had taken a pillow in her lap, had wrapped her arms around it. Her head canted to one side as she stared at the screen. She barely shrugged.

"Your mom used to like the Sox. I took her to a game once," he said.

She didn't answer. He looked at her, at her hair that gathered in pretty waves around her face.

At six o'clock the following evening, he settled into a folding chair. The basket came around and, not wanting to look cheap, he threw two bucks into it. Then Russ folded his arms over his chest and listened while someone spilled their guts.

When he agreed to come to these meetings he had figured, a couple meetings, a few weeks. A month, tops. But here now it was October, and Ronnie seemed determined to keep coming. The guy was like a Clydesdale, dragging a load. Didn't occur to him to maybe give it a rest. And what was Russ supposed to do? How do you tell your best friend that the meetings for dealing with his son's death are making you lose your mind?

He crossed his arms the other way as the woman talking said, "Pass." A few chairs to her left was Nachalah. He looked at her and they made eye contact. She blinked a long blink, like she was saying hello. His face warmed and he looked down at the table.

After the meeting Ronnie lingered by the door, black windbreaker zipped up, hands in his pockets.

"You saw the news about the silver factory," he said. It wasn't a question. Of course Russ had seen it, it was all over the paper.

Russ nodded.

"It's something, isn't it?" said Ronnie. "Factory closes, lays us all off. And then, after we lose Aaron, after we can't help him no more, they decide to turn the place into a rehab center."

Russ stared at the scuffed linoleum floor, his lower lip pinned under his front teeth.

"You see what the paper said?" Ronnie continued. "That it's gonna be *a medical campus*? That's what they said, serving all of western New England. Hey, you know what? I hope they can help some other people's kids, I really do. If they can save one family from—" he said, and stopped.

"Course it'll be a bunch of new jobs, too," he went on, "although probably not too many machinists." He laughed, the sad way. "It'll be, I don't know, nurses, I guess? I suppose that's a big deal for Greenfield, isn't it. A medical campus in Greenfield. How about that."

Russ walked Ronnie to his car and then climbed slowly into the 4Runner. As he started to pull away, he saw Nachalah, purse strung over her shoulder, waving a hand like she wanted to say something. He rolled to a stop and put down the window.

"You doing okay?" she said.

"Uh, yeah," he said, and looked at his hands on the steering wheel.

"Should we get a coffee?"

He thought he should probably get home. Flor had Molly and everything. He glanced at Nachalah.

"Alright, sure," he said.

"Meet you there."

He got to McDonald's before her. There was a line at the drive-thru, but it was quiet inside. He ordered a coffee and sat down at the same table as before. There was one guy by the window, eating a value meal.

When she slid into the chair across from him, milkshake and straw in her hand, he said, "Your, uh, boyfriend's not expecting you? For dinner?"

She belly laughed. "I'm gay," she said.

"What?"

"Gay. Lesbian. I like girls. And no, no one's expecting me for dinner."

Russ blinked. Are you kidding me. What was he supposed to say now.

But she didn't seem to notice, her fist wrapped around the straw as she tapped the end on the table until the wrapping tore, then she poked the straw through the lid.

"How you been?" she said, and took a long sip.

"Uh."

"Yeah, I can see it," she said, wiping her mouth with the side of her hand.

"See what?"

"You got a lot on your mind."

"I'm fine," he snorted, and lifted his coffee. Then set down the cup and said, "Why are you so concerned about me anyway?"

She cocked her head. "This is how it works," she said.

"What."

"The program."

He blinked at her.

"Other people did the same thing for me. I wouldn't even have stuck with it if other people hadn't helped me figure it out."

He kept looking at her, blank.

"You don't know what I'm talking about? This is the twelfth step."

"What?"

"The twelfth step, you know we read the steps at the beginning of every meeting? This is the twelfth step, carry this message to others."

He squinted.

"I'm doing my twelfth step," she said. "It's not like it ends. It's not like you finish and wash your hands and say I'm all done. The twelfth step is you reach a hand back to people just starting the program. Which is what people did for me, and I've done for other people, and now I'm doing it for you."

His mouth opened. This was why she asked him to coffee.

She had paused but when he didn't say anything she started talking again.

He would finish his coffee and go. He took a big swallow, scalded his tongue. What was that, what did she just say? There she goes with the higher power.

"Bull crap," he said, shaking his head.

She stopped and looked at him. "What?" she said.

"That's bull crap, the god stuff. Give me a break. How can anyone believe that? The priests are god's messengers? Please."

Her forehead creased.

"But what they're actually doing, c'mon," he sniffed, "you know what they're actually doing is they're touching little boys."

She looked at him, and a shadow of understanding crossed her face. He saw it. He saw the change in the way she regarded him. His chest started pounding. She knew. He had just revealed his story to her.

He had never told anyone. In his whole life, he had never told anyone what happened to him. His heart pounded. And now this Nachalah, she knew.

She was looking at him, her eyes sad. He should go; he should just get up and go. He glanced over his shoulder, then back at her.

"You know," she said, holding his gaze, "we can all break the cycle."

When Russ, pale, climbed out of the car, hit the button to shut the garage door, and came into the kitchen, Flor was sitting at the table. She had her reading glasses on, the register of her daisy checkbook open in front of her. The TV was on in the living room.

"Where were you?" she said.

"Ronnie's meeting."

"That finished at seven."

He put his keys on the counter. "So?" he said.

All he wanted was to watch TV, could he just watch TV and relax for one second? But of course Molly was there, on his couch, her skinny legs crossed at the ankles while a movie played on the screen. What movie was this. Mel Gibson, an old one. Did she even want to watch this.

He lowered himself into the hardback chair by the front door and unlaced his work boots, pulled one off his foot.

You know what he wanted. He realized it all at once, a revelation.

A beer.

He blinked as he pulled off the other boot, set it neatly beside the first. That was it. He needed a beer.

He hadn't had a beer in, Jesus, ten years. No, more than ten years. Of course he needed a beer. A guy is entitled to a beer every ten years.

He stood up and drifted through the living room to the bedroom. Slowly he put on his sweatpants. When he came back out to the living room, he stood for a second by the couch, looking at Molly, her chin slumped on her chest. On the TV someone fired a gun, and it went to commercial.

"Do you even want to watch this?" he said.

She shrugged but didn't look at him.

He sat down beside her. Imagine just going to the fridge and grabbing a cold one. He could put his boots back on, run out to the package store; it wouldn't take fifteen minutes.

He looked into the kitchen. Flor was getting up from the table, putting her checkbook in the basket on the counter.

"I'm going out to the store," he said quietly, "then I'll come back and watch with you."

This time she turned her head and looked at him. Long lashes, olive-brown eyes. She looked at him and said, "My mom doesn't like you."

He froze.

"What?"

"My mom doesn't like you."

"That's not a nice thing to say."

"Why doesn't she like you?"

"I guess you'd have to ask her."

"Well, I can't ask her right now, can I?" she said. "You don't know why?"

"No," he said, "I don't."

He glanced over the back of the couch into the kitchen. Flor had started putting away dishes.

"I'm going to the store," he said, and nodded.

When he stood up his legs quivered. Around the other side of the couch, he slipped his feet back into his boots, leaving the laces undone. In the kitchen he grabbed his keys off the counter.

"Where are you going now?" said Flor.

"I'll be right back."

When he pulled into the plaza on the western reach of Main Street, there wasn't a car in the parking lot. Closed. It was closed. It was after nine and the damn liquor store was closed.

He parked in a spot by the check-cashing place. The glow from the streetlight fell on the empty passenger seat as he stared straight ahead, his breath heavy.

He was trembling. His whole body was shaking.

In the window the lettering said We Buy Gift Cards.

———

It was just before four o'clock the following afternoon, when Flor was arranging chicken thighs in a Pyrex, that the doorbell rang. Molly was sitting motionless in front of the TV, her back to Flor and the kitchen. She didn't move at the sound of the doorbell.

Flor came out of the kitchen and looked at the back of her granddaughter's head. Wiped her hands and pulled open the door. On the step stood a girl with a pierced nose, her arms full of files. Flor frowned.

"Hi there, are you Flora?"

"Who are you?"

"Nachalah Rosen, DCF."

"DCF," Flor repeated.

"Department of Children and Families."

"I know what it stands for."

"We always check in on the domicile after a custody transfer; it's completely routine. Can I come inside?"

———

The guys had closed up, the chain-link gate shut and padlocked. Russ, last one there, had locked the office door and was out in the parking lot, the hatch of his 4Runner thrown open.

He'd always kept supplies in here. He had a full-sized spare tire on a rim. He had jumper cables, tie-downs, a come-along. Ice scraper with brush. Now he had this grill—he could cook right out of the hatch if he had to. Up front he had the US road atlas, purchased years ago, for their first trip to Maine. A large flashlight, the kind cops use. And under the seat, his .22.

Of course he knew what guys were buying today. They were getting Glocks. And they were buying accessories, bigger clips, extra rounds. You could get those things in different colors. As if that's what you needed, your firearm in a special color. If push comes to shove, you need to protect yourself. Who's going to be faster? You, fumbling around with your damn accessories, or me, with a simple .22? See, you get my point, he thought, slamming the hatch shut.

Just then a red pickup truck came rolling into the empty lot. The engine flipped off and Russ heard the click of the e-brake. A kid hopped out. He was short and square, wearing a maroon hoodie, the tongues of his sneakers sticking out over his jeans.

He looked at Russ.

"Do you work here?" he said.

"What do you need?"

"I'm looking for someone," he said, coming toward him. "I don't know his name. But he has a stepdaughter named Casch."

28

"Date of your last period?"

She stared at the uniformed woman sitting across from her.

"Date of your last period?"

Casch didn't say anything.

"If you don't know, then you can just estimate."

"Why would you need to know that?"

The woman lowered her pencil.

"A comprehensive exam is part of the admit process," she said, and raised the pencil. "Date of your last period?"

Casch stared back at her.

"Okay, we'll skip that. Have you ever accessed mental-health services?"

Pause.

"No."

"Ever experienced sexual assault?"

Who the fuck are you? she didn't say. "No," she said.

When the cops first brought her in, Flora had posted bail. They assigned her a court date for a couple days later. She had stood in the courtroom, beside the lawyer she just met, facing an American flag, as someone read her charges aloud for everyone to hear. Disturbing the peace. Possession of a Schedule I substance. Resisting arrest.

"Sentenced to ninety days in the Greenfield County House of Corrections," said the gowned man. His name was etched into a copper placard that sat out in front of him. They cuffed her right then.

"Remove your clothes."

"What?" said Casch. The woman was pushing out her chair and standing up.

"Remove all clothing from your person."

What if she said no. She looked around the tiny room, at the cinder block walls. There were no windows. There was a heavy door behind the woman. She looked at the door while the woman stood there, arms folded. She wore black cargo pants with a nylon belt. A holstered firearm.

Neither of them spoke. The only noise was the buzzing of the lights.

Casch felt a cough come up her throat. It bought her thirty seconds. She coughed. Raspy, raw.

Finally, slowly, she started to undress. When she was naked and shivering, the woman said, "Face the wall, squat, and cough." The mandatory cough set off real coughing. Casch crouched there, trying to shield herself from the woman's eyes as the hack came up her throat. Her bare feet were cold but sweaty on the shiny floor.

Afterward she handed Casch a pale blue uniform and gigantic white underwear and bra.

"Any items found on your person from this point forward must be county-issued or will be considered introduction of contraband. That's a felony," she added, picking up Casch's own clothes with a latex-gloved hand. She sealed them into a plastic bag.

Casch was assigned to C-11 and handed an extra uniform, sheets, blanket, and a rolled-up pad—her mattress, it turned out. And a thick manual, *Inmate Handbook.*

"You're responsible for knowing the rules in the handbook and complying with them," said the male officer who deposited her in C-11. The door clicked shut.

"Ah, fuck," said the woman on the lower bunk, raising her head to look.

That night Casch lay there listening to officers calling out numbers, the numbers echoing. There were other voices, too, that were shouting and echoing. She pressed her eyes shut. People kept shouting and the sound rebounded in her temples. Did they make the place this way on purpose, every sound amplified? She could hear every movement. Everyone rustling. Everyone breathing, flushing a toilet, clinking something onto a metal surface. Upstairs, downstairs, all of it echoed in her head.

She shivered and pulled the thin blanket to her chin. The smell was old cafeteria, recirculated air. She pressed her eyes shut. The lights were still on, and the fluorescent glow shone in her face. She didn't know what the woman on the bottom bunk was doing—Thompson was her last name, Casch had heard an officer call her that—but for a second Casch thought about getting up and switching off the light.

Then it was like two hands slipped around her neck.

She could not control the lights.

She lay that way, eyes open, shivering on the papery mattress, as the light pressed into her face. All night the lights stayed on and the sounds echoed.

———

By early morning she was full-blown sick. She knew how it went now. After the coughing came the shitting, the puking. And the fear down your throat. The fear because you don't have what you need to feel okay.

"Of course I get one with withdrawals," said Thompson, staring into the underside of the upper bunk, when the shitting started.

The metal toilet, which had no seat or lid and jutted out from the base of the metal sink as one single fixture, was barely a couple feet from the bunk. Just a couple feet from Thompson's head. Whenever they weren't on count—meaning headcount, meaning stay in your cell till the officer calls it over, which seemed to take place at least seven times a day—whenever they weren't on count, Thompson rolled her eyes at Casch and got up and left her to shit alone.

The feeling that her skin had peeled back lasted longer this time. It didn't come then go but lingered, like her bloody red muscles were scratching against the sheets, against the nothing mattress, chafing on the metal underneath.

Her head drowned in the noises. She heard the TV down on the unit; she heard the static of an officer's radio; she heard one girl burp ten cells over. In the noises she saw flashes of the kids. There was Molly. There, Dean. One of them, then the other, then both of them.

"Mom. Mom!" They peered at her, needing her. "Mom!"

"Where are you, Mom?"

"Please, Mom."

"Oh, Molly, Deanie," she whimpered, her eyes shut tight. Sobs came up her chest.

"Shut *up*," said Thompson. "At least you're not in state. You know how much worse they got it in state prison?"

Casch didn't know how many days it was like that. It went on, it went on. How could you know, anyways, how long it was? How could you know, when your mind was half gone, when the lights stayed on? She didn't know how long it was, but she knew it was longer than before. Had to be. Because even with all the lights on, it was never so dark.

Then it stopped. The shitting stopped, the coughing stopped. And she lay still. Her lips were dry and her muscles were gone. Her shrunken body disappeared inside the blue uniform. She was all thirsty bones.

But her mind was there. Her mind had returned. Awake. And searching.

What the fuck had she done. Look what I've done. This is what you've done.

How long had she left Molly and Dean? How long were they alone? What happened? Who found them? Did they call for help? How long were they alone—wondering where she was, thinking she abandoned them. Molly and Dean, abandoned. She abandoned them.

That's what you did. You abandoned your children.

She couldn't breathe. That's who she was, that's who she was now. How long did they wait for her to come home?

She could see them perfectly, Molly paging through a kids' detective book, Dean holding Otis in his arms. The two of them walking on that trail with Topher, Topher showing them a flower, and Dean reaching up and taking his hand. And Topher standing there, casually holding Dean's hand.

Dean, in his truck pajamas, asking Casch to tuck him in. Wanting her to stay with him while he fell asleep.

But where was she now? How many nights had she been gone? Please, god, let them be okay. She was crying. She hadn't appreciated that being under one roof with your children is the greatest thing you can ask for.

"I love you, Molly. Can you hear me? I love you, Dean, Deanie, I love you. I love you. I'm sorry, I'm so sorry—I love you so."

She sobbed on her stomach without making a sound until the spit coming down her chin made a dark circle in the pillow-case.

The CO opened the cell door and stood looking at his clipboard.

"Abbey, Casch," he said, peering in.

"What."

"Caseworker meeting."

"What?"

"Your caseworker meeting is now."

She rubbed her face. Slowly she sat up and climbed down. On the wall between the bunk and the cell door was a sort of mirror. Reflected about as good as a spoon. But for a second she saw herself. Sunken eyes, rash around her mouth. She looked away and followed the officer out.

The TV was blaring out on the unit. A few women in blue uniforms sat, expressionless, on couches that were made of gray rubber and bolted to the floor.

They passed the guard station. Behind the semicircle desk sat a shrimpy guy in uniform, his face pocked with acne. He glanced from the computer screens as Casch and the officer passed by.

Just before the huge sliding metal door was a tiny office. It had one plexiglass wall that looked out onto the unit. The door was open. The officer pointed and Casch went in.

The woman at the desk wasn't wearing a uniform; she wore a suit jacket. A laminated ID hung around her neck. There were papers in front of her, a file open.

"Have a seat," she said, and when Casch sat down, the woman smiled. "I've looked through your case," she said.

The office was no bigger than C-11, and Casch could smell the woman's shampoo. She wore a cream blouse under the jacket. She had a mole on her neck.

"A powerful thing that we often forget is that we can *choose* to be happy," the woman said, interlacing her fingers on the desk between them. She wore a wedding ring, Casch saw. A diamond. It was gray and cloudy in the flat light, but it looked to be a pretty decent-sized rock.

"What I want to make sure you understand," the woman was saying, "is that you are calling the shots in your own life. You may have done some bad things in the past, but you get to decide where you're going in the future. Isn't that powerful?"

The woman paused, nodding to herself. On the wall behind her was a small laminated sign that said:

LISTEN TO LEARN
AND
LEARN TO LISTEN

"What I'm saying is, you can choose to give up this lifestyle."

"Lifestyle," said Casch.

"That's right. And to help you do that, we have some programming available here that I want to point out to you. The key thing I'd like to highlight is we have volunteers leading twelve-step meetings. Now, I see that you're a mother," she said, looking down at the file, "and I want you to know that participating in a twelve-step will make it more likely you'll regain custody of your kids. This is something we strongly—"

"What."

"—because judges look favorably on—"

"What did you say?"

"Excuse me?"

"Regain custody of my kids?"

"That's right."

She whispered, "Who has custody of my kids?"

"Custody of your kids has been transferred to"—the woman shuffled the papers—"it looks like, your son, his father? Your daughter, it says, maternal grandmother. That would be your mother?"

"Are you, they can't, that's not—"

"The state has deemed you an unfit guardian," the woman said, straightening in her chair. "Now let me just circle back to this point about participating in our programming—"

There was a pounding in her ears. She had lost Deanie to his dad. And Flora had *custody* of Molly. Meaning *Russ* had custody of Molly.

There was no air in here, the cinder blocks came in at her. Russ had Molly.

"Can I make a phone call? I need to make a phone call. Can I make a phone call?" she said.

"Y-es," the woman said, looking at her like she was dumb, "all inmates have access to the unit telephone."

Casch stood at the back of the unit clutching the heavy black receiver, sweaty fingertip trembling as she punched the silver numbers. She did it wrong, had to start over. Finally it rang. She heard Flora's voice, "Hello?"

"Mom?" she croaked.

But a recording began to play. *"Will you accept a collect call from a correctional—"*

Casch pressed her eyes closed. This is the loser you are now.

The recording finished.

"Yes," said Flora.

"How's it going there?" Casch whispered.

"We're making do," Flora said. But she said it like a question: We're making do?

"How's Molly?"

"She's . . . what do you want me to say? She just sits there, stares at the TV."

"What time is it? Is she there? Is she back from school? Let me talk to her."

"All right," said Flora. "One sec."

There was rustling, then quiet. Then came Molly's small voice. "Hello?"

"Baby, it's Mom."

"Hi, Mom."

"Baby, I'm so sorry," she started to say. But then she started to cry. She could not let Molly hear. She cried silently. She hunched toward the phone. She could not let anyone see; no one could see her cry.

"It's not going to be long like this, okay?" she said, mucus gathering at the back of her throat. "I'll be there to pick you up before you know it."

"In three *months*," said Molly.

Casch's eyes were closed. "Yeah, that's right." She cried silently, swallowing. "How's school, baby?"

"Okay."

"What are you learning about?"

She could hear Molly breathing, but she didn't answer.

"Baby, are you okay? I need to know, are you okay? Do you get what I mean? Is anyone, is anyone? Is anyone—are you okay?"

"I'm okay."

Casch let out a breath.

"But you know you can tell me anything, right? If you're not okay, you can tell me."

Molly didn't say anything.

"Listen, Molly, you got to listen to me. Listen really good, okay? Okay? Molly?"

"Okay."

"Baby, you have to stay away from Russ. Stay right by your grandma, whatever you have to do, stay away from Russ. Lock your bedroom door when you sleep. You understand? You get me? Stay away from him."

"Mom, I want to come home," said Molly, and she started to cry.

"I know, I know, baby. Molly, sweetie, you just got to promise me, you promise me? You stay away from Russ? Molly?"

"I promise," she said, so quiet Casch could barely hear.

"I'm sorry, I'm so sorry, it's my fault, it's my—" said Casch, shaking her head, but the words dissolved.

That night on the papery mattress, one thought played on loop. Nothing mattered except Russ could not touch Molly. Russ could not touch Molly. Molly could not be at Russ's. If Russ touched Molly . . .

At last she screamed. It echoed.

"KNOCK IT OFF," said Thompson. "You know they'll put you in the hole if you don't shut the fuck up."

But she kept hearing it. You'll never get your kids back; you'll never be anything. She kept hearing it. It wasn't her voice. She didn't know whose voice it was.

"FUCK THAT VOICE," she yelled, she screamed it. "WHAT-EVER THAT VOICE SAYS I SHOULD DO THE FUCKING OP-POSITE."

"Now bitch is talking to a voice," said Thompson.

The following day during count, staring at the wall, she realized that the thing about jail is that it's you with you. And Thompson. Meaning it's you and your thoughts. You think about everything and then when you finish you start over and think everything again. Does Molly hate me. Does Dean have his Spider-Man shirt. Does Molly have her notebook. Do they both hate me. You deserve for them to hate you. She would never undo this. I hate myself. She wanted to get high—see, you'll never be anything. And there it was, that voice. You'll never be anything. Was she a crazy person? Do other people have that voice? It wasn't her voice, whose was it? She didn't know. But if it wasn't her own self, then it should just knock it off. She never listened to anybody, why should this be any different.

Fuck you, voice, she thought. If she could just _____. The unfinished thought hung there. Being a single mom, it was always one step forward, two steps back. Or in this case two hundred steps back. How are you ever supposed to do better. But she had to, somehow she had to. For Molly and Dean. For Molly and Dean, if they didn't hate her guts when she got out, which they probably did, but it didn't matter, for them she would figure it out. She would figure it out. She would get through this. She would get to the other side. Back to normal—no, fuck that, better than that. Normal was falling apart. She would do better; she would figure it out. If anyone could do it, it was her. Where did that thought come from?

If anyone could do it, it was her.

Flora put money in her canteen account. Which meant Casch got an order sheet, and she went down the list, checking off things she wanted. She spent time with that list. She read every item. Potato chips, vanilla wafers, graham crackers, Oreos, popcorn, Pop Tarts. There was ramen. There was a pizza kit you could cook in the microwave down on the floor. There was hot sauce. There were Jolly Ranchers. Plus cough drops. Tylenol. Carmex. You could get sweatpants and a sweatshirt—those were expensive. You could get shampoo, conditioner, lotion. Down the side of the sheet, she saw there was a list of cosmetics. Her forehead wrinkled. You could get liquid eyeliner, an eyelash curler.

This explained how some of the girls managed to look—

normal? Managed not to look like her sorry ass? Apparently that was how they kept their chin up or whatever.

Knock yourselves out, ladies, she thought. You can have your liquid eyeliner. I'll be fixing myself ramen.

When Wednesday came around and the officers called commissary, everyone hustled into line. Afterward Casch toted her order, which had been prepacked into a gray mesh bag, back onto the unit. One of the COs looked at her supplies, the yellow box of vanilla wafers on top, and said, "Junkie's finally getting hungry?"

When she got back to C-11, the bottom bunk was bare.

"Thompson?"

She stared at the place where Thompson had always been. Then she grabbed her little mattress, with its sheets and blanket, and put it on the bottom bunk.

Sat herself down.

Then took her canteen bag and spread everything out on the bed. She looked over all of it, the bright colors, the different-sized packaging.

If anyone can do it, it's you.

She remembered now where those words came from. It was Marylouise. That's what Marylouise said to her when she was pregnant with Molly. Marylouise saw it in her. Marylouise knew she would take good care of her baby even before Casch did. Sometimes all you need is one person who believes in you. One person believing in you can save your life. When Casch had gotten into nursing school, Marylouise had said, "I'd invest in you any day."

Casch felt the shame tighten her chest.

She'd robbed Marylouise.

But she would make it right. She had done some shitty things, and she would make it right. *If anyone can do it, it's you.*

She had herself a red Jolly Rancher.

The caseworker lady apparently signed Casch up for whatever thing she was peddling, because the following day a CO came to her door, looked down at a sheet of paper, and said, "Abbcy, Casch?"

"Mm."

"Your twelve-step is now."

"What?"

"Twelve-step meeting."

"Do I have to?"

"No."

"Then leave me alone."

He walked off. Of course he didn't care if she went. What difference did it make to him if she went to some meeting? He didn't care if she rotted in her cell; he made that clear every time he called her name. She shook her head into the pillow. She thought of the caseworker lady, the mole on her neck. Saying you can change this *lifestyle*, saying judges look favorably on—

She got up. She pushed open the door, which was the color of pancake batter, and peered down the hall.

"Hey? Hey? I'll go to that meeting."

It was off the unit, in a room the officer referred to as the library. There were low bookshelves underneath huge mirrors. The smell was different, Casch noticed, as she and the other women filed in, it didn't smell like cafeteria. Two ladies in normal clothes were sitting at the head of a plastic folding table. Casch and the others sat down.

"Hi girls, how we doing today?" said the one wearing a crewneck sweatshirt. It had a collar sewn inside the neck. A couple of the other jumpsuited women sort of nodded at the question. I mean, how do you think we're doing? No one said that. The woman with the collared sweatshirt cleared her throat and started reading from a sheet in front of her.

One entire shelf was stocked with identical brick-colored copies of the Holy Bible, Casch saw. Another shelf was *The World Book Encyclopedia 1991*. While the woman read, Casch looked at the titles of the other books. If she were here, Molly would read every title.

"Does anybody want to start?" the lady at the front of the table was saying, looking around. Casch kept her eyes low.

"Angie, addict," said someone to Casch's left.

"Hi, Angie," said both women at the front of the table, in unison.

"I'm just really hoping I can stay sober, is all, because of my baby girl."

"Thanks, Angie."

There was a pause.

"Alice, alcoholic, addict," said the woman across from Casch, raising four fingers off the plastic table in a sort of wave. She had large holes in her earlobes; she must have had gauges. They made you remove all jewelry at intake.

"Hi, Alice."

"Okay, so where I am today is someone's really messing with me and I'm just, you know, trying to keep it cool, right? Because I only got two weeks left—"

Casch's eyes dropped to the table. Only two weeks, I have two and a half *months*. I can't do this, she thought. She'd been holding her breath; she let out a breath. How long was the meeting. She looked at the clock, at the second hand ticking. Every time it ticked it wobbled and fell back a tiny bit. Oh my god. But it couldn't be more than an hour, right? And now less than an hour, because how long had they already been here?

Casch looked at Alice, at the scar over her eyebrow.

". . . and I know these catty bitches ain't worth my shit," Alice was saying, her hands resting on the table, clenching, the knuckles turning white, "but I would just love to get, like, one good clean swing at her, you know? That's all. Yep. That's it."

"Thanks, Alice," said the lady in the collared sweatshirt, shifting in her chair. "I see we have a newcomer today," she said, and looked straight at Casch.

"Me?"

The woman nodded. "Want to introduce yourself, dear?"

"Uh, Casch. I'm Casch."

"Hi, Casch," said both women in unison. They said it without hesitating on her name, which she gave them credit for. Then they kept looking at her.

"Do I have to say something?" she asked, sitting up straighter, heart quickening. "What am I supposed to say?"

"Anything on your mind."

Her first thought had been, How do you get out of saying something? She was silent for a couple beats. But then, maybe because she hadn't talked to anyone—had hardly said a word since she'd been here—she surprised herself. She began talking.

"One thing I just started thinking about," she said slowly, her voice quivering a little, "like, today, this morning, or last night, I guess it was? Whatever, time is weird. I started thinking about,

I'm supposed to pay my debt to society? That's what I'm doing here? Because, ha. What did I ever do to society besides bring people their fucking fried shrimp platters? And get them extra napkins? Right? And then get canned for a broken foot?"

The words came out louder than she'd expected.

"Meanwhile, you know, the doctor gave me those meds. And then the cops put me in here? When what I actually need is a tiny bit of fucking help? But never mind, no, you know what? I'll be all right without help from any-fucking-body. So, yeah, don't worry about that."

She wasn't sure how much she should say—probably nothing, she should probably shut her mouth right there. But she went on.

"The officers laugh at you," she said, "and don't get me started on them with the older lady, every single one of us knows who I'm talking about, who thinks she's going to some dance. Won't stop talking about a dance, the only time she said anything to me she asked to borrow my car to go to the dance. And what do the officers do? Smirk at her. Please tell me how a woman with gray hair who thinks she's going to a dance is locked up in here, getting her ass laughed at by the jerk-off officers? Can someone please explain that to me? And every officer thinks they're doing god's work, which to them apparently means treating you like you're worthless. I have as much right to raise my kids, have a house, whatever, as the next girl.

"Actually, it did feel good to say that," she said, and paused for a second before adding, "wish I had a cigarette."

They returned to the unit, the officer escorting them through cinder block halls, their small group of prisoners waiting in front of a sliding door and then, when it opened, shuffling down a ramp, then waiting at another sliding door, which opened onto the unit.

Casch had fallen into step beside Alice, their identical slippered feet padding along the polished floor.

"Hey, did I hear you say you been here a few months?" said Casch after the door rattled closed behind them. They stopped just past the guards' station, where they would split off to their cells.

"Eight months, dude."

"Did you know someone named Jasmine? She would've come through a little while back."

"Oh, yeah, I know Jasmine."

"You do?" said Casch, lifting a little at the connection. "Do you know where she went?"

"Yeah, Chittenden. State prison. They're not gonna let the Black girl stay in county. County is for white girls."

And Casch stood frozen as Alice walked off.

When she got back to C-11 there was someone on the top bunk.

"What up, girl, I'm Clarise," she said, lifting her head.

"Hi?" said Casch, surprised, because it was so un-Thompson-like. "I'm Casch."

"Cash?"

"C-A-S-C-H."

"That's got to be the coolest name I ever heard."

"Thanks," she said, shaking the hand the girl offered out to her and looking at the baby face up there in the bunk.

"This your first time in here?" Clarise asked.

"Why you asking?"

"Cause I never saw you before."

"Oh." Casch lay down on her bed. "You been in a lot?"

"Oh yeah."

They were quiet for a while. Casch took her Jolly Ranchers from the locker under the bed. Pulled out a red one and spun it in her fingers.

"Hey, Clarise?"

"Yeah?"

"You want a Jolly Rancher?"

Clarise leaned out and looked at her. "Oh my god, thank you," she said.

Casch took out another one, and they both unwrapped the loud crinkly plastic.

"I wish I had something to give you," said Clarise from above.

"No worries."

"No, this is exactly how it should be," she said, leaning out again. "We take care of each other. Some of the girls get that and some don't. Actually, you know what?"

Casch didn't say anything. She could hear Clarise rustling.

"I do have one thing," she said. She came climbing down and sat herself, cross-legged, on the floor. She whispered something so softly that Casch couldn't hear.

"What?"

"Klonies. Klonopins."

"Really?"

Clarise nodded.

"I have to have 'em. I will lose my shit if I don't have 'em. Like, I can go without almost anything, you know? But this is the thing that takes the edge off."

Casch resisted the urge to ask how she got them in here.

"A lot of girls have pills," Clarise was saying. "You know girls are sucking back happy pills all day."

"From the med line, though, right?"

"Some of them. But the COs are hooking some of them up. Which I think is shady. I don't want to be owing anyone a favor, you know what I mean?"

Casch nodded.

"So I just put 'em in a tampon," she said, grinning. "In this world, if you need something, you take care of it yourself."

"I agree."

"Man, I got lucky getting you for a bunkmate," said Clarise.

Casch almost laughed. Clarise leaned back on her hands, cheeks dimpling as she smiled. "Anyway, listen," she said, her face getting serious again, "I will share these with you."

"What?"

Clarise nodded gravely. "I will share with you. When I have one, you get one."

Casch's mouth opened.

"What's mine is yours," Clarise went on.

"Thank you," Casch said, phlegmy, trying not to cry, because this girl was really going to give her half of what she had. "You need those," she said. "You just told me how much you need them. You got to keep them for when you really need it."

"I'll get my boyfriend to bring more," she shrugged.

"I appreciate it. I really do," said Casch, shaking her head. She was going to get her kids back. "I'm all set."

She and Clarise made ramen that night. While they waited at the microwave, another girl came over and Casch recognized her from the meeting.

"Casch, you know my girl Angie?" said Clarise, looping her arm around Angie's waist.

"Everyone knows me because of Steve," said Angie to Clarise.

"Angie's boyfriend killed that woman," Clarise explained, her voice sad.

"Back in the spring?" said Casch.

"Yeah."

"Do you know Rick?" she said, looking at Angie, whose hair was streaked pink. Casch couldn't remember Rick's last name, or maybe she'd never known it. "Rick who works at The 99," she said.

"Oh, for sure," said Angie. "I've known him my whole life. His sister's my best friend."

The microwave beeped and they put in the second ramen cup.

"We were gonna quit those pills," said Angie, though Casch hadn't asked. "Me and Steve, I mean."

"Oh, yeah?"

"Yeah, we'd stopped going to our dealer and everything. We said we're gonna stop; we promised each other. I mean, you can't have two people both with a two-hundred-a-day habit, you know? You can't, you can't get that much money, believe me, we tried. We promised each other we were gonna stop. I didn't know Steve had this other connect. He was getting pills from that woman. I guess he met her through work. Wasn't sharing with me. And then, I mean. Well, you know. It was in the news every day."

Casch nodded and they were quiet. She wanted to ask what Angie herself was in for, but she held back. You don't want to be asked that, and no one else wants to be asked either. She did look at every single woman, though, and wonder why they were here.

"Steve wasn't like that," Angie was saying. "This is what I been trying to tell people. I know girls with boyfriends that'll swing at them. I know girls with boyfriends who'll swing a bat at them. That wasn't Steve. He was, like, shy. A softie. That's what I been trying to say, that when you want those pills, you aren't even yourself no more."

Casch stared at her. The microwave beeped.

"Which is why I'm like, I don't want those pills," Angie continued. "I mean, of course I want them, who doesn't want them? You never felt so amazing in your life. But at the same time, no. Keep those shits away from me. No, thank you. I got a baby girl; I'm done with all that."

Casch nodded her head.

She and Clarise talked until morning. Clarise narrated most of her life, though Casch didn't mind. There wasn't that much to tell. Clarise was only nineteen. When she first got into pills she got a job stripping. She couldn't believe how much she made.

"You ever done dates behind Bintliff's?" Clarise asked.

"No."

"You can make a hundred and fifty in five minutes," she said, her voice soft in the fluorescent light.

"You know what's messed up for me?" said Casch after the silence. Her eyes were closed. "I lost everything, you know? I lost everything. I lost my kids. And I still want to get high."

Clarise didn't say anything, and Casch thought she must have fallen asleep. But then, from above, a small voice said, "You know, we're only human."

29

T he following night Casch waited in line for the phone. You were supposed to follow the fifteen-minute limit, but a lot of the girls ignored it—which Casch wasn't even mad about. What do we have besides these calls? She had told Flora not to bring the kids to visiting hours. She didn't want them seeing her this way, remembering her like this. She would see them when she got out, in sixty-eight days.

In eight days she would be done with her first month, she thought, leaning a shoulder against the wall. Then she would be into month two, and when that was over, she'd be on her last month. She had counted and recounted the days so many times she was driving herself crazy. She would be out before Christmas. There was a newspaper on the floor, and she grabbed it. It was a week old, but who cares. Her eyes went down the front page.

Pharma Co Unveils "Miracle Drug"

Springdale, CT (AP) – Olson-Abrams Pharmaceutical, LLP, has announced the development of a drug it says will save "hundreds of thousands, if not millions" of lives. The medication is a reformulation of buprenorphine, widely used in the treatment of opiate addiction.

"We are proud of this innovation and excited about its potential to help those who struggle with addiction," said the company's chairman, Dr. Richard Olson, who holds a majority interest in the family-owned company.

Yet some experts decried the company's move into the addiction rehabilitation market. "Buprenorphine saves lives by preventing cravings and overdose," said Dr. Angela Sue, specialist in addiction
CONTINUED ON PAGE 6

Casch thumbed to the back.

MIRACLE DRUG CONTINUED FROM PAGE 1

medicine at Mass General Hospital. "Such medicine should be freely available to anyone who needs it," said Sue.

Casch's pulse had sped up as she read. Now there was a click, and the woman who'd been talking hung up the phone. The next woman, who had frizzy blondish hair—Casch hadn't seen her before—stepped forward. But after only a second, she hung up. Apparently no one had answered. The woman slinked up the hall.

Casch tucked the newspaper under her arm and lifted the warm receiver. She had a phone card from canteen now, which meant she didn't have to dial collect. She punched the numbers off the card and dialed her mother's house.

"Hello?" The recording started to play but Flora didn't wait for it to finish. "Hello, Casch? Oh my god, Casch? Casch?"

"Mom, I'm here, what is it?"

But Flora said so much so fast, squealing into the phone,

that Casch couldn't understand. Her heart spiked to a million; it knocked around her chest. What happened? What happened? *What happened to Molly?*

"Mom, what is it? CALM DOWN and tell me what happened, MOM? CALM DOWN."

Flora was gasping on the other end of the line. "It was just a couple hours ago," she said. "I got home from work, Russ left a note on the counter."

"And what did it say?" Casch's pulse thudded in her neck. Where was Molly? What did Russ do? *What did Russ do?*

"He's gone."

"What, where's Molly?"

"Molly? She's right here," said Flora, and she started to cry. "I can't believe it. I can't believe it," she sniffled. "Abandon his wife right when I'm taking care of my granddaughter, can you believe it? It's just like your daddy. Your dad left me right after you were born, and I was never the same."

The following afternoon she lay in her bunk, listening to Clarise quietly croon Whitney Houston. Clarise had asked roundabout questions first until Casch realized she was offering to sing.

Which could have been a real downer. Was she now going to have to listen to Clarise's weak Whitney imitation until eventually she'd have to tell her to shut her piehole because we are trapped together in this nine-by-twelve box and I'm just trying to keep from losing my mind, bitch?

But no.

Casch had figured Clarise was going to do the obvious stuff—"I Will Always Love You," the corny stuff—but instead she was all "Shoop Shoop." And damn if her voice wasn't pretty.

Obviously she was no Whitney. But for the Greenfield County House of Corrections, she wasn't bad. And it was the most beautiful thing Casch had heard in twenty-three days.

Just now Clarise was singing "I'm Every Woman" as quietly as she could to keep from echoing. Casch almost smiled as she stared into the underside of the upper bunk.

Russ is gone? Russ is gone. Russ is gone forever?

She was afraid to believe it. Maybe he would change his mind. Maybe he would come barreling home in his shiny SUV just in time for Flora to cook him dinner.

But maybe. He was gone.

That was when the officer opened their door.

"Visiting hours," he said, looking in.

"Oooh," said Clarise, her legs appearing over the side of the bunk. She climbed down and went to follow him.

"You too," he said, looking at Casch.

"What?"

"Do you want to see visitors or not?"

She sat up, not all the way or she would've hit her head. Did Flora bring the kids? She'd told her not to. Casch had told her to just wait—

But the idea that Molly and Dean were here, that she could see her children, that she could hold them in her arms, made her so excited that her feet trembled as she slipped her feet into her canvas shoes and went.

She and the other women stood in a line in a hallway for what had to be forty minutes. No explanation for the delay, they just had to stand there, all of them jumpy and chattering even though the officer told them to shut up. Then, at last, there was the mechanical click of the door unlatching, and the hum as it slid open, and the officer leading them, and another officer opening a set of double doors that let into a bright room.

All of a sudden it was chaos. Women saw their visitors and ran to them even though they were supposed to line up and wait to be called. Someone was reading last names. Casch was scanning the room—which was full of kids, kids waiting to see their mothers. She was looking, looking.

But she didn't see Molly. She didn't see Dean. She looked for Flora, here by herself? At last she realized they weren't there. It was some mistake. She had no visitors.

She was the last one standing up front after everyone had gone to a round table to see their people. Clarise was with her boyfriend toward the middle of the room. Casch tried to act like it was fine, it was no big deal. Like the disappointment wasn't choking her throat so she couldn't let go of her breath.

Then she saw him. Standing in the back corner, looking toward her, his hands in the pockets of his jeans.

And now she was crossing the room. She was hurrying around other people's kids who were saying, Mom! Mom! She was skirting the women who were lifting their babies in joy. She was almost tripping over a box of board games as she ran all the way to the back corner, where Topher wrapped her in his arms.

When he finally let go, after their tears had run together, he went over to the vending machines along the wall. She watched. She watched him press buttons and swipe a white card. He pressed buttons and swiped, buttons and swiped, until it looked like he had gotten one of everything—potato chips and pretzels and cheese sandwiches and cookies and peanut butter cups and lemon-lime sodas. And Topher came back to her, his arms full.

———

"The field got busted," he told her as they ate.

"What, you did?" She studied him with thirsty eyes, taking in his dark hair and the stubble along his jaw. His maroon hoodie, unzipped, with the sleeves pushed up. His calloused hands, his sturdy forearms. And the chain around his neck peeking out from the collar of his black T-shirt.

"I wasn't there, none of us were there. We'd just finished harvesting. It was right after that."

She dropped her voice. "You got the weed out?"

He nodded.

"All of it?"

"Yeah."

She stared at him.

"But that's—it," he said. "Obviously we can't grow there anymore."

"So what are you gonna do?"

"Well, I'm okay for a while," he said. "But I guess I was thinking, I don't know. I might look around for jobs. It probably all pays shit, you know? But I thought, I'd just see."

She broke a smile as he popped a pretzel in his mouth.

"And if you thought, if you thought, you and Molly and Dean might be, uh, wanting to hang out, with me, I could look closer to down here. I mean, I don't have to be in White River."

"You didn't give up on me," she said softly. "I told you to fuck off and you didn't give up on me."

"No. I—"

"Topher?"

"What?"

"I'm sorry for being an asshole."

He exhaled a laugh. "I just been worried about you is all."

"I was too messed up to realize," she said, "you were looking out for me."

His eyes lifted.

"Which is why, actually," she said, swallowing, "I was thinking about it, and actually, I wanted to say, thank you."

He smiled and it lit his eyes.

"You're welcome," he said softly.

For a moment they were both quiet. She started eating again. She finished the sandwich and opened the peanut butter cups.

"Actually," he said, "I also wanted to say something. Which is that I love you."

"I love you too. You think I'd be dreaming about just anyone's grandma? I friggin met your Gram in my dream."

"You did?"

"Yeah, I did. And I think she really likes me."

The following Tuesday Topher picked up both kids, and he and Molly and Dean were waiting together at a table when she came into the big room. Casch trembled as she rushed to them and pulled Molly and Dean into a hug. Molly felt skinny—Casch pulled back to look at her. Her daughter was so lanky and tall, like she'd grown two inches.

"I miss you so much, baby," she said, her voice cracking as Molly stared at her. Maybe Molly would never forgive her. Casch swallowed. She looked down at Dean. She knelt so she was at his eye level.

"I miss you, baby."

"I miss you, Mom," he said, frowning, hunching away from her. Her chest went tight. Slowly she stood and hugged Topher, the only one of them smiling. He squeezed her.

"You guys hang here, I'll get us some snacks," he said.

"What about our game?" said Dean, and Casch saw there were UNO cards spread across the table.

"Your mom can play for me," said Topher.

"Okay," said Dean, but he looked doubtful.

"It's okay, baby," said Casch, "let's play."

"Yeah, Dean, it's fine," said Molly, shrugging, sitting down. She was wearing a teal pullover jacket that Casch didn't recognize.

When Topher came back to the table with sodas and candy, Dean tore open the red sleeve of Skittles and spilled them across the table onto the floor. Molly immediately started picking them up.

"It's your turn," said Molly when she had picked them all up. "Mom? Your turn."

For a while they played UNO and sipped their sodas, Casch and Topher sharing one hand of cards.

"UNO," said Molly.

They put the cards back in the box and the kids went to look for another game. For a second Topher and Casch sat without saying anything, and he took her hand.

"I saw a job posting," he said. "I think I might apply for it."

"Really? What is it?"

"It's with the state forest—they're, actually, looking to hire veterans."

Their eyes met and she broke a tiny smile.

The kids came back with checkers. But they had only just gotten the board set up and started playing when an officer shouted that visiting hours were over. Guests were to remain seated, inmates to file out.

Casch kissed Topher. She hugged and kissed Molly. "I love you so much," she whispered.

When she hugged Dean, he said, "I want to come home." His chin puckered as his eyes filled with tears, and he scrunched his face and turned away from her.

"I'm sorry, baby," Casch whispered, trying to swallow her own tears. "I'm sorry, I'm so sorry." She tried to reach for him, but an officer came by and nodded at her. She trembled, holding her breath as she turned to go. Molly looped an arm around her brother.

30

Six Months Later

Topher was late on the Saturday morning when he was supposed to plant snow peas with the kids. In Flora's kitchen Casch stood washing dishes, steaming tap water turning her hands pink as she scraped last night's lasagna from the corners of a Pyrex. Then the doorbell chimed and her back straightened. Topher wouldn't ring the bell.

"I'll get it," she called, peering into the empty living room. She pulled open the door.

Gabi was on the front step, a box of donuts in her hands.

"Yo! Hey!" said Casch, grabbing her into a hug.

"I thought I'd spread some Easter weekend cheer." Gabi grinned.

"You're amazing, c'mon on in. Guys, donuts!" she called as she led Gabi to the kitchen. Molly and Dean appeared in a second.

"Hey, hey, manners," said Casch as they tried reaching before she'd even set the box down. "What do you say?"

"Thanks," said Molly.

"Thanks," said Dean, taking a jelly one. He ate it while cornering Otis and picking him up.

"He doesn't like that," said Molly. "Don't hold him like that."

"Yeah, he does."

"Why don't we let your mom visit with her friend?" said Flora, appearing in the doorway. "Deanie, Moll? Why don't we start clearing out the garden while you wait for Topher?"

"Where *is* he?" said Molly.

"I don't know, but let's wait outside."

Dean dropped Otis, and Flora herded him and Molly out through the slider, pulling it shut behind them.

"You finish your midterms?" Gabi asked as they sat down at the table. She broke off half a chocolate glaze, her fingernails painted glossy green, and took a bite.

"Barely. I had to memorize about three thousand anatomy words."

"I'm proud of you, girl," said Gabi, leaning back in the chair.

"Thanks. The program director told us the rehab place that's going in the old silver factory will hire a lot of people, not just nurses. She said there'll be jobs in peer support."

"What's that?"

"Meaning, I could eventually get a job because I've been through it, and use what I learned to help other people get back on their feet."

"That would be incredible."

"Right?" said Casch. "But you know I need to get out of here," she added quietly, gesturing with her head. "I'm dying to have our own place again, and now Topher's all talking about buying a house, and I'm like—"

"Really? He has the money?"

"I don't know, I guess so. But I'm like, that's not how it's supposed to happen."

"What do you mean, not how it's supposed to happen?"

"I've always taken care of myself."

"So maybe that's the thing you have to learn," said Gabi.

"What is?"

"That nobody does it all on their own. Everyone needs help."

Casch felt her shoulders soften. "Thanks," she said. "I needed to hear that."

"Anytime."

"You know what I been doing when my mind starts going all crazy," said Casch. "I been thinking about the graduation party I'm throwing for you next month."

"What!" said Gabi, sitting forward.

"You think I'm going to let you get all fancy with a *business* degree and not even celebrate you? I'll be the one in the front row shouting loudest."

"You'll have to fight my mom for that," said Gabi, smiling big.

"Your mom hasn't seen my swing. Anyways I can at least dish out some cake to our kids."

"Well, I won't argue with that." Gabi leaned all the way forward, her voice dropping as she said, "Hey, I heard some gossip."

"Oh yeah?"

"Yeah, it's about Jay. You still don't know why the change of heart, right?"

"No," said Casch, staring at her. A couple months after she'd been released, out of nowhere Jay had offered her primary custody of Dean. They would have to go through a whole review process with the state to make it official. "But I'm not going to question it," she said. "Why, what did you hear?"

"Well. Two ladies from that insurance company came in the restaurant last night. Sat at the bar, got a little tuned up. And, turns out, Jay doesn't work there no more. His ass got fired."

"Shut up."

"They said he had a pissy attitude. No one wanted to work with him."

Casch laughed. So Jay was out of work. He was broke—and he'd handed off his son to her.

Not that she was surprised, she thought. Of course she wasn't surprised. Suit yourself, Jay. Yes, I will raise my son.

"You want to know the funniest part?" said Gabi.

"What?"

"They told me to apply for his job."

"What! That's amazing. Oh my god, imagine you get Jay's job, that's incredible."

"Nah," said Gabi, waving a hand, "there's an opening in the financial aid office at school that Frankie told me to apply for; that's what I really want."

"That's cool," said Casch, blinking, picturing it. "Maybe you can help me figure out how to afford all this tuition?"

"Exactly. Imagine I get paid to do that," said Gabi, plucking the other half of the chocolate glaze from the box.

"Wow, your nails are looking sharp."

"Just got 'em done," Gabi grinned, and she flashed the green polish and the tiny frogs on the thumbs.

It was almost noon when Gabi left. Casch stood in the kitchen, staring at the pansy clock on the wall beside the door to the garage. The kids were still out back, and no word from Topher.

For weeks after Casch had gotten out, back in December, she hadn't called her friend. Why would Gabi forgive her? But then they had run into each other at school, and suddenly Casch was fumbling through an apology.

"I forgive you, girl," Gabi had said. "I forgive you." And Casch had wanted to cry.

She had started writing a letter to Jasmine on sheets of lined notebook paper. It was slow but she would finish it. Still, though, she had not gone to see Marylouise—she would, someday. She would be honest about what she did, and maybe Marylouise would never forgive her. And who could blame her. But Casch would pay her back, eventually. Every penny. Casch closed her eyes.

A couple nights ago, after the kids were in bed, Flora was pouring herself a drink when Casch came to talk to her. Flora saw the serious look on her face.

"What? What's wrong?" she'd asked.

At first Casch couldn't say it. She had wiped her eyes and tried again.

"Mom, I needed you so bad," she whispered.

"What?"

"You know when. I came to you for help," she whispered. "I needed you. I needed you to choose me over Russ."

For a moment it hung in the air between them—not the weight of the past, which was always between them, but the significance of Casch having said it out loud. She had spoken the words.

"Well, I can't change that now," Flora croaked, "and I'm doing good for you and the kids now, aren't I?"

Casch, exhausted, had wiped her eyes and nodded. "I had to tell you," she said. "I needed to say it."

In the kitchen now, she opened her eyes. For a second she stood frozen. The lasagna pan was still in the sink. She went over and finished washing it. She dried her hands on the plaid dish towel.

294

Then she looked at the pansy clock, its skinny black hands ticking in circles over the flowers. The ticking was the only sound.

Sometimes you want it. The feeling comes up your throat, and you just want it. Because you remember how good you felt.

Her chest started thumping.

She would go outside. She would go outside and see what the kids were doing. She glanced around for her shoes. How long does it take to forget that feeling? Do you ever forget?

But just then she heard the front door open and close, and his steps through the living room.

"Hey," she said softly, as he appeared in the kitchen's open doorway. It always felt like the whole house changed when he came into it. He was grinning from underneath his hoodie. But in a second his face changed.

"Hey, you okay?" he said, reaching for her hand.

"Yeah, I was just—" she started, but didn't finish.

There was a pause and then he said, "I got something to show you guys today."

"What? No, the kids'll be bummed. They're waiting to do the garden."

"I don't think they'll be bummed. C'mon."

Her van was on its last legs now, and they couldn't all fit in the Ranger. So the four of them piled into Flora's Mercury. Topher got on the highway heading north.

"Where are we *going*?" said Molly from the back.

"You'll see."

It was an hour before he took an exit for White River Junction, then drove a county road and made another turn and went up a long hill. He turned at a gravel driveway where a For Sale sign was stuck in a muddy lawn.

Casch looked at him. He was smiling but wouldn't look at her.

"This was my Gram's cabin," he said when they climbed out. "Her and my grandpa built this. There were people living here till recently, but it got foreclosed."

The kids, unimpressed, stared at the log cabin that had one broken window. Overhead, the sky was a stubborn gray.

"Why are we here?" said Molly.

"I want to buy this place. It could be for us, for all of us."

"*What?*"

"That's just an idea," said Casch quickly, her eyes big as she looked at Topher.

"Why don't we have a look inside?" he said. "There's keys in a lockbox. I got the code from the realtor."

When he pushed open the door, and Casch smelled dust and mildew, Topher said quietly, "It's the same. It's exactly the same."

The kids squeezed past them into the room. There were scuffed pine floors and windows along one wall. The space was empty except for a black cast-iron stove. A giant pipe rose from the stove's rear and went up through the ceiling.

"That was ours," said Topher, stepping forward and opening the firebox. "This was our stove."

Casch could see that the thing was full of ash. The kids looked at it for a second, then continued into the next room, their voices bouncing off the bare walls.

"Are you smarter than a plywood box?" Topher said, turning to look at her. For a second they caught eyes. Then he was running a finger along the wall. "The insulation is shit," he said. "We were always freezing. But I guess we can put up with that, right? Until I can do new insulation?"

"Topher, do you have the money for this?"

He looked at her.

"Yeah, I do, I have the down payment. I had a bunch saved from, you know. And now I have a pay stub and everything. And there's a thing for first-time home buyers."

"Is that enough? You need credit—you have good enough credit?"

"I think so. Your mom also offered to co-sign."

Casch felt a wave of unease.

"I don't think we'll need that, though," he said, watching her face. "She just offered because she wants to help."

They drifted into the kitchen. The refrigerator was the color of buttermilk, and there was an old gas range. By a side door that led out to the backyard was a squat washing machine. Molly and Dean were opening cupboards.

"I heard something," said Dean. "There's something in the cupboard!"

"Probably a mouse," said Topher. "Actually probably a whole city of mice. C'mon, let's check out the upstairs."

The kids snapped the cupboards shut and the four of them trooped up the narrow staircase. At the top was a bathroom with curling linoleum and a stained tub. There were three little bedrooms, and they all peeked in the first two. Then, pushing open the last door, the floorboard creaking beneath him, Topher said, "This was mine."

The tiny room had dark wood flooring and a crooked shade over a single window. Casch watched Topher's face. Molly slipped past them and opened the closet. At last Topher turned away.

The backyard was mucky but big, with an umbrella clothesline whose ropes were wet and sagging. The four of them squished across the grass until it sloped downhill to a cluster of trees, then to a marshland. There they stood facing the cattails. The stalks were pale and dry from last season. But the marsh was loud, birds chirping and flitting around.

"Red-winged blackbirds, mostly," Topher murmured.

"Hey, look at this," said Molly. She was squatting and pointing at a tiny yellow flower. "This is a trout lily," she said.

"Look at all of them!" said Dean.

Casch looked where Dean was pointing and saw that the same flowers were growing all along the edge of the marsh, so small she would have stepped on them. She bent and looked at one blossom, barely the size of her thumbnail. It had yellow petals that curled back toward the stem. And then there were a hundred more.

Maybe this could happen for her, she thought, her eyes on the trail of flowers. She glanced up the hill toward the house. Maybe she could have this.

The kids tried walking around the marsh, but thick briars kept them from going very far.

"There's a trail through these woods," said Topher, "or there was when I lived here. We can try looking for it next time—and we'll wear better shoes," he added, eyeing their soggy sneakers.

Finally they walked slowly back toward the house.

"We could plant snow peas here," said Molly.

"Big time. My Gram was the garden kingpin. Look, you can kind of see the outline of her old plot right there. She'd be out here talking to the tomatoes. Actually, you know what? You guys could each have your own garden—but that means you got to take care of it."

"I don't know how," said Dean gravely.

"That's cool, I'll show you."

Topher locked the front door and shut the keys back into

the lockbox. As they walked up the gravel toward the Mercury, Molly fell in step beside Casch.

"Mom, are we actually going to live here?" she asked.

"I'm not sure, baby," said Casch, looking at her. "Did you like it?"

"Yeah, I did. I know which room I want."

"Oh, do you?" she smiled.

"Yeah, I do. So don't mess this up, okay?"

Casch stiffened. She glanced at Topher and Dean, getting into the car.

Then she looked back at Molly.

"I'm only human," she said, "and I'm doing the best I can."

She and Molly looked at each other for a second. Then Molly let Casch take her hand and squeeze it. They got in the Mercury. And the April sun burned through the clouds as they drove back to Greenfield.

Acknowledgments

This book was called *G City* from a time before I wrote the first sentence. In the midst of the brainstorming for a new title, Jenny Katz suggested "untended" over iMessage on the morning of Wednesday, May 8, 2024. Later, *The Untended* was the unanimous pick by all voting parties.

Fletcher inspired me and read my drafts, too.

Two writers helped incubate this book in its earliest pages: Patrick Bensen and Jordan Hall.

People who let me ask them questions or otherwise taught me things that helped me write this book: Krysty Walsh, Caelie LaRochelle, Lindsey Robinson, Evan Bogart, Sean Fogler, Kenny Chartrand, Joanne Mange, Ella Thorne-Thompson, Kerri Santos, Anna Marzullo, Colin Bergeron, and many others.

Taylor, Matt Mitchell, and brothers Dylan and Alex provided inspiration.

Getting Wrecked: Women, Incarceration, and the American Opioid Crisis by Dr. Kimberly Sue was a valuable resource.

Over a span of more than five years, many different people read drafts and contributed through their reflections: Lynn Tryba, Pegi Touff, Carl Vigeland, Lindsey Fletcher-Lynch, Roger Lynch, Chris Buelow, Jenna Garvey, Jamez Ahmad, Helen Leung, Russell Horning, Brit Weber, Bob Saul, Roy Andrews, Peter Millard, Kate Lindroos Conlin, Bethanie Beausoleil, Poppi Kelly, and Steve Kelly, who passed before it was published.

An earlier draft of this book included more about the lawsuits aimed at the pharmaceutical companies, and on that topic I had help from Peter Merrigan, Jeff Gaddy, Meredith Reeves, Michael Touff, and Katherine Touff.

The people I met at the Bread Loaf Writers' Conference include, but are not limited to, Cleyvis Natera, Liz Harmer, Jesse Donaldson, Ravi Howard, Angela Boyd, and the members of the Robert Frost Moth Sorority: Stephanie Wobby, Natasha Rao, Jennifer Christman, Maia McPherson, Pamela Worth, Margaret Albee, and Tamar Shapiro.

Riana Pizzi, who assigned this to her book club two years before it was published and then invited me to their thoughtful discussion. Book club members: Anemone Benedetti, Jessica Dacus, Wendy Ferris, Renée Greenfield, Amelia Leonardi, Kate Sweetser Owens, Liz Aguirre Shurman, and Nunia Mafi Silver.

Jenny Katz stepped out of the universe and became the raddest creative compatriot a creative could ask for.

Kyra Kristof helped me design and print bound copies in 2021 so that it was real.

Rachael Ingraham, Kate Stevens, Maria Millard, Malika Amandi, Phil Gordon, Courtney Deary, and Uyen Doan.

Uncle Jack, who stepped up to hold this dream with me.

Uncle Pete, who taught me to box and then, thirty years later, met me at the gym every week.

Mom, who raised me in G City and appears in these pages as the driver of a Prius who gives Casch a crisp twenty. Dad, who died early but first raised me in G City and appears in these pages as Russ's boss, manager of the scrapyard. My brother, who read this book when it was still called *G City* and called it fire. My ancestors, and especially great-grandfather *zayde* Isador Kramer, who arrived in Greenfield in the early twentieth century and opened a scrapyard.

About the Author

Photo credit: Cara Totman

MATTEA KRAMER is a writer and researcher who has been published in *The Nation* and has appeared on MSNBC. She lives in Amherst, Massachusetts.

Looking for your next great read?

We can help!

Visit www.gosparkpress.com/next-read or
scan the QR code below for a list
of our recommended titles.

SparkPress is an independent boutique publisher
delivering high-quality, entertaining, and engaging
content that enhances readers' lives, with a special
focus on commercial and genre fiction.